Sinister Returns

RACHEL FITZJAMES

Copyright © 2026 by Rachel Fitzjames

All rights reserved.

No part of this publication may be reproduced, distributed, or transmitted in any form or by any means, including photocopying, recording, or other electronic or mechanical methods, without the prior written permission of the publisher, except as permitted by U.S. copyright law. For permission requests, contact the author.

ISBN: 978-1-967700-11-0 (Paperback)
ISBN: 978-1-967700-10-3 (Ebook)

Library of Congress Control Number: 2025926850

The story, all names, characters, and incidents portrayed in this production are fictitious. No identification with actual persons (living or deceased), places, buildings, and products is intended or should be inferred.

Book Cover by Maldo Designs

A note to readers

Each book in the Spruce Hill series features on-page, open-door steamy scenes, along with swearing and some degree of suspense. There may be a limited amount of on-page physical violence as well as the threat of peril facing one or more characters. Specific content in this story that might be of concern to readers includes fatphobia in medical settings, light kink (bondage play), arson, and a brief on-page physical assault (including choking). As a general reassurance, no animals or children are ever harmed in my books.

For more details, please visit my website at or use the QR code below.

*To all the readers who just want
a castle with Belle's library inside—no,
it's not too much to ask.*

Contents

1. Chapter One — 1
2. Chapter Two — 16
3. Chapter Three — 24
4. Chapter Four — 36
5. Chapter Five — 44
6. Chapter Six — 53
7. Chapter Seven — 65
8. Chapter Eight — 76
9. Chapter Nine — 85
10. Chapter Ten — 99
11. Chapter Eleven — 106
12. Chapter Twelve — 116

13. Chapter Thirteen — 123
14. Chapter Fourteen — 133
15. Chapter Fifteen — 143
16. Chapter Sixteen — 151
17. Chapter Seventeen — 161
18. Chapter Eighteen — 170
19. Chapter Nineteen — 180
20. Chapter Twenty — 187
21. Chapter Twenty-One — 196
22. Chapter Twenty-Two — 205
23. Chapter Twenty-Three — 212
24. Chapter Twenty-Four — 223
25. Chapter Twenty-Five — 231
26. Chapter Twenty-Six — 242
27. Chapter Twenty-Seven — 251
28. Chapter Twenty-Eight — 263
29. Chapter Twenty-Nine — 272
30. Chapter Thirty — 281
31. Chapter Thirty-One — 289
32. Chapter Thirty-Two — 296
33. Chapter Thirty-Three — 306
34. Chapter Thirty-Four — 316

35.	Chapter Thirty-Five	324
36.	Chapter Thirty-Six	332
37.	Chapter Thirty-Seven	344
Epilogue		351
Also by		355
Acknowledgements		357
About the author		359

Chapter One

CHARLOTTE

As a librarian, I tried to accept everyone. My job was to create a safe, welcoming space for the community as a whole and part of that was meeting people where they were.

But I *really* despised doctors.

In truth, I hated everything about hospitals, from the weird antiseptic smell to the incessant beeping to the too-bright lights, but doctors were definitely at the top of the list.

The whole sanctimonious, condescending, fat-shaming lot of them.

Despite countless injuries and appointments over the years, I'd met only one exception so far—Libby Bardot, who'd been my favorite babysitter when I was a kid. Instead of restoring my faith in her professional colleagues when she became a doctor, though, she just made the difference more glaring when I measured them up against her awesomeness.

Every other doctor I'd ever met had let me down. I was sure tonight would be no different.

With my head tipped back so I could stare blankly at the stained ceiling overhead, I tried to pretend I was anywhere other than perched on a vinyl table in a curtained-off section of the Eastman Memorial emergency room. I'd already been waiting there for nearly an hour after a nervous tech took an X-ray of my wrist, but I had yet to speak to anyone with the authority to tell me if it was broken and send me on my way.

Nothing said wild Saturday night like listening to the guy with alcohol poisoning to my left barfing into a trash can and the grandmother on the other side assuring her granddaughter she was right as rain. From what I could discern through the curtains, the woman needed a couple dozen stitches and had bled through three kitchen towels already.

My ice pack slipped to the floor with a wet plop just as my phone vibrated with yet another text from my best friend, Penelope.

I'd ignored the last seven after telling her yes, I was *still* sitting here, but apparently she was done waiting for a response. Just as I slid off the paper-covered exam table to grab the ice pack, my phone rang. Even on silent, the buzzing of the vibrations was annoyingly loud, and I struggled to hop back up with only one hand to assist me before answering the call.

"Pen, like I told you an hour ago, I'm still waiting for the goddamn doctor," I hissed into the phone, just as a tall, impossibly handsome man in dark blue scrubs and a white lab coat strode purposefully past the curtains.

When he overheard my comment, he arched one arrogant brow at me without so much as a smile.

I muttered, "I have to go," and shoved the phone awkwardly back into my pocket.

"I'm the goddamn doctor, though most patients just call me Dr. Thorne," he said calmly. "And you must be...Charlotte Whitmore?"

I clenched my jaw for a count of three and then inclined my head. "Yup, that's me."

The man being ridiculously hot did not lessen my distaste for his profession. If anything, it only annoyed me further.

His ice blue eyes swept over me, top to toe, with such barely veiled disdain that I bristled immediately. Gilded hair of a shade somewhere between light brown and honey blonde fell past his collar in casual waves that shimmered gold in the obnoxious overhead light, though a few silver strands decorated his temples.

Seated as I was on the table, we were nearly eye to eye, so he had to be over six feet tall. A faint shadow of stubble clung to his jaw, and I wondered if he was almost finished with a shift or just coming in.

"How broken am I, Doc?" I asked to distract myself from admiring the rest of his physique.

Why a man this beautiful had to choose a career I abhorred was beyond me.

He turned the iPad in his hands around to show me the X-ray. "The good news is your wrist isn't broken at all, just sprained. The bad news is that soft tissue injuries can often take longer to heal than an actual fracture. It may be several weeks before it's recovered enough to resume normal activity."

"Lovely," I grumbled, causing his eyes to snap to my face.

Startled, I stared straight back at him. He was probably used to being fawned over and appreciated.

All I wanted was to get the hell out of there.

"In the meantime, ice, rest, anti-inflammatories. I'll get you fitted for a splint before you go. I can recommend a physical therapist here at the hospital if you'd like. PT would help speed up your recovery."

I didn't even live in the city, so I muttered, "I'll find someone, thanks."

"The intake nurse didn't say how you injured the wrist," he stated. His tone was even, but his gaze was still sharp on my face, like he could see straight through to the inner workings of my mind.

"That's because I didn't tell him."

Something flickered in his eyes before he glanced back down at the screen. "Any previous injuries to that wrist?"

"Um." I frowned, thinking back. "I'm pretty sure that's the one I sprained in tenth grade. And again a few years ago."

"Pretty sure?"

Rolling my eyes, I said, "Look, I've had a lot of sprains over the years."

"Are you an athlete, Ms. Whitmore?"

"No, I'm a librarian."

Though announcing my profession to random men usually resulted in a naughty librarian joke—I often wished they'd at least try to be original—he just studied my face as though he was looking for something.

Maybe doctors didn't joke. More proof they were terrible.

I sighed. "I have hypermobile joints, which makes me particularly injury-prone. Can we move on with this so I can get home before dawn?"

There wasn't a chance in hell that I would tell him I'd sprained my wrist testing out Pen's bondage cuffs before her next date with her new girlfriend. She broke a nail halfway through spacing them along the spindles of her headboard, left to go file it down without uncuffing me, and then her roommate came home with our dinner for movie night at their apartment.

I loved Grisham almost as much as I loved Pen, but the decision to tickle me while I was half restrained was not his brightest move. I'd wrenched so hard against the cuff that something in my wrist popped and sent excruciating pain radiating through my arm.

At first, I'd tried to brush it off with a bag of frozen peas and some ibuprofen, but when the swelling got worse instead of better, I caved and let them drop me at the ER, refusing their offers to accompany me inside.

Just when I was about to apologize for snapping at him, the doctor set his iPad next to me on the table and nodded to my wrist. "May I?"

"I'm all yours."

The second the words were out of my mouth, I froze in abject horror. Dr. Thorne, however, didn't even crack a smile. He just swept his cool gaze over my features again before turning away to sanitize his hands.

Oh. My. God. If Pen had heard that, I would *never* live it down.

By the time he turned back, I hoped the heat in my cheeks wasn't visible, but he didn't bother glancing back at my face. Gently supporting my wrist with one hand, he lifted away the melting ice pack. When my gaze caught on the strands of gold—and the occasional silver—mixed into the waves of his hair, I forced my eyes back down to my wrist.

Big mistake. I sucked in a sharp breath when I saw how terrible it looked.

Deep purple bruises crept under the ice-pinkened skin. It had swelled to the size of a tennis ball, and a deep red scrape delineated exactly where I'd yanked against the edge of the cuff. Not even pink marabou could cushion that.

"The bruising and inflammation make it look worse than it is," he said quietly. "Have you taken any painkillers yet?"

The pad of his thumb brushed lightly along the uninjured skin just beyond the scrape. I had to remind myself to breathe normally—not because it hurt, but because the motion was somehow both blindingly erotic and immensely sweet.

I blinked away from the sight of his hand on mine, staring down at the melting ice pack instead. "Um. I took ibuprofen a couple hours ago, right after it happened."

"You can alternate that with acetaminophen. Try to stay on top of the pain for the first few days."

"Right," I mumbled, finally glancing back at his face.

After another moment of inspecting my wrist, he lifted his gaze to mine and said, "Anything you say to me is protected by doctor-patient confidentiality, Ms. Whitmore. If someone hurt you, a lover or partner, you can tell me. We can connect you with resources for help."

A strangled laugh burst from my throat. "Oh, god no, I am *very* single. Believe me, it was nothing like that. It was just a stupid accident."

Maybe I imagined the quick flash of interest in his eyes at my idiotic declaration before he glanced back down at the injury, but I was mortified nonetheless. My only excuse was that it had been an extremely long day. It probably would have been lovely, were it not for the emergency room trip I'd ended up with instead.

Of course, Penelope would almost certainly insist it was worth it when she heard about Dr. Hottie.

When the gorgeous doctor himself looked up again, there was an odd mix of stern disapproval and unexpected concern in those pale depths. "If you're sure. I'll go get the splint and we can get you out of here."

Even though he was only gone for two or three minutes, my mind wandered into dangerous territory during his absence. I imagined telling him what had really happened, watching his expression grow incredulous at my explanation, then receiving a lesson from the hottest doctor in all of history about safe bondage play.

My face flamed when he walked back into the room with a black wrist brace. Aside from a tiny quirk of one golden eyebrow, he didn't comment as he lifted my hand from my lap. His fingers were callused, rough against the sensitive skin of my wrist, but his touch was still surprisingly gentle.

"You'll need to take it easy for several weeks," he said, his voice low as he bent over my wrist to secure the brace.

"Okay."

"No lifting heavy books."

"Okay," I repeated, kicking myself immediately for sounding like a dolt.

For the first time, his eyes brightened as he glanced up at me, not quite amused but almost. "I hope you're right-handed?"

Recognizing that my brain was going haywire from his proximity, I just nodded. He took a half step back and offered his left hand to help me off the table. I clasped his palm in my good one, slid down until my feet hit the floor, then stumbled immediately against him like the clumsy oaf that I was. With his other arm, he caught me at the waist to steady me.

Either the man was a furnace or my skin was still hot with embarrassment. My mind raced with how, exactly, I might avoid telling Pen about any part of this experience.

"Right. Thank you," I mumbled.

"My pleasure, Ms. Whitmore. Please take care of yourself."

His voice was low, the rumble of it skittering along my veins. I looked up at him, surprised to see his lips curving into a semblance of a smile, then he let go of me and stepped away. The intake nurse met us in the corridor outside, ran me through the discharge paperwork, and sent me on my way.

The cool evening air was refreshing as I burst through the doors, especially against my flushed skin, but spring around here was unpredictable at the best of times and the temperature had taken a nosedive since Penelope dropped me off. I found a bench in the courtyard on the opposite side of the hospital from the busy emergency room and texted her that I was finally done.

After ten minutes passed without a response, I tried Grisham. I called both of them as the half hour mark approached, but there was no answer.

"If you two are doing shots right now, I'm going to destroy you both. Slowly and gruesomely," I growled into Pen's voicemail.

"Do you enjoy the cold?"

I jumped, startled, as Dr. Hottie walked into view. He'd changed into faded jeans and a beat-up leather jacket, looking no less attractive than he had in his scrubs and lab coat.

If anything, he looked even hotter.

My lips twitched. "No, but my friends were supposed to come back to get me and I'd rather be out here than inside. I'm sure they'll be here soon."

Though I expected him to continue on his way, he sat down on the other side of the bench, leaving a respectful space between us. A half smile tugged at the corner of his mouth as he said, "Then I'll wait with you."

"That's really not necessary."

"You shouldn't be sitting out here alone in the dark."

I scoffed and gestured with my splinted wrist at the courtyard lights. "It's not dark. I'm fine here. You can go."

"Or," he said, lips twitching, "the goddamn doctor will make sure you're safe until your ride shows up."

Closing my eyes, I sighed heavily and wondered if the Earth might swallow me up to save me from humiliating myself any further. The doctor's low chuckle didn't help to stave off the heat rising in my cheeks again.

"I'd apologize for that comment, but as a general rule, I can't stand doctors," I admitted, refusing to look at him.

Instead of taking offense, he gave a short laugh. "Can't say I blame you, having met more than my fair share myself. There's definitely a higher-than-average proportion of assholes in the bunch."

I glanced at my phone, which lay silent on my lap, then peered down the street as though by some miracle, Penelope might cruise up to the curb at that very moment. I'd never even used a rideshare app before, and the thought of sitting out here to download one and figure it out in front of Dr. Hottie was not attractive in the least.

After a moment, he stood, shrugged off his leather jacket, and gestured for me to sit forward on the bench. "You're shivering. Here."

"Oh, no, I'm fine. It's really not that cold," I protested, but my fingers were going numb.

"It really is. I run warm, and you've been out in the cold longer than I have."

At the commanding note in his voice, I leaned forward so he could settle the jacket over my shoulders, tugging the collar until the residual warmth from his body enveloped me. My breath caught for a beat as I glanced up at him, then he stepped away and sat back down on the other side of the bench.

"You really don't have to wait with me, Dr. Thorne. I'm sure they'll get my messages any second now."

"Please, call me Sawyer. My shift ended with you," he said.

"Sawyer," I repeated softly, then made the mistake of meeting his eyes, shining with a sincerity that swayed me toward not despising him on the grounds of his profession.

"I promise you're safe with me."

Though I was too smart to take that at face value, I blew out a breath and nodded. "Okay. If you're sure you have nothing better to do than sit here in the cold."

"Nothing at all. You should text your friends with my name, though, just to be safe." His pale eyes danced under the street lights.

"I will. I'm also a black belt in karate," I warned him.

He smiled like he didn't quite believe me. Since I was lying through my teeth, I didn't take his skepticism personally—but I'd read enough thrillers to know all the ways this could go. Sure, I loved a good romance novel, but I liked to be prepared for a variety of situations.

Which made me wonder about the statistics regarding doctors who were also serial killers, then about whether there were rules against doctors dating patients.

Exhaustion was clearly getting to me.

Dr. Hottie—Sawyer—smirked at me and nodded toward my phone. "Go on, then."

I snorted and fired off yet another text to Penelope with the doctor's full name and a dire warning that she'd better be on her way to the hospital.

Hopefully she'd see it before I turned into a headline on the evening news.

Sawyer laced his hands behind his head and I tried to ignore the way his biceps flexed against the sleeves of his black t-shirt. Between the worn leather jacket that smelled like some kind of woodsy, masculine shampoo and the heat simmering in my core at his casual display of muscles, my tension eased little by little.

"Is there a doctor in particular who ruined your view of the rest of us?" he asked, looking for all the world like he didn't even need a jacket. "Or are we all just generally disappointing?"

I choked on a laugh. "A bit of both, I suppose. When I was a kid, I twisted my knee rollerblading, and after I suffered through the pain for months, waiting for it to get better, my mom finally made me go get it checked out. The doctor told me it was growing pains. I'd already been my adult height for two years."

"Oof."

"Yeah. Once I hit college, I went in for an ear infection and the advice was, 'Have you tried losing weight? Maybe if you exercised more and ate fewer carbs, you could reach your goal weight.' It was *his* goal weight, not mine, utterly ridiculous for my frame, *and* not related to my ear infection in any way."

Sawyer glanced over at me, his jaw tight. "A medical professional said that to you?"

"Yes."

"Who was it?"

I blinked at him in surprise. "Did you just pull a *who did this to you?*"

"I don't know what that means," he replied, frowning at me.

"It's a—you know what, never mind." I wasn't about to explain beloved tropes or the dark romance genre to this man. "Anyway. Just some dickhead doctor."

He fell silent for a long moment. "I'm sorry, Charlotte."

"Not your fault," I said, shrugging off the sincerity I heard in his apology. "I guess you're not as terrible as others."

For a second, he was silent, then warm laughter spilled out of him and I forgot all about the cold. "High praise coming from you."

"It is," I replied tartly, and he laughed again.

My phone vibrated on my lap and I almost dropped it onto the concrete as I fumbled to check my messages. Penelope had *finally* gotten my texts and was two blocks away.

"Is that your ride?" Sawyer asked.

"Yeah. She'll be here in a minute. Thank you for waiting with me," I said, reluctantly slipping the coat from my shoulders.

Sawyer rose to his feet again, and it was probably overkill, but when he offered his hand, I took it. "I'll wait until you're safe in her car. Take care of yourself, Charlotte," he said with another half smile. The expression took him from stern to sexy at lightning speed.

I handed him the coat. "You too, Doc. Thanks for the company."

When I glanced back after crossing the courtyard to meet Penelope at the curb—where she hopefully wouldn't catch a glimpse of Sawyer—he was leaning against the side of a silver sedan, looking like sin personified in his leather jacket and jeans. His hair shimmered under the streetlights, falling across his forehead as his lips curved in a smile that looked entirely unlike the cold doctor who'd stumbled onto my irreverent phone conversation.

He raised a hand in farewell, so I shot him a smile and slipped into the passenger seat of Pen's car. My wrist still ached, my frustration with my friends was at an all-time high, and I missed the warmth of his jacket, but as we drove back to the apartment, the smile lingered on my lips.

Maybe the night hadn't ended quite as badly as I'd anticipated.

Chapter Two

SAWYER

I CHECKED MY WATCH for what had to be the seventh time in the past five minutes, rushing to finish my charting so I could officially end this shift and make it to the restaurant on time for my meeting. Once I finally saved the file and swiveled away from the computer, I knew I was cutting it dangerously close.

That didn't stop me from slowing my near-jog to a stroll as I passed the physical therapy suite on my way out of the hospital, ever hopeful that I might catch sight of a certain blonde former patient. She'd been a breath of fresh air that night—the flash of stubbornness in her eyes, the dry sense of humor, the adorable rambling—and god knew I needed more breathing room in my life.

I told myself I wasn't disappointed when there was no sign of her, as there hadn't been for the past week.

The lie rang hollow.

With only a few minutes to spare, I hurried down the sidewalk from the hospital toward the restaurant where I was meeting Dr. Bardot. As I gave my name to the hostess and followed her directions toward a booth along the wall, I tried to slow my heart rate and calm my nerves.

This wasn't exactly an interview, but it certainly felt like one. And I hadn't wanted a job this badly since I accepted the position I was now leaving, the one I'd given my notice for months ago without anything new lined up. My last explosive argument with my father—in front of what felt like half the senior staff of Eastman Memorial—had been the final straw.

"Dr. Thorne, so good to see you." As she rose and shook my hand, I met the warm brown gaze of the woman I hoped would be my new employer.

"Dr. Bardot. Thank you for meeting me here. But please, call me Sawyer."

"Sawyer it is. And you can call me Libby." She gestured for me to sit as she settled back down on her side of the booth, her smile wide and friendly. "Are you just coming off a shift?"

"Yes, sorry I'm late. We were slammed all afternoon."

She waved off my apology as the waiter came to deliver glasses of water and menus. "You're right on time. I hope you don't mind if I eat while we're talking. I didn't have time for lunch and I'm starving."

"Of course. I'm ready for dinner, too. I'm sorry you came all this way. I could have come down to meet with you."

"Don't worry about it. I wouldn't have suggested meeting here if I wasn't willing to come up in person. Your schedule is far more chaotic than mine." She flashed a grin. "Which is why I'm hoping you'll agree to come work with me at the clinic. I'd like to officially offer you the position."

Relief coasted along my limbs at her words. This was what I'd been afraid to even hope for.

After meeting her a couple months back, when her brother-in-law came in through the emergency room while I was working, we'd hit it off and my respect for her had only grown with everything I learned about her clinic. I'd expressed interest in the job about a month ago when she reached out to me, and we'd spoken on the phone twice already.

The truth was that I was tired, exhausted on a cellular level. Emergency medicine had been my dream, and I loved it, but working at the same hospital my father practically ruled over had sapped my enthusiasm for the job.

I should have known diverging from the path he intended for me wouldn't be enough to get me out from under his thumb.

"I accept," I said simply, my lips twitching when she raised her fists in a silent cheer.

"Are you sure you don't want to come see the clinic in person first?" she asked. "Not that I want to scare you off, because

I really need you, but it's quite a change of pace from a city hospital."

I shook my head. "Nothing I might see there would change my mind."

"Okay, then. I'm not going to be the one to talk you out of it."

The discussion turned to logistics after the server came by to take our orders. When she chose a cheeseburger for herself, I decided to have the same.

"Tell me more about the clinic," I suggested, watching as her eyes lit up.

Libby Bardot might not have gone into emergency medicine, but the woman thrived on a challenge. I had a feeling we'd get along beautifully.

"We're a bit of a cross between an urgent care clinic and a regular medical office," she said, "though it started out more as the former. Having to travel half an hour to a hospital wasn't ideal for Spruce Hill residents in many cases, so we got a lot of minor injuries—stitches, X-rays, that kind of thing. Gradually, we gained more and more patients looking for primary care, even though there are a few other doctors with offices in town."

"Do you still take walk-ins?"

She grinned. "Yes, and we get enough of them to keep your days nice and varied. Major emergencies are sent to Eastman or the hospital out in Sodus, but your skills will absolutely be put to good use."

Fuck, why did it feel so good for a practical stranger to recognize what I needed in my day to day life?

Because your father never gave a shit?

I shook off the thought of him and his opinions on my career. "It sounds perfect. Just what I'm looking for, really."

"Excellent. So, when can you start?" she asked.

"I, ah, gave my notice a couple months ago, so I'll have to finish out my scheduled shifts over the next couple weeks, but I should be able to start the week after that, if that works for you?"

"Wonderful," she breathed. "You have no idea how desperate I am. We've had to double-book appointments most days and I've been covering six days a week for the last two months. It's been...a lot."

"I'm glad I can help, though I'll have to find a place in Spruce Hill. The commute would be rough, but if I have to deal with it until I find a rental, I'll make it work."

"No, no need to commute. I know just the place," she said, her eyes alight. "Nice street, close to the clinic, quiet neighbors. The owner is the husband of one of our nurses and I know he'd be open to a short-term lease while you're getting to know the town."

"That sounds perfect."

"I'll email you the info. You're sure you won't miss living in the city?"

I laughed. "Positive. I should have gotten away from this place years ago. I'm ready for something new."

She smirked. "Well, it will certainly be a change."

When I first talked to Libby about the position, I'd researched Spruce Hill in depth. It wasn't far from the city, but I'd never been there. Hell, I'd barely heard of it before Libby's email showed up in my inbox one day. Based on the small town's website, it sounded like the setting of a Hallmark movie. Nestled between Lake Ontario and the Finger Lakes, it was an idyllic but bustling little area.

And maybe that was exactly what the doctor ordered.

A home, a yard, hobbies, and a fulfilling job working with a doctor I admired—I'd be able to have it all. Hell, I'd even have time to date. As I imagined going out on Saturday night instead of working or trudging home to sleep before my next shift, an image of my librarian popped unbidden into my mind.

Maybe I'd even have a family one day. I'd given up on that idea so long ago, I wasn't sure how to process it, but there'd be plenty of time for that.

When I gave my notice at the hospital without another position lined up, it was a moment of impulsivity, yes, but the peace it brought was immediate. I'd figured I could take a bit of time off as I looked for something new, but when Libby reached out to me?

The whole thing felt serendipitous, especially the timing. This was a perfect solution for both of us.

"I'll forward you the details on the rental, but I won't be offended if you want to look for something else. There are plenty of options in town," she said, finishing the last bite of her cheeseburger.

"I appreciate that. I think I'd like to get the lay of the land before making any permanent decisions about living arrangements, so a short-term rental sounds perfect."

Her responding grin was radiant. "We can't wait to have you join us."

"Believe me, I can't wait, either."

That was the understatement of the century.

By the time Libby and I finished lunch and shook hands over my official job offer, it felt like I'd shrugged off the crushing weight of the past decade. Those boulders I'd been carrying, both personal and professional, crumbled to dust. I was moving forward, finally making further progress in my determination to choose my own path.

I could only imagine my parents' reaction to the news. With any luck, they wouldn't find out until I was gone.

My one-year contract was waiting in my email when I got home from the restaurant, along with a listing for the rental house. It was a far cry from my current apartment, but everything I'd told Libby was true.

I *needed* a change. One bigger than just switching up my lunch choices at the hospital cafeteria or running on a treadmill in my apartment building's gym rather than along the city streets when I had time for exercise.

I needed room to breathe. I needed to get out from under my father's thumb, to finally accept that my life belonged to me and me alone.

Christ, I hadn't been this excited about anything in years.

Even if I flinched every time my phone rang after giving my notice at the hospital, afraid my father had finally heard I was leaving Eastman Memorial for greener small town pastures, he stayed miraculously silent as the weeks went by and hope swelled in my chest with every passing day.

I finished out my shifts with a growing sense of relief and a blossoming feeling of anticipation, but I continued to make excuses to pass by the PT offices whenever I had a free moment. If fate smiled upon me and sent Charlotte back to the hospital, that was the most likely place for her to be.

Unfortunately, she never showed up.

If I'd known I was leaving the city when I said goodbye that night, it might have prompted me to at least give her my contact information before she got in her friend's car, but maybe it was all for the better that she didn't return to the hospital.

A fresh start was what I needed, not a connection that threatened to drag me right back to the city that was my father's domain.

Even if the fantasy of her being part of that fresh start was utterly enticing.

Chapter Three

CHARLOTTE

"I still can't believe you didn't at least give him your number," Penelope grumbled from the other end of the couch.

I threw a piece of popcorn at her head, which promptly led my new foster puppy, a chocolate lab mix I'd named Spoon, to leap off my lap after it. "He's a medical professional. I was his patient, thanks to you two. Sorry I didn't throw myself at him for your entertainment."

Somehow, I'd managed to avoid this conversation after returning to Penelope's apartment last Saturday, probably because I looked exhausted and pathetic from my jaunt to the emergency room. After bringing over dinner tonight—their treat—and supplying a boatload of snacks for movie night at my house this weekend, they'd latched onto the topic of Dr. Hottie himself.

Now, there was no escaping it.

Grisham frowned thoughtfully. "I don't think there are rules about that, especially after you're discharged. It's not like he's the one giving you a physical exam each year," he mused, then bounced his eyebrows at me. "Though I'm sure he'd be happy to."

"You two are the worst," I grouched, scooping up the puppy with my right arm when he ambled back toward me. "He probably wasn't even interested in me."

"Impossible," Penelope declared. She was eternally loyal, which lessened my irritation over rehashing the night of the injury yet again.

"Chuckles, you're gorgeous. Have you seen your rack? Any dude who's into women would give his right arm to get into your pants. Unless you think he bats for the other team, in which case I need you to break my wrist right now."

I refrained from throwing popcorn at Grisham only because the puppy was finally dozing off on my lap. "Thank you both for your votes of confidence, but since I'm not planning to stalk him at the hospital, I'll probably never see him again."

"Should've jumped him then and there," Pen muttered beneath her breath as she turned on the movie.

"Not every guy is like Brent," Grisham said, his tone so gentle I actually flinched.

Pen hit pause and froze, still staring toward the TV, as though if she didn't move, I wouldn't see her there.

"Guys, we don't need to rehash this..." I started.

Grisham met my gaze and held it. "He was an epic douche-canoe who lied to your face and broke your trust over and over again. He scarred you, but he's not worth living your life alone just to avoid future pain."

"Jesus," I muttered, rubbing my sternum.

"He's right," Penelope chimed in. "Brent the Bastard shouldn't be the reason you don't trust hot dudes anymore, Char."

It was more than that and they both knew it, but Brent *had* been the catalyst for my very long dry spell. During a time when my gut was telling me something wasn't right, I'd ignored it, stomped down that feeling, and it blew up in my face.

Spectacularly.

It had been four years and my heart hadn't recovered—not because I was madly in love with him, but because something inside it had broken when his deceptions were revealed. I'd tried to patch it up, went on a few dates a year ago to quash the nagging from my two best friends, and when that blew up in my face, I retreated again.

"And how was your date with Clara last night?" I asked Penelope, determined to turn this conversation away from both my encounter with the hot doctor and my sordid past.

She shot me a disgruntled glare. "Beautiful and romantic, but she's leaving for Europe next week for some kind of world tour. She'll be gone for three months. Who does that?"

"Artists?" I suggested. Clara was a free-spirited painter who might actually have crossed the impossibly high threshold of being *too* free-spirited for Pen.

"People with money to spare?" Grisham added.

"Whatever. I'll rock her world for another week, and I assure you, she will miss me while she's gone."

Grisham and I exchanged a look, trying not to laugh at Penelope's tone. She loved hard and loved frequently, which was something we both adored about her. No matter how we teased her about her big heart, it was the absolute best thing in the world.

I, on the other hand, was verging on confirmed spinster at this point. Never before had I wished I could be more like Penelope than when I thought about Dr. Hottie. What would have happened if I'd given him my number? Or, better yet, asked him to take me back to his place instead of waiting for Pen to pick me up that night?

I wasn't sure what he'd do with the opportunity to persuade me into telling the truth about the injury, but I imagined it could have been extremely enjoyable for both of us.

What's done is done, I told myself as I pulled a blanket over myself and Spoon, leaving just his little head peeking out. The illusion of a stern, sexy doctor was probably better than the reality, after all. Maybe he was actually the arrogant bastard he'd seemed at first.

In the end, I would treat the experience as exactly what it was—a memory to pull off the shelf on lonely nights.

At least it was something.

MORNINGS AT THE LIBRARY were my favorite, when the whole world was quiet. It was every childhood daydream come true for me, being alone in the silence, surrounded by books. All I needed was a rolling ladder and a mysterious prince, and the fantasy would be complete.

I flipped on the lights, tucked my tote bag into my office drawer, and checked the overnight return chute connected to the parking lot behind the building.

Back when I first started here as head librarian, a kid had returned a book with a child support check stuck inside the front cover. Both he and his mom, who had a chronic illness resulting in medical debt that made every dollar vital, had been frantic until I found it and got in touch with them. Ever since that incident, I'd taken to carefully inspecting each book and holding onto any surprises found within.

With memories of a certain very attractive doctor at the forefront of my mind, I sorted the returns, fanning through pages for any errant items left tucked inside.

When I lifted up the last book, a receipt fluttered to the desk. It hadn't been caught between the pages, which meant it might have been in one of the other returns or simply stuck between two books piled on a table at home somewhere. I picked it up and studied it for a moment. People often used receipts or scraps of paper as bookmarks, so it wasn't that unusual, but I tried to check for significance before throwing anything away.

The print was so faded I couldn't even make out where it came from, but just before I crumpled it to toss into the trash can, I noticed something written on the back.

It was a list of a handful of businesses, starting with The Hideaway, a seedy bar on the outskirts of town. I wasn't much of a barfly, but the place closed down almost a year ago after some kind of kitchen fire. The next name was a bowling alley I'd been to once with friends in high school, followed by a laundromat called Suds & Fold.

There were two other names scrawled so illegibly that I couldn't make out a single word. At the end of the list, Montrose Farms was circled—I remembered taking field trips there for apple picking back in elementary school.

There seemed to be no rhyme or reason to the names on the list, nothing obvious to connect them, but I tucked it into the file folder I'd created for just that purpose in case someone came looking for it.

Patrons began to trickle in shortly after I unlocked the front doors, then I lost myself in the comfort of my work and forgot all about it.

Two days later, mid-morning brought in my senior activity group, which consisted of a handful of older, retired town residents who'd finally agreed to show up each week if I stopped badgering them.

They loved it. They just didn't want to admit that I was right.

For the most part, I left them to their own devices as they played chess or chatted over coffee in the library's event room. I fetched a dozen magazines for Mr. Bauer and brought a cup of tea to Mrs. Garcia so she didn't have to set aside her knitting, but otherwise I kept myself busy with regular library business.

David and Pop, two of my favorite humans in Spruce Hill, were ensconced in thrifted armchairs by a window that morning instead of playing chess. Though I'd never ask outright, I was almost positive they'd moved in together a few months after I first started the group.

I couldn't help but smile at my accidental matchmaking.

When I had a free moment, I grabbed the book I'd ordered for Pop from the Oakville Library and headed their way.

"Another fire?" David asked in a low voice just as I reached their table.

My breath stalled painfully. Before my parents' divorce, my father had sworn up and down that he'd attend my very first dance recital. Instead, he stayed home watching TV and fell asleep with a cigarette in his mouth. The entire house and all our belongings had been engulfed and destroyed, but Dad managed to stumble out to safety. For weeks, he lied about how it happened, until my mom finally got the truth out of him.

She filed for divorce the next day. The fire wasn't the only reason, but it was the final straw.

Without Dad, we had to move into a more affordable rental in town, down the street from both Libby and her future husband, Mark. Losing the house had been awful, but that rental might have been the best thing that ever happened to me, because I gained far more than I'd lost. Honorary family through Mark and his brothers, Libby, and an example of true love in Mark's parents.

I still couldn't sleep if I caught a whiff of smoke in the air, though, not without checking the entire house top to bottom.

Struggling to shake off the memories, I gave a tentative smile when David caught sight of me over Pop's shoulder. "Sorry to interrupt. I just wanted to bring this over so I don't forget."

"Thank you, Charlotte. You're a gem."

"I wasn't trying to eavesdrop, I promise, but...there was a fire?"

Pop reached up and squeezed my hand firmly. These two men had lived in Spruce Hill their entire lives; they knew everything that went on, the good and the bad. They were well aware of my experience with fires.

When neither of them spoke, I said, "It's okay. Please just tell me."

Still looking hesitant to share, Pop nodded. "Last night. The old tobacco warehouse has been around since before I was born. Another local landmark gone up in flames."

"Friedrich's son works in insurance." David tipped his head toward Mr. Bauer. "He said the coverage on the place was astronomical."

"No amount of money can replace history," Pop replied.

"You said 'another,'" I mused. "Have there been more?"

David lifted a scolding finger my way, though his eyes twinkled like always. "Nothing for you to concern yourself over. Just a couple of old men speculating when we have nothing better to do today."

I grinned. "Right. No chess?"

"We've taken to playing in the afternoons at home," he replied. I didn't miss the tender look he sent toward Pop, nor the responding softness in Pop's brilliant blue eyes.

"That's great. I hope you two will keep coming to the group, though." I lowered my voice and leaned in to add, "You know seeing you makes my day."

They both laughed and assured me they would be here no matter what. Though I was tempted to ask more about the fires, the library served as a safe space for everyone—inserting myself into private conversations was not a good look for a librarian, and I'd already intruded as far as I could.

Still, as I headed back to the checkout desk, I couldn't help but wonder at the coincidence of them discussing a fire the same week I found a list topped by a business that burned down.

It might be nothing more than happenstance, but what if it wasn't? My gut churned with the same unease I experienced when I smelled smoke.

I'd have to do a little digging of my own. Nothing calmed that disquiet like research into the source. Once I was assured it was just a coincidence, I'd stop worrying about it.

Between helping library patrons and the usual interruptions that made up my work hours, I scoured the internet for details on each name on the list. Most of the results were just websites for the businesses themselves, along with articles from the local newspaper reporting the kitchen fire at The Hideaway.

One of the others had closed down after a fire as well. Suds & Fold, a laundromat south of town, had burned to the ground due to faulty wiring six months back, and Al's Discount Warehouse had to be the overnight blaze David and Pop were discussing. After finding a news article about it, I looked back to the list and wondered if it was one of the illegible names written there.

Historic or not, that place had been a big part of my childhood because they had the best prices on school supplies. As a single parent, my mom knew how to bargain hunt like a professional. I hadn't realized the building was so old, though.

Each of the businesses on the receipt—the names I could read, anyway—were located in a building that had been standing for the better part of a century, but they shared very little in common besides that. Spruce Hill itself had been settled in 1794, so it wasn't like there was a shortage of historic landmarks all over town. Al's and The Hideaway, as far as I knew, hadn't exactly been kept up to code over the years. They were the very definition of dilapidated.

Even the three businesses related by destruction were scattered throughout the list, not topping it. The bowling alley was still in business, though, which left the farm at the bottom. That place had been closed down for years after the family who owned it moved down south.

I was missing something.

I'd ignored my instincts before to catastrophic ends—I wasn't inclined to do that again, especially not with fires involved. And my gut said this was more than a coincidence.

Eventually, I was forced to set my research aside to run story hour over in the children's section, and by the time I'd swept up the last graham cracker crumb from the giant clock rug, it was nearly closing time.

I tidied up the circulation desk and my office, made sure the receipt list was safely tucked into the locked filing cabinet, and decided to let the information percolate.

Maybe in the coming days, I'd be able to find a connection between those businesses, or maybe I'd be able to glean something new when whoever had lost the list came into the library to claim it.

Or maybe...maybe it was just a random note used as a bookmark. If David and Pop had spotted a trend surrounding destructive fires, it was impossible to know how many others might have noticed. It was entirely likely some other library patron had just been noting down coincidences they came across.

Either way, it was a mystery, and no one knew research like a librarian. Eventually, I'd stumble across a real connection—or run out of leads and have to call it quits.

Only time would tell.

Chapter Four

SAWYER

"YOU CANNOT BE SERIOUS about this."

Dr. Sylvester Thorne, world-renowned neurosurgeon and first-rate pompous ass, stared at me like I'd just announced I was joining a monastery and giving away all of my worldly possessions instead of taking a good job in a nearby town. He'd been my father for thirty-seven years; he should have known by now that when I told him I'd made a decision, there was nothing he could do to sway me from it.

In fact, our very public fight at Eastman a few months ago should have driven that home, but apparently I was in for a potential repeat.

Remembering how my new boss recognized the nuances of my particular career choice and respected those needs gave me the strength to draw a deep, calming breath before responding to my father.

"I am very serious about it, Dad, and I'd appreciate it if we could stop rehashing the matter. Unless you're going to help me pack boxes for the movers, I've got shit to do."

He barely hid a sneer at the thought of using his million-dollar hands for something other than surgery. "Your mother is concerned. We've never even heard of Spruce Hill."

"Whether you've heard of it or not, it exists. An entire town full of people doesn't just disappear because you haven't met them."

"There can't possibly be a medical facility worthy of a Thorne there."

That was the crux of practically every argument we'd had for the past decade or more—*worthy of a Thorne.* Was it distinguished, award-winning, renowned, prestigious enough for the family name?

Inevitably, my choices never quite lined up with what he wanted.

I pinched the bridge of my nose. "I realize this probably comes as a shock to you, but people everywhere are deserving of quality medical care, Dad."

"After everything you threw away to choose emergency medicine over surgery, you think you'll be content with some backwater clinic in the middle of nowhere?" he asked, arching a silvered brow like I might suddenly see his wisdom and agree.

"Yes, as a matter of fact, I do."

Middle of nowhere or not, the clinic offered enough variety to keep my interest, but enough stability to allow me to finally explore everything *else* life had to offer. Really, I should be thanking my father for being the final prod to take this chance, one that might finally allow me the freedom to have a home, maybe even a family, out from under his thumb.

"Your mother had lunch with Veronica the other day." He dropped the information gleefully, like he hoped I'd burst into tears at hearing it.

Veronica.

My ex-fiancée of over a decade, the woman who'd lied and manipulated me until she realized my decision to go into emergency medicine was final, then cast me aside when my parents threatened to disinherit me over a career choice unworthy of the Thorne name and reputation.

If he hoped for tears or outrage, he'd be sorely disappointed.

I still wondered if the breakup was yet another manipulation on their part, like the three of them thought the risk of losing a fiancée clearly more in love with my family's wealth and status than my actual self might finally set me straight.

Incredulity gave way to a thousand questions.

"Why is Mom still having lunch with her?" I asked, finally settling on the most pertinent.

His sneer intensified. "She's practically a member of the family. Just because you ruined your relationship doesn't mean she ceased to exist for the rest of us."

Of course they'd kept in touch. I wondered if they'd written her into their wills yet.

I braced my hands against the kitchen counter and dropped my head, counting my breaths until I thought maybe—just maybe—I could look my father in the eye without punching him.

"One day, a seat will open on the board and your name won't even be mentioned, not if you're living in some hick town in the middle of nowhere," he said, sounding exactly like the elitist asshole he was.

"Good thing I don't want a seat on the board, then," I replied. "Nor have I ever. Now, if you don't mind, I have to finish packing."

Whatever he muttered in response, it was nothing the outside world would ever hear from Dr. Sylvester Thorne's lips. No, he saved his sarcasm and vitriol for his utter disappointment of a son.

I made good money, but that was never the endgame for Sylvester Thorne. Prestige, reputation, power—real or imagined—those were the things he valued, and his only son choosing the emergency room was an insult of the highest order. I thrived on working through the unexpected, never experiencing two days exactly alike, and my father hated that.

In his mind, we were the cowboys of the medical world, and he and his cronies were the upper crust.

"I'll text Mom the address once I'm settled. You two should come down for dinner sometime," I said brightly, knowing full well it would never happen.

If looks could kill, I'd have dropped dead then and there with the glare he directed at me.

"Of course," he spat. "Don't forget you'll need to attend the charity gala, whether you're on staff at Eastman Memorial or not. I'm taking your mother to the Bahamas for our anniversary and someone has to represent the family."

Since I couldn't remember the last time my parents went on vacation—hell, the last time they'd spent any quality time together, period—that was one obligation I was willing to fulfill.

Not for his sake, but Mom deserved something nice.

After all, she'd been putting up with his stodgy ass for over forty years, hosting fancy dinners for all the cronies with god complexes my father liked to surround himself with. Once I was old enough—bright enough, articulate enough—I'd been expected to play the role of his perfect heir at each of those dinners.

Fortunately, I was clever and willing to perform like a circus monkey until the last possible second, when I chose emergency medicine over neurosurgery. I thought my father was going to have an aneurysm then and there.

Too bad I wouldn't have been the neurosurgeon to fix it for him. Hopefully he'd started training some other underling to carry on his legacy after I defected.

"I'll be there," I assured him.

"It's black tie."

I huffed a laugh. "I do understand the term. After all, you raised me."

"Not very well," he countered under his breath. When I didn't rise to the bait, he gave a frosty smile. "Your ticket will be at the door when you arrive."

I smirked back at him. "I'll be bringing a date, so make sure there are two tickets waiting. I would hate to embarrass the family name by making a scene."

"A date?" he sputtered. "Who?"

I didn't have a date lined up at all, but I couldn't resist the urge to rile him, especially after he had the nerve to bring up Veronica.

Unbidden, an image of the woman with the sprained wrist popped into my mind. There was no reason why the deliciously curvy blonde with her mysterious injury should have distracted me, lingering in my thoughts long after she left that night, but I just couldn't get her out of my head.

Something about her utter lack of respect for my profession only made me want to win her over that much more.

If she had told me how the injury had come about, I might've tried my luck, gotten a phone number or at least confirmed the interest was mutual. I was almost positive it was, but there hadn't been enough time or opportunity to be certain.

When a woman was cagey about an injury, it was never a good sign. In the end, I let her walk away.

I'd regretted it ever since.

"You don't know her," I replied, forcing the memories down as I taped the flaps of a box of kitchenware. In fact, he would probably hate her on sight—her intense disdain for doctors would throw him into an absolute tailspin. I almost laughed aloud at the idea of shutting them in a room together.

But in the end, it didn't matter. I might never see her again, so I'd have to find someone else to bring to the gala.

When I lifted my gaze back to my father, he was glowering at me, his jaw clenched so hard I wondered if his sparkling white smile could possibly still include all his own teeth. We locked eyes, a fresh round in the neverending battle of wills, until his lip curled and a temporary détente was declared once again.

Not because he admitted defeat, but because he'd long ago deemed me an unworthy adversary.

"I'll see myself out," he said stiffly.

I inclined my head, not that he was waiting for my agreement, then watched as he turned on his heel and left my apartment for the last time.

Relief, swift and comforting, washed over me when the door clicked shut behind him.

I packed two more boxes before retreating to the sofa, where I dropped my head against the cushions and sighed. The movers would be there the next morning, leaving me with little to do besides try to get a decent night's sleep and drive myself to Spruce Hill tomorrow.

This would be the fresh start I should have sought years ago, when Veronica left me practically at the altar.

The only reason I'd stayed at Eastman was because accepting a residency outside the city before the wedding would've tipped off my parents too early. I spent months keeping my plans under wraps to avoid the inevitable blowup as long as possible.

Fat lot of good that did me.

I deserved this move. A new life, a second chance, an escape from Sylvester Thorne's shadow.

Forcing Veronica from my mind allowed the blonde back in. Charlotte, the sassy librarian who couldn't stand doctors, who looked even more gorgeous wearing my leather jacket, who lied to my face about having a black belt in karate.

Charlotte, with glittering green eyes the color of a deep forest, that smart mouth with its perfectly kissable lips, those little flashes of challenge that stirred my blood. Then that horrified look on her face when she blurted she was all mine.

With my apartment packed up and nothing else to occupy my mind, I closed my eyes and let the memories replay. I'd probably never see the woman again, so those memories would have to last a lifetime.

Dammit, I should've at least gotten her number.

Another opportunity missed, but I couldn't turn down the one before me. Everyone at the hospital knew exactly who I was, knew my parents and my past. It hadn't been easy to ignore the gossip, to pretend my family didn't exist, but I'd managed.

Now that I had a chance at something new? I was excited to take it.

Chapter Five

SAWYER

When I finally stood before my new home in Spruce Hill, studying it from the sidewalk out front, I told myself it wasn't so bad. The pictures, obviously taken at least a decade ago, made it seem like it was in slightly better shape, but it was a rental, so it didn't need to be perfect. If I hadn't been in such a rush to find a place, I might've searched harder. The little two bedroom ranch would do for now.

The movers had just left, though I'd had to put some of my furniture into storage until I found a place to buy. Spruce Hill wasn't that far from the city, but the two were different as night and day, including the real estate markets. Even with a slight drop in salary, I could afford a whole lot more in this small town than I could in the city.

There were some new loft apartments and condos being built at one end of town, which I'd considered putting a deposit on, but I wanted to get a feel for the town first. I signed the contract for a year at the clinic—beyond that, I needed to be sure this was the right place for me.

Libby's recommendation of this rental had convinced me to give it a try. Having seen it, though, it didn't seem likely she'd been inside.

Not in recent decades, at least.

The couple who'd lived there since 1976 had just moved into some kind of senior community across town. As far as I could tell, very little had been updated since they first bought this place. Their son, my new landlord, had repeatedly said I was welcome to make any changes I wanted as far as the carpets or paint colors.

Somehow, I doubted a coat of paint would solve the issues, but it'd suffice for now.

The fact that my father would be absolutely horrified by the shag rugs was enough to convince me to give it a shot. While I had appreciated the low maintenance nature of my apartment in the city, my new job would allow for more time to take care of things like a house and a yard.

My gaze drifted to the other houses on this end of the street, settling on the powder blue Victorian whose driveway sat on the other side of a tiny strip of grass beside mine. That was more my style than this little bungalow. It had been years since I'd put any thought into that kind of thing, though—the last time I considered house-hunting had been in the weeks before Veronica broke off our engagement.

I didn't start at the clinic until Monday, so I had plenty of time to get settled in. With one last glance at the house next door, I grabbed the final bag of groceries from my front seat and headed inside.

Once those were put away, I poured myself a glass of whiskey to toast this new direction my life had taken. Twilight fell outside the dining room window as I sipped at my drink and stared out into the yard.

The grass was getting a little long, weeds creeping up along the edge of the driveway. There was a lawnmower in the shed out back, and something in me thrilled at the prospect of mundane chores, of caring for my own space—of having *time* to care about those things.

This would be a positive change, a new life with time for things like homeownership and dating.

For the first time in a very long time, I was ready to look to the future.

B Y THE END OF the weekend, I had managed to make a serious dent in unpacking and organizing the little house. It took several trips to load the trash and recycling bins by the detached garage, just in time for trash night. After a break to eat my leftover takeout from the night before, I headed back out with the cartons to roll the bins to the street.

As I was walking back up the driveway, though, I heard a stream of muttered curses coming from next door. Despite the falling darkness, there were no exterior lights on, so I could barely see where the increasingly profane litany was coming from.

"Excuse me? Do you need some help?" I called, crossing the narrow grass median between our driveways.

The woman gave a startled shriek and tripped over her trash can, crashing straight into my chest as a motion light on the side of the house finally flickered on. I caught her just before she sent us both sprawling to the ground.

For a second, we blinked at each other, squinting in the bright light. Something hard and scratchy hit my ribs and I realized—somewhat belatedly—that it was a black wrist brace.

"Dr. Hottie?" she whispered finally, her green eyes wide with shock.

"Hottie?" I repeated, but my confusion quickly faded as a broad smile stretched across my face. "Mystery Sprain? Now this is a delightful surprise."

Finally, a stroke of luck. What were the chances she not only lived in Spruce Hill, but right next door?

Her expression was priceless, a startled mixture of joy and horror, which I very much hoped was due to her realization that she'd used that particular nickname aloud and not a reaction to seeing me again.

For my part, I was over the moon. At least, I was, until she set her hands to my chest and took a pointed step back.

"What are you doing here?" she asked suspiciously.

I gestured back toward my house. "I just moved in. I took a job working at the clinic in town, actually."

"At the clinic," she repeated. "You're going to work with Libby?"

I swept my gaze over her. She'd been wearing something simple that night at the hospital, leggings and a t-shirt, and tonight I was fairly sure she was in pajamas. Her hair was tied up in a bun, highlighting those green eyes that haunted my memories—though they were narrowed on me like I'd offended her with my very presence.

Noticing my perusal, she crossed her arms over her chest, lifting her breasts against the fabric of her top. I tore my eyes away and focused on her adorable scowl.

"Yes, Libby hired me a couple weeks ago. I start Monday," I said finally, since she'd been waiting for an answer. "You two know each other?"

Charlotte wrinkled her nose at me. "Everyone knows everyone in Spruce Hill."

"I'll take that as a yes."

"Yes. She's my primary and the only doctor I go to if I can help it. She used to babysit me when I was a kid," she replied.

"Huh." The realization that this was probably not such a coincidence began to dawn on me.

"Huh? What does that mean?" she demanded.

"Nothing," I said, lifting my hands in a calming gesture. This pretty librarian looked ready to bite my head off if I put a foot wrong. "Libby suggested this particular rental when I took the job offer, that's all."

I could practically see the steam rising from her head when she growled, "Of course she did."

"She never mentioned you lived next door." I seemed to recall something about quiet neighbors, though. Curiosity struck me as I studied her. "Does *she* know how you sprained your wrist?"

"No, she does not, and I'll be keeping it that way, thank you very much."

My lips twitched. "Interesting. So there is at least one exception to your rule of hating doctors," I mused.

"One, yes."

Charlotte's chin lifted as she said it—she probably meant the gesture in defiance, but I took it as a challenge. Another slow smile spread across my face, though her eyebrows drew immediately downward in response to it.

This was going to be fun.

"Good. I look forward to doubling that number," I said smoothly.

She made a sputtering sound at that, so I cleared my throat to keep from laughing and looked at the trash bin she'd been trying to wrestle down the driveway one-handed.

"I'll take care of this. You're supposed to be resting that wrist, Ms. Whitmore," I called over my shoulder as I wheeled it to the curb. "It's only been three weeks."

When I returned for her recycling, she eyed me cautiously. "You remember when I came in."

I allowed myself a grin once I'd turned away. "I do, yes. It's not every Saturday night that a beautiful woman shows up and refuses to explain an injury, let alone referring to me as *the goddamn doctor.* Most people want to confess their darkest sins to an authority figure, but among those who don't, they generally just lie," I pointed out as I strolled back toward her.

"I've never been a very convincing liar. How do you know Libby?"

"We met at Eastman a few months back."

She nodded. "When Milo got hurt. Right."

"Everyone really does know everyone here, huh?"

"I grew up in the house next door to Libby's husband, Mark. Milo is his brother. And how did you end up working at the clinic?"

"A few weeks before you came in, she reached out to see if she might be able to lure me away from the city, and since I've been in need of a change of scenery, I jumped at the chance."

Charlotte hesitated for a beat. "And she really didn't mention me living here? The hospital sent her a report, so she knew we'd met."

My smile faded. "I swear to you, she did not. I didn't even know you lived in Spruce Hill."

She cocked her head at me for a beat. "Okay. I believe you."

"I looked for you," I admitted. "I thought I'd lost my chance at seeing you again when I left the city."

Those eyes, dark as the deepest forest at midnight, moved over my face before she spoke again. "You wanted to see me again?"

"Very much so."

"Oh."

It was just a tiny breath of sound, but it shot straight through me like an arrow. Maybe it was a trick of the light, but it looked like her body swayed toward me, like maybe she was drawn to me in the same way I was drawn to her.

"I told you you're safe with me, and I meant it. That didn't end when you got into your friend's car, Charlotte. If you live here in Spruce Hill, why were you at Eastman?"

"My friends live in the city. I was there for movie night." Then a grin lit her features more brightly than the motion light. "I've gotten six free meals out of it so far."

"Very impressive. Does that mean your friends had something to do with this mysterious accident?"

"Oh, Doctor, I am far too clever to fall for that little trick," she said, sounding every inch the prim librarian despite wearing what I now saw were flannel pajama pants covered in bluebirds. When she caught the way my gaze dropped to the little birds, she batted her lashes at me. "And now, I have a date with Netflix. Welcome to the neighborhood, Doc."

"It's Sawyer," I called after her as she turned back toward her door.

She was draped in shadows by the time she looked over her shoulder at me. "Welcome to the neighborhood, Sawyer."

Chapter Six

CHARLOTTE

I was still reeling when midnight rolled around. What were the chances?

Penelope was going to flip when she found out about this. She and Grisham had been teasing me almost nonstop about putting my foot in my mouth in front of the hottest doctor on the planet.

The second they saw him in person, it was over.

I couldn't believe he moved in next door to me. It was either a sign from the universe or my worst nightmare come true. Something about him had me blurting out all sorts of embarrassing truths—what if I couldn't keep a lid on that?

The house beside mine had been empty since Mr. and Mrs. McCallum went into some kind of senior housing earlier this year. Their son, Lee, owned a gorgeous house in the next town with his husband, so he only came by to mow the lawn, except when he was able to get one of the teenagers down the street to take care of it. I'd been enjoying my little bubble here at the end of the dead end street for months, and I still wasn't completely sure how to feel about Dr. Hottie moving in next door.

"His name is Sawyer," I said aloud.

Spoon twitched at the sound of my voice, but he didn't stir from where he lay draped across my lap. I stroked his floppy ears and stared up at the ceiling, thinking about the way Sawyer's eyes had coasted over me in my ridiculous pajamas.

The weird part wasn't him looking, though. It was the way that pale blue went a little molten, even when his gaze caught on the silly bluebirds.

He'd looked *interested,* just like at the hospital when I blurted out that I was single.

Oh, god. I hadn't given another thought to him being a serial killer after he waited with me for Pen to show up that night, but now he knew exactly where I lived.

What if I was wrong?

No, that was impossible. Libby was the best judge of character I'd ever known. If anyone could sniff out a serial killer who also happened to be a drop dead gorgeous doctor, it would be her. She'd hired him, so she must have been sure he could be trusted.

"Come on, Spoon. It's time for bed."

I carried the sleeping puppy upstairs, set him gently into his crate at my bedside, and climbed under the covers. There was more to life than ogling smoking hot doctors, but surely a little idle fantasy never hurt anybody?

Because hot *damn*—Dr. Sawyer Thorne could inspire a lifetime of fantasies.

IT WASN'T REALLY SHOCKING that I didn't run into Sawyer during the days that followed, even if he lived next door. I'd be the first to admit I was a consummate homebody. Even that fateful movie night at Pen and Grisham's place had been the exception rather than the rule. I'd only ended up there because I knew Spoon would be coming up from a rural shelter down south the following week, which effectively shifted movie nights to my house for a while.

The only surprise was that I was actually *disappointed* by not seeing him. Not even a glimpse of shirtless lawn mowing.

Not that I'd been harboring *that* fantasy since the minute we ran into each other again.

Still, with a book sale coming up and a calendar of events to prepare for at the library, my days were busier than usual. In a rare moment of free time, I remembered my plan to conduct further research on the list of businesses from the book returns, but then a third-grader needed my help finding the next installment in his favorite series, and it fell to the back of my mind again.

Finally, on Thursday morning, I stepped out of my house at the exact moment Sawyer exited his. Across the width of the driveways, our eyes met and held, locking me in place. My pulse kicked into overdrive and a tingle zipped along my skin.

"Good morning, Charlotte."

What was it about the way he said my name? That low, commanding rumble reverberated inside me as I fought down a shiver. "Good morning, Sawyer."

He didn't move any closer, but his grin flashed in the morning sun. "How's the wrist?"

"It's fine." I kicked myself for the stupid answer. "How's the clinic?"

"Wonderful, actually. I'm still settling in, but I think I'm going to really enjoy my time in Spruce Hill."

The words were benign enough, but they sounded almost—flirty? My eyebrows drew down as I tried to interpret what he might have meant by that statement, and Sawyer shook his head, still smiling.

"I need to get to work. Enjoy your day, Charlotte."

"You too," I mumbled, watching him slip into his subtle-but-expensive silver car.

All the way to the library, I cursed my unending curiosity—and my inexplicable disappointment over not running into him sooner—for tempting fate and causing that awkward interaction.

The next evening, Penelope was supposed to meet me for a drink at The Mermaid, a trendy restaurant and bar on Main

Street about three blocks from my house, while Spoon spent the night at the vet after being neutered. I was already sitting at the bar, sipping something that was a more vibrant shade of blue than could be found in nature, when Pen texted to say she got stuck at work and wouldn't make it.

After banging my forehead against the gleaming wood in front of me, I sat back upright just in time to see Sawyer walk through the doors with Libby and her husband, Mark.

Libby waved and whispered something in Sawyer's ear before he made a beeline toward me, but she and Mark followed the hostess over to a table in the far corner instead of joining us at the bar. I narrowed my eyes at the pair of them, then an unfairly hot doctor filled my view.

"Hey there, Mystery Sprain. This seat taken?"

"My friend just canceled on me, so it's all yours," I replied, waving magnanimously.

He sat beside me, ordered the evening's special small batch IPA from the bartender, then reached out and brushed his thumb across my forehead. I stared at him in shock until he dropped his hand.

"You were hitting your head when I came in. Just making sure you didn't injure yourself again," he said with a broad grin that threw me completely off balance. When he saw my expression, probably looking as dazed as I felt, he smirked. "What? Do I have something on my face?"

"No," I said slowly, "you just...this is a far cry from the stern doctor routine I got from you at the hospital."

Sawyer thanked the bartender when she slid his drink across the gleaming surface of the bar and tipped his head at me, flashing a sinful smile. "Oh, you mean Dr. Hottie? Or was it *the goddamn doctor?* It's hard to keep them all straight, and now you're adding Stern Doctor to the mix?"

I flushed at the reminder that I'd called him Dr. Hottie right to his face when he startled me in the driveway the other night.

"Though I suppose they're not mutually exclusive, depending on your particular tastes," he added.

Attempting to control my expression, I drew in a long, slow breath, then admitted, "You were a bit of both, to be perfectly honest."

I did not add that my *particular tastes* appreciated both traits equally, but he seemed to read it in my face. The heat blossoming in my cheeks threatened to set us both on fire, along with the bar itself.

Another fabulous headline: *Local librarian ignites latest blaze with her humiliation.*

"You liked Stern Doctor, did you?" he asked, looking very interested in my answer.

"I'm afraid I can't dignify that with a response."

He flashed a grin before taking a drink. "Another mystery, I see. So your friend canceled on you—the same friend who didn't come pick you up at the hospital?"

I made a face. "Yes, Penelope. I love her to death but she's not the most reliable person I know. I was already here, though, so I figured I'd finish my drink before I head home."

"Well, I'm sorry to crash your party."

"Are you?" I asked, arching a brow. "You were pretty quick to ditch Libby over there."

"No, I'm not sorry at all." His smile widened, shifting him from stern to scorching. "Every time I run into you feels like fate is moving me around like a little chess piece."

"That's not fate, it's just life in a small town. You'll get used to it eventually."

He laughed, the sound rough but soft as velvet. "Well, I appreciate your neighborly insights, Charlotte. So, you said you're a librarian. Here in town?"

"Yup. The library is just up the street."

"Is that what you always wanted to do for a career?"

Maybe it should've seemed nosy, but instead, he just sounded curious. "Yes, pretty much. Books are my refuge. What about you, did you always want to be a doctor?"

"No." A shadow crossed his eyes before clearing. "I wanted to be an astronaut until I turned thirteen."

I grinned. "Did you really?"

"Yup. But my father is a surgeon and by the time I hit high school, it was clear there was no other path he'd approve of. I love what I do, don't get me wrong, but it's hard to tell, looking back, how much of it was what I wanted and how much was what I was told to do."

"I'm sorry," I said softly.

"Don't be. I wouldn't have met you if I'd been up in space."

Laughter bubbled up from my chest. "Very true. How do you like working with Libby?"

His expression shifted, revealing a deep kind of contentment that stretched across the space between us. "It's been amazing. I think this new job, the new town, will both be a wonderful change for me."

"Is she as big a pain in your ass as she is mine?"

"Not at all," he replied, laughing. "She's been great. I'm definitely not going to complain that the house she suggested led me to seeing you again, Charlotte."

Heat crept along my cheeks again and I tried to brush it off with a joke. "Yeah, you could've done worse in the neighbor department."

"Much worse," he agreed. "Besides, after watching you wrestle that trash can, I think you need a closer eye on your activities while you're supposed to be taking it easy."

"I can take care of myself, you know."

"I absolutely believe that. But you're really not going to tell me how you sprained that wrist?"

Maybe it was the bright turquoise alcohol edging into my bloodstream, maybe it was that reckless smile on a face that had looked so serious in our first encounter. Whatever the cause, I leaned in so that my breath brushed his ear and whispered, "Not in public."

Those pale blue eyes sharpened on my face. "Is that an invitation, Charlotte?"

Something about my name in that low rumble sent a delicious quiver through me. I held his gaze for the span of a heartbeat, then another, and nodded. I was almost never impulsive when it came to humans—agreeing to take in a puppy or two at a moment's notice, maybe, but not relationships and certainly not sex.

"Yes, I think it is," I said.

Those crystal blue eyes heated, scanning my face for a moment, then he rapped his knuckles on the bar. "Let's get out of here, then."

Then reality sunk in, just a little bit, and I corrected, "An invitation to join me for dessert at my place. Not for sex. I mean, not a hookup. That is—"

His gaze shot to mine as I slapped my hand over my mouth to contain the ridiculous tumble of words trying to escape.

"Duly noted, though now I have to wonder why you think that would be my assumption."

My confidence faltered and I looked back at the neon blue drink in front of me, though I could still feel his gaze on my face. I bit my lip in silence.

"Charlotte," he murmured, leaning toward me. "Tell me what you're thinking."

"I can't."

It was the truth. I felt tongue-tied and awkward, like I'd taken my shot and missed by a mile.

"Were *you* thinking about a hookup?" he asked finally. His expression was gentle, but his eyes were still molten when I finally made myself glance his way.

"Maybe. Yes." *Fuck my life.*

"Just now? Or at the hospital that night?"

My face felt ready to catch fire again. "Both."

"I need you to listen very carefully. I'm interested in you. Very much so."

My body jerked in surprise. "You are?"

"Of course. I told you I hoped to see you again, because I'm the idiot who didn't give you my number before you left that night. But while I'd be tempted to take you up on the offer of something casual, if you made it, I think it might be a mistake."

I flinched and dropped my gaze. "Oh."

His fingertips brushed my chin, lifting my eyes back to meet his. "Because I think we have the potential for more and I don't want to blow my chances by encouraging less."

"More," I repeated.

"Yes. Much more."

I couldn't tear my eyes away from his, captivated by what I saw there. "Oh."

His lips twitched. "So I think it's important that we take our time, get to know each other first. I work with Libby, you two are friends, we're now neighbors. Those are complications that suggest proceeding with caution so I don't fuck things up for you."

For me. Not for himself. Something about that was immensely comforting.

"Okay." I blew out a breath. "So...dessert?"

"Dessert. Is that your first drink tonight?"

I blinked at him. "Yes. It's not very good, actually. Why? Do I sound drunk?"

"No, though you do have an endearing tendency to blurt out things I'm not sure you mean to say aloud. Some people do it when they're under the influence, but it seems to be standard for you."

"No kidding," I muttered, but his rumbled laugh made me feel somewhat better.

"Did you drive over here?" he asked, motioning to the bartender for his check. When he had her add my drink to his tab, I opened my mouth to protest, but one of his Stern Doctor looks shut me up.

Remembering that he'd asked a question, I said, "No, I walked. Didn't you come here with Libby and Mark? They won't mind if you leave?"

"Good. I walked over, too. Libby's directive when we came in and saw you was something along the lines of 'do me a favor and make sure Charlotte gets home okay.' Somehow, I don't think they'll miss me."

"That conniving little sneak."

When I turned my glare back toward their table, both Libby and Mark studiously avoided my gaze. I didn't have time to dwell on wondering why, exactly, she thought she could play matchmaker with me and this gorgeous man before I felt him moving at my side.

"I'm not sure I'd be brave enough to call her that to her face, but I'm also not complaining if she's the driving force behind me finding you again," he said, lips quirking.

"Oh." Warmth crept up from my belly, as though I'd sucked down the entirety of the neon blue liquid in my glass.

He tucked several bills into the vinyl folder the bartender had left, stood, and held out his hand to help me down. I took a second to study him, from the sincerity in his eyes to the smile tugging at one corner of his lips.

This might be a mistake—in fact, it probably was—but sometimes too much peace and quiet was counterproductive.

I took a deep breath and laid my hand in his.

Chapter Seven

SAWYER

CHARLOTTE WAS NERVOUS.

No matter how sure she'd sounded, her entire body radiated anxiety as we walked the three blocks home. Her shoulders curled inward, her steps floundered enough that she tripped over a crack in the sidewalk at least twice, and every trace of the talkative woman from the bar faded into silence. Whether she was wary of men in general or me specifically, I couldn't quite tell, but the overwhelming desire to earn her trust hit me straight in the chest.

I didn't want to make a scene on the sidewalk, especially when I was new in town and every one of our neighbors had probably known her since childhood, so I didn't stop walking when I leaned down to murmur in her ear.

"You are safe with me. Always."

Her green eyes, almost black in the twilight, lifted to mine. With her left wrist still encased in the splint, she held my hand with her right, and I squeezed her fingers in reassurance. After a second, her face lit with a brilliant smile.

"I believe you," she said. "I don't know why, but I guess I do. I figure Libby would have suspected something if you were a serial killer."

A laugh burst from my throat. "If you thought I might even *possibly* be a serial killer, you sure as shit shouldn't have invited me over for dessert. Christ, you shouldn't have stuck around with me that first night, either."

She hummed a little and shrugged. "I like to live dangerously, what can I say?"

"Do you really?" I replied, smirking at her.

"No. Not at all."

I burst out laughing and she grinned up at me.

Tonight's outfit was different from the first two times we'd met, a twirly dress that looked like something from decades long past. Yesterday morning had been something similar, though I hadn't had time to appreciate it. If this was her work wardrobe, I committed myself to lingering in my doorway like a creep in order to catch her every morning. The skirt was full, swishing outward from the generous curve of her hips, and it wasn't until we passed under a streetlight that I noticed there were little books printed across the fabric.

"This dress is absolute perfection," I told her.

I could have sworn she inserted a bit more sway into her step so the skirt brushed against my leg with each stride. "It's a favorite of mine."

"I can see why."

We're just having dessert, I reminded myself when my palms itched to slide up her bare legs and under those layers of fabric.

The neckline was modest, but it exposed her collarbones almost all the way to her shoulders. Her hair was twisted up into a knot, and under the street lamps, I caught a peek of a crescent moon tattoo just below the nape of her neck.

"Don't get too used to it," she replied. "I like to play up the book theme for work, but usually I dress for comfort. I only wore this tonight instead of yoga pants because I was supposed to meet Penelope and didn't have time to change after work before heading out again."

"I quite liked the bluebird pants, anyway," I said, grinning when she rolled her eyes at me.

When we got to her door, she reached into a pocket hidden within the folds of the skirt and pulled out her keys. I followed her inside, slipped off my shoes on the mat where she left her simple black flats, and tried very, *very* hard to stop ogling her when she skipped up the three stairs to the kitchen in front of me.

"Watch out for dog toys. I would have picked up if I'd known company was coming," she said over her shoulder.

"You have a dog?" I asked.

The house was completely silent around us and I wondered what kind of dog didn't greet its owner at the door. She gestured for me to sit at the small table by the kitchen window, where a tiny bud vase holding a sprig of hyacinths perched on the sill, their soft aroma drifting throughout the room.

"I'm fostering a puppy, but he was neutered today and is staying overnight. There was a little more bleeding than they expected, so the vet wanted to keep an eye on him. His name is Spoon."

"Spoon," I repeated. This woman never ceased to mystify me.

I watched as she removed the brace from her wrist, washed her hands and the lower half of her left forearm at the kitchen sink, and dried her skin with a towel. From where I sat, I didn't see any bruising and the swelling appeared to have gone down. When she tossed the towel aside, I gave a low hum and crooked my finger at her.

"It feels mostly better. Just twinges now and then if I reach for something too quickly," she said as she came toward me. "I haven't had time for PT, but I found some exercises online."

"That's good. That was where I looked for you, you know," I replied as I took her hand in mine and gently inspected her range of motion before running two fingers along the injured area.

"You did?"

I hummed a confirmation. "I made excuses to walk by the physical therapy suite, hoping I might see you again."

"What if you had?"

"I would have remedied the fact that we didn't exchange contact information, right after I asked you to dinner."

Her pulse jumped against my fingertips. Though I knew I should let go of her, she shifted closer and hope flared inside me. Instead of releasing her hand, I bent down to press a featherlight kiss to the delicate skin of her wrist.

A sigh ghosted past her lips when I lifted my head again. I studied her face for a moment, gauging her reaction. Pink crept along her cheekbones and her eyes had turned a deep forest green.

"Your eyes change color. It's incredible."

As I'd intended, it gently broke the fragile bubble of intimacy. I wasn't ready to face the intensity of the attraction between us, and I wasn't convinced she was, either. The only thing I could do was give us time—after all, it was only my first week in Spruce Hill. I couldn't risk antagonizing not only my new neighbor, but my new boss as well.

"My mom always called them mood ring eyes," she replied, her tone light but the words just breathless enough to assure me she wasn't immune to this pull.

"Fascinating," I murmured.

Her blush deepened as she cleared her throat. "I have chocolate or strawberry ice cream, which do you prefer?"

"I'll have whatever you're having." I sat back as she pulled the cartons from the freezer.

"Then I hope you appreciate the decadence of a scoop of each," she teased. "With chocolate sprinkles on top."

Though she managed to get bowls down from the cupboards without an issue, the sprinkles were tucked away on a higher shelf, requiring her to stretch up on her tiptoes. I told myself that I jumped into action to keep her from leaning any weight on her wrist, which was likely still too weak to support her, but as soon as I was standing behind her to lift the container down, I knew it wasn't true.

She froze as my hand settled lightly at her waist, then her body swayed back against mine as I reached up to grab the container and set the sprinkles on the counter. When the full curve of her backside pressed into my groin, my grip tightened and I growled against her ear.

"You are a dangerous little thing."

She laughed, barely more than a swift exhalation, and turned to face me, still caught between my body and the counter. "I don't think I'm the one who's dangerous," she replied.

"You want me."

It was a statement—I had no doubt of her desire, not anymore—but Charlotte held my gaze for a long moment before responding. "Yes."

"And I want you. More than I've wanted anything in a very long time. But we shouldn't rush into this."

The reminder was more for myself than for her.

When her expression dimmed slightly, losing that dazed flare of lust that I found absolutely intoxicating, I felt a pang of regret. I dropped my forehead to hers, trying to regain some semblance of self-control.

"You're right," she said, placing her hands against my chest until there was space between us again. "So let's enjoy our dessert."

"And then it's story time," I reminded her.

With a dramatic sigh, she scooped the ice cream, spooned on the sprinkles, and handed me a bowl. "You might be disappointed, you know."

"Never."

Her expression was still skeptical once we were seated at the table, so I decided to break the ice before asking her to reveal her secrets.

"So Libby is the one doctor you like. Now that I've gotten to know her, I see why."

Charlotte's eyes narrowed. "Yes, she's the exception."

A grin crept across my face. "And yet here I sit, treated to a decadent bowl of ice cream. With *sprinkles*. Does that make me an exception too?"

"You," she said, pointing her spoon at me, "are a menace."

"Come on, Charlotte, you can tell me the truth," I cajoled.

She looked grumpier and more adorable by the second. "Have you ever told a woman to lose weight? To reassess her diet and exercise even if she came to you for a problem completely unrelated to her weight?"

"No. Studies have shown that being overweight is not a sole indicator of poor health. Blanket recommendations like that in healthcare can be very damaging. Every patient has individual needs and healthy norms."

"Then I guess you're an exception, too."

Even after she pointedly turned her attention to her bowl, I studied her carefully. She was beautiful and vibrant and yes, curvy and full-figured. "You're gorgeous and I hate the thought of anyone telling you that you need to change because of their own bias."

The blush in her cheeks deepened, but she shrugged it off like she didn't believe me.

Challenge accepted.

It might not happen tonight, but I *would* convince Charlotte Whitmore of just how outrageously attracted to her I truly was.

We finished the ice cream without any mention of her injury, so I leaned back and laced my hands behind my head, waiting patiently for her to speak.

"Fine," she groused. "You want a story? Here it is. My friend Penelope just started dating this woman who's around my height, though she's very petite. Pen bought some fuzzy pink bondage cuffs and wanted to make sure they'd work for Clara."

"Fuzzy pink—okay," I said, blinking in surprise. This was not anywhere close to what I'd expected her to say.

"We were supposed to be having a movie night, but while we waited for her roommate to get back with dinner, she asked if

I'd help her test the cuffs out so she didn't make a fool of herself in front of her girlfriend."

My lips parted at the images supplied by my imagination. "Go on."

Charlotte scowled. "Well, Pen broke a nail and left me with only one wrist attached to her bed frame while she went to fix it. Then her roommate, our other friend Grisham, came home with the takeout."

"And?"

"And when he spotted me cuffed to Pen's bed, he thought it was a good opportunity to tickle me. I yanked my arm trying to twist away, and..." She gestured vaguely toward her wrist.

The picture of Charlotte bound to a bed with fuzzy handcuffs melted away as I recalled examining the injury, her delicate flesh bruised and swollen. I forced the memory away, focusing on the way she sank her teeth into her lower lip while waiting for my response.

I studied her closely. "Are you interested in bondage like your friend, Charlotte?"

"I've never really tried it," she admitted, the words tumbling out like she couldn't stop them.

"But you want to?" I guessed.

I heard the hitch in her breath, saw that sweet blush spreading across her cheeks and chest—I wanted to explore just how far it stretched. Her lips parted as the tip of her tongue peeked out and I swallowed back a groan.

"Yes. I read a lot of that kind of stuff. I just...I've never been with someone I trusted to know what they're doing."

Reaching across the table, I took her hand and stroked my thumb over her knuckles. "I see. Do you trust me, Charlotte?"

"Are you—I mean, do you know what you're doing? With bondage?"

"Yes, I do." I held her gaze as I said it, then repeated softly, "Do you trust me?"

A sigh whispered over her lips, then she swallowed hard. "I'd like to."

"Good," I replied, squeezing her hand. That was more honesty than I'd expected. "Then we'll work on building that trust as we get to know each other. Trust is vital when it comes to that kind of play."

"Trust is hard for me," she admitted.

A small smile tugged at my lips. "I gathered that. But why exactly didn't you want to tell me how you got hurt at the hospital?"

For a long, drawn-out moment, she was silent, then she lifted her chin. "You were all stern and disapproving already. I was afraid if I explained it, you'd lecture me on safe bondage play and I'd die of embarrassment, looking like an even bigger idiot than I already did."

"Oh, Charlotte," I drawled, unable to resist when she was looking at me like that, like she was throwing down a gauntlet that would lead to the most pleasurable contest imaginable.

"You couldn't look like an idiot if you tried, and I wouldn't have lectured you."

"No?" she asked incredulously.

That sass nearly crumbled the last of my resistance, so I tugged her hand until we were both leaning across the tabletop, our faces only inches apart. Heat flared in her eyes even as her grip on my fingers tightened.

"Of course not," I whispered. "But once you were officially no longer my patient, I definitely would have offered to demonstrate."

Chapter Eight

CHARLOTTE

All the air in my lungs escaped with an audible whoosh at those words, low and rumbly and full of temptation. Only a rim of pale blue still showed in his eyes—the rest was all pupil, dilated wide as he gazed steadily back at me.

This felt like some kind of test, a line in the sand, and his words echoed back inside my head.

We shouldn't rush into this.

I hated that he was right. Dating in Spruce Hill was hard enough, given that running into an ex around our small town was all but inevitable. Avoiding Brent had taken a whole lot of maneuvering for nearly six months until he learned to stay out of my way. With Sawyer's new job in the mix, that made it even more risky to explore this attraction between us without forethought, along with the fact he was living next door.

At that moment, though, I wanted to toss caution to the wind, throw myself into his arms, and let the chips fall where they may.

God, his *do you trust me* echoed in my brain like a ping pong ball.

Was I that transparent? Could he tell I had those hangups Brent left me with? I understood the importance of trust in kink situations, having read plenty about it in books, but this seemed deeper, like he wanted me to trust him on a more personal level.

And I wanted to give him that.

I'd never tried any kind of bondage before. The extent of my experience was listening to Penelope's exploits secondhand and my extensive reading history. I didn't know what it was about this man—the stern demeanor from the hospital, the strength he exuded from every pore, the strange fact that I *did* trust that I was safe with him—but the dark promise in his voice made every nerve ending tingle.

I clenched my thighs together beneath the table, fighting the rush of desire that only intensified with every second in his presence.

The knowledge that he was right about moving slow should have lessened the potential sting of rejection. Instead, it was the fact that he'd straight up told me he wanted me that was the real balm, though I was still annoyed by the idea of waiting. Before I could grumble at him, though, he nodded toward my left arm.

"That wrist needs a full recovery, first of all," he said, one corner of his mouth tilting upward. "I won't do anything to risk your health or safety."

My response was an indignant *hmph,* which only made his smile widen. Then he lifted our joined hands to brush his lips slowly across my knuckles, and my breath stalled in my lungs.

"In the meantime, are you free on Sunday? Maybe we could have lunch together."

I blinked at him. "Yes. Sure."

His grin was almost a smirk, like he enjoyed his effect on me. Hell, I enjoyed his effect on me, so I couldn't really complain. When he turned my hand over to press a kiss to the inside of my wrist again, everything inside of me tightened with anticipation.

"I'll come get you around noon. Your choice of restaurant. I'll need your local expertise to introduce me to the best spots."

"I—okay."

He winked at me. "Good. It's a date."

Once he'd released my hand, we both stood, and I busied myself with putting the bowls into the dishwasher. He waited until I turned to him again before holding out one hand, palm up. I took a single step closer, then another, and laid my hand in his.

Each movement he made was slow and measured as he drew me closer to his body, giving me every chance to protest or pull away, but I desperately wanted to press up against him.

"I'd like to kiss you goodnight, if you're okay with that." His voice was low, hypnotic.

I shivered but nodded quickly—probably too quickly, if his wry smile was any indication.

Without another word, he lowered his head, brushing his nose along the edge of my jaw before his lips captured mine. It started off light, not tentative but sweet and searching. When my fingers clutched at the front of his t-shirt, he growled into my mouth and hooked his hand around the small of my back, pressing my entire body flush against his.

Any doubts that he wanted this as much as I did were erased as my hips ground into the hard length of him behind his zipper.

By the time we came up for breath, I was convinced he'd just ruined me. Not in the Regency heroine sense, obviously, but I'd never even *liked* kissing all that much.

Now? The bar was forever raised.

My pulse skittered wildly. My skin felt heated and I was sure my lips were swollen. My whole body radiated need, thrumming with it.

"Dangerous," he whispered, the word wafting across my flushed cheeks.

With obvious effort, he stepped back. The hand that had been on my back squeezed my hip as he moved away, like he needed one last caress before the connection was broken. My chest heaved as though I'd run for miles rather than just soaking up this man's intense dedication.

"Thank you for dessert, Charlotte."

I didn't think I'd ever get used to my name on his lips, the soft purr of it in his deep voice. My own quavered slightly as I said, "You're very welcome, Sawyer."

As I led him down the stairs to the side door, he reached out and brushed one fingertip over the moon inked at the top of my back. This dress didn't display any cleavage, but I felt naked in the most delicious way possible when he touched my bare skin. I expected him to comment on the tattoo, maybe, or to lean in and taste it the way his expression said he wanted to when I turned to face him.

Instead, he let his hand fall and took another deliberate step onto the driveway. "Goodnight," he said softly.

I had to clear my throat before I could return the sentiment, then he headed toward the side door of his house and disappeared inside. If not for the rapid drum of my heartbeat and the way I could still feel his mouth on my own, I might have thought I'd dreamed the entire evening.

Sawyer's car was still parked in the driveway when I got home from the vet the next morning with Spoon, who was eager to return to his usual puppy antics. I lifted him down from the back seat, awkwardly clutching a cone of shame under my other arm.

"You leave those stitches alone or you'll have to wear this," I warned him. "And no jumping."

"Will the humiliations never cease?" lamented a deep voice from next door.

I turned with a smile, but it fell away when I saw Sawyer lounging against the doorframe wearing nothing but a pair of gray cotton pants that hung loosely from his hips. When I realized his lawn was freshly mowed, I almost swore aloud that I'd missed my chance to see it. On the other hand...

Holy. Shit.

The man was glorious, lean and sculpted through the chest and shoulders. His belly was a little soft, which only made me like him more, and the curling hair across his chest shone almost golden in the morning light.

"This must be Spoon," he said, straightening to walk toward us. "How old is he?"

Forcing myself to stop gaping at his bare chest, I replied, "Almost ten weeks."

To my surprise, Sawyer knelt down in the grass beside the puppy in order to keep him from jumping up for attention, presenting me with the broad muscles of his back and shoulders.

More fodder for my daydreams.

"Don't jump, little guy, you'll tear your stitches. What a cutie you are," cooed the stern doctor, carefully rubbing Spoon's belly when the puppy rolled over. I blinked in surprise, but when Sawyer shot me a boyish grin over his shoulder, everything inside me went gooey and soft. "What? I love dogs."

"He'll be up for adoption soon."

Sawyer flashed a regretful smile. "I don't think I can handle a puppy quite yet. My schedule here is much better than at the hospital, but I know how much work puppies can be. He deserves a family that won't have to crate him all day."

"I understand completely. One of the library volunteers runs a doggy daycare in town, so they let me bring my fosters over while I'm at work for a hefty discount. It works out perfectly."

"Daycare, huh?" he mused, carefully prying Spoon's sharp puppy teeth away from his hand. "I hadn't thought of that. How long have you been fostering?"

I leaned back against the hood of my car, watching the two of them. At least, I pretended to watch them both, but my focus was drawn back to Sawyer's muscles shifting as he played with the puppy. "Almost six years."

Sawyer lifted his head to smile at me. "Aren't you tempted to keep them?"

"I did, once."

Interpreting my expression correctly, Sawyer stood. His eyes softened with such sympathy that my chest ached. "I'm sorry, Charlotte."

"It was a long time ago. My dad had just died, which was its own kind of mess for me to deal with, and this senior dog came up with the transport. He had a congenital heart defect. We knew it was unlikely anyone would adopt him, so he lived out his last few months with me." I swallowed down the memories, along with the tears threatening to break free.

"I'm sorry about your father, too, then," he said gently.

I shook my head. "The world's better off without him. Angus was the true loss."

Sawyer looked like he wanted to ask questions, but he seemed suddenly aware of his state of undress. Glancing down at his bare feet, he gave a rueful smile. "I swear I wasn't watching out the window for you to get home."

"Liar," I muttered.

He laughed, his face lighting up with it, and I just barely managed to catch Spoon in my free arm before he jumped to try to lick Sawyer's face.

"I should get him inside. Have a good afternoon, Sawyer."

Before I stepped around him, though, he lifted his hand to cup my cheek. He didn't move in to kiss me, which was both a relief and a tragedy, just swept his gaze over my features as though trying to memorize my face.

"I'll see you tomorrow for lunch," he said softly, letting his thumb brush across my lower lip.

A tremor ran through me at the barely-there caress. "I'll be here."

With one final ear scratch for Spoon, Sawyer smiled again and strolled back to his house. I didn't bother to glance away from the muscles of his back, watching intently as a pair of delicious dimples peeked out just above the waistband of his pants. By the time he turned back to wave before going inside, my face was aflame.

If his expression was any indication, he didn't miss that fact.

"We are in big trouble," I whispered to the wriggly puppy tucked under my arm. "Very, very big trouble."

Chapter Nine

SAWYER

WITH ABOUT TWO MINUTES to spare, I showed up at her door on Sunday, trying to remember the last time I'd been so nervous before taking a woman out.

Never. I'd *never* felt this strange clutch of anxiety before a date.

Then again, I hadn't had the time or desire to actually date after the fiasco with Veronica. In the years that passed, I kept strictly to short flings or one-night stands, unwilling to lead myself into another situation like our engagement. Most of the women I'd been with hadn't even known I was a doctor, and they certainly hadn't learned who my father was.

Everything was different this time around.

Before I lifted my hand to knock, the door swung open. Charlotte stood before me in a lightweight sage sweater that brought out her eyes and a pair of black dress pants. Her hair fell in loose waves around her shoulders.

"Hi," she breathed.

My lips curved into a smile. "Hi. You look beautiful."

I didn't miss the way her eyelashes swept downward as she turned to lock the door, nor the pretty pink flush in her cheeks. Maybe she wasn't used to being complimented.

I'd take care of that.

"Where are we headed today?" I asked, leading her toward my car.

"The Mermaid. You didn't get to try their food on Friday, and it's my favorite restaurant in town."

I opened the passenger door for her, but before she could slip past me, I brushed my thumb over the color highlighting her cheekbone. "I'm looking forward to it."

Her lips parted, then she hurried to slide into the seat.

Baby steps. I could do that. However long it took to win her trust, I was prepared to work for it.

The drive to the restaurant was over practically before it began, but the day was chilly enough that I wasn't going to suggest we walk. Besides, once we were shut together in my car, her soft floral scent wafted over me like a harbinger of the warmer weather promised by the local forecast.

She opened her door the minute I parked in the lot beside the restaurant, but she didn't pull away when I curled my hand around hers. Once we passed by the mermaid statues guarding the front entrance, I shifted my hand to the small of her back and she leaned into my touch as we followed the hostess to a booth.

While I studied the menu, I felt her gaze on my face and lifted my eyes to meet hers. "What's your favorite thing here?"

"Dessert," she said, then bit her lip like she was remembering our conversation from the bar on Friday.

"You like sweet things, do you?"

A shaky breath trembled past her lips. "Sometimes."

She made me want to throw caution to the wind, but I clenched my fist beneath the table and reminded myself not to rush things.

"Should we skip lunch and just get dessert, then?" I asked.

"Absolutely not," she replied immediately. "The stuffed mushrooms are almost as good as the desserts. And the truffle parmesan fries are to die for."

The server returned to take our orders, and the conversation shifted to local history when I noticed some of the artwork lining the walls. Even though I'd grown up less than an hour from this town, I'd never heard any of the stories Charlotte told throughout the meal—from pirates on the Erie Canal to rum-runners during Prohibition, the role this area played in the Underground Railroad to the tragic tales haunting the Spruce Hill Lighthouse.

I'd never been so attracted to the cadence of a woman's voice before. The underlying enthusiasm in the way she shared knowledge was as much a turn-on as the excitement sparkling in her emerald eyes.

By the time we finished our desserts—strawberry shortcake for her and cheesecake for me, though we stole bites from each other's plates—I knew there'd be no avoiding this thing that was blooming between us.

Afterward, Charlotte needed to get home to check on Spoon and keep him from getting too rambunctious as he healed, so I walked her to the side door, wondering all the while if she wanted me to kiss her again before I left her there.

I didn't have to wonder for long.

She turned, dropped her gaze for a split second before sweeping those long lashes back up, and lifted up on her toes to kiss me. I let her take the lead this time, resting my hands lightly on her hips as she treated me to a kiss sweeter than any dessert I'd tasted.

When she drew away, her cheeks were pink again and her eyes hazy. I wanted to follow her inside and explore her flushed skin, but I forced myself to step back.

"Dinner this week?" I suggested, my voice low and rougher than intended.

Her nod was immediate. "I'll check my calendar and let you know when I'm free."

I couldn't help it—I dropped my head to brush my lips over hers one last time, then said, "Good. I look forward to it."

Slowly, reluctantly, I stepped backward toward my own house as she let herself inside and threw one last smile over her shoulder.

Dangerous.

The word bounced around inside my mind throughout the rest of the day and straight into Monday morning as I drove to the clinic. I was standing by the front desk after updating charts for my last couple appointments when my gaze caught on the newspaper lying on the counter.

I hadn't picked up the Spruce Hill Gazette since moving in—I was actually shocked the town had a newspaper still in circulation—but a headline about a fire at an old warehouse in town caught my eye. No one was injured, but the building was a total loss.

Maybe there *was* enough going on in Spruce Hill to warrant a newspaper.

"How are you holding up?" Libby asked as she appeared at my shoulder, a bright smile on her lips. "Enjoying small town life?"

"So far, so good. I'm treated to a lot more gossip here than in the city, though. This morning alone, I've heard more juicy tales about who's sneaking around with which neighbor than if I spent an afternoon watching soap operas."

She laughed. "You better get used to that. Word travels fast around here. Speaking of neighbors..."

"Yes, please, let's talk about neighbors."

"How's the house?" she asked brightly.

"I wondered when you'd get around to bringing this up. Surely you're not meddling in the affairs of mere mortals, Dr. Bardot?"

"Who, me?" She pressed a hand to her chest and batted her lashes.

I narrowed my eyes at her, but her grin only widened. "Did you know we'd met when you suggested the rental?"

"I might have seen your name on the report the hospital sent over," she hedged. "The owner of the house is Aaron's husband, and since Aaron is my best friend's brother, I liked the idea of keeping it in the family."

Aaron was one of the nurses at the clinic. Though I knew he lived in Oakville with his husband, I hadn't realized that husband was my new landlord.

Small town life really would take some getting used to.

"So I promise Charlotte wasn't the only reason I suggested it. But I figured both of you could use a decent neighbor, right?" Libby asked, looking like the very picture of innocence.

"Uh huh."

She patted my shoulder when Aaron gestured to room two, where her next patient was waiting. "You'll benefit from having someone who knows the town inside and out right next door, and Charlotte will have someone to keep an eye out for her. It works out great for everyone."

I rolled my eyes at her, but I was still smiling when I walked in to greet my next appointment.

"Mr. Rockford? I'm Dr. Thorne, it's a pleasure to meet you."

The older man huffed a laugh that turned into a cough, though he recovered before I reached his side. "Please, call me David. Nice to have some new faces around here."

As I ran through my exam, he regaled me with stories about Spruce Hill's history that even Charlotte hadn't mentioned—probably because he'd lived through them and she hadn't. He told me about having to drive half an hour or more for stitches for one of his grandchildren after old Doc Hawkins retired, emphasizing every few minutes what a blessing Libby and this clinic had been for the town.

"Plenty of bad apples out there," he said, eyeing me closely. "Not just quacks, but arrogant bastards with no bedside manner to speak of."

I looped my stethoscope around my neck. "Don't I know it."

"Not you, though," he mused.

"I appreciate that." Though my voice was solemn, a smile tugged at one corner of my mouth.

"Dr. Bardot would no sooner hire a bastard than she would a quack," he continued. "We're glad to have you, Dr. Thorne. Spruce Hill might not be glamorous, but it's home, and we appreciate those who serve this community. Thankless work sometimes, I imagine, so thank you."

The warmth that swept through my limbs rendered me speechless for a moment, but the old man winked and patted my shoulder—he must've been at least my height in his prime, though he now was slightly stooped—as he preceded me out toward the reception desk.

Was this what it was like to be part of a community? To be valued for my own contributions rather than my family name?

That feeling lingered throughout the day, until I sat down in the break room to have a sandwich for lunch and found a text from Charlotte, when it intensified even further. I couldn't remember a point in my life where I'd smiled as much as I had since moving to Spruce Hill.

Got your number from Libs because I'm a creeper like that. Would you mind dinner at my place instead of going out?

Would I mind? It sounded better than any restaurant on the planet. *Works for me.*

Weds? Say, 6 pm?

I confirmed that I'd be there, grinned when she sent back a photo of Spoon snuggled up under a blanket, and returned to work with a spring in my step. That fact didn't escape Libby's notice.

In truth, I suspected very little escaped her notice.

"I hope it was okay to give her your number," she said between patients. "I actually refused, figuring I should ask you first, until she told me she'd storm the clinic unless I sent it over. She's here often enough as it is."

"It's fine. I should've given it to her myself, but I wasn't thinking." My smile faded as her last statement sunk in. "Why is she here so much?"

"Poor spatial awareness, she likes to say. She's one of our frequent flyers. Fortunately, it's usually nothing serious."

It wasn't anything Charlotte hadn't admitted herself at the hospital that night, but the sudden thought of someone causing even minor injuries to her twisted my gut like a vise. I remembered her awkward announcement about being single in the ER—and my reaction to it—but I needed to be sure.

"Has she been seeing anyone?" I asked, trying to brush off the clutching sensation in my chest as indigestion.

Libby sobered immediately. "No. And if I thought for a second someone was hurting her, I'd take care of it myself," she said fiercely. Her usually warm expression darkened with the implied threat.

I'd already accepted that Libby Bardot was one of the most brilliant people I'd ever met—no matter what my father thought of small town doctors—but my respect for her increased tenfold after that simple statement. The idea that so many others had Charlotte's back was more of a relief than I expected.

When the clinic's receptionist, an older woman named Molly, told her that room three was ready, Libby flashed me a smile and disappeared down the hall.

The days passed quickly, though the clinic's pace was blessedly slower than Eastman Memorial's emergency room. Libby had been running the place alone since she opened it several years earlier, but it hadn't been easy on her own. With two doctors available, we could see more patients and allow for more days off for each of us.

The schedule currently involved us each working a rotating four days a week along with alternating Saturdays. Last week had been something of a trial run to get me acquainted with the clinic and its operations, so this weekend would be my first Saturday shift.

On Wednesday, we finished up our last appointments just after four—another novelty for me, having enough time after work to get groceries or go for a run, to make a nice dinner or go on a date. It felt like the luxury it was, this free time that would take some getting used to.

Libby, who seemed to know everything about everyone, wiggled her fingers at me when we reached the parking lot.

"Enjoy your dinner with Charlotte," she called.

I laughed as I got into my car. At least she hadn't told me to leave her the hell alone. That seemed like a good sign, until I remembered the expression on Libby's face when she said she'd take care of it herself if anyone was abusing her friend.

Maybe that had been the only warning she was inclined to give.

Fortunately, I had no intention of hurting Charlotte in any way. And if she wanted to try a little bondage, I knew enough to keep her safe, unlike her friend's roommate.

I got home with time to shower and change into a dress shirt and jeans. Charlotte had sent a text telling me to come through the gate into the back yard, reminding me to make sure Spoon didn't escape. I grinned, grabbed a bottle of wine I'd purchased for the occasion, and crossed the short distance to Charlotte's house.

Though I didn't hear anything from the other side of the privacy fence, I kept one foot in the gap as I opened the gate in case the puppy came hurtling toward me. I glanced around, but the yard appeared empty. A small gazebo draped in strings of fairy lights housed a round picnic table set for dinner.

Hyacinths of all colors lined the inside of the fence, perfuming the air with a scent I'd forever associate with Charlotte herself. I latched the gate behind me and walked around the corner of the house just as she came through the back door with Spoon tripping along behind her.

"Oh, hi. Good timing," she said, waiting until the puppy had cleared the screen door before letting it close behind them. Her arms were full of containers and serving utensils, but she shook her head when I held out a hand to assist, even though she wasn't wearing the brace.

I shot her a stern glare and she winked, so I let it go.

"What can I do to help?" I asked instead.

Eyeing the bottle of wine, she grinned. "Go find us some wine glasses? I'm sure there are some in a cupboard somewhere. If not, you'll unfortunately soon find out that I am a basic bitch and will happily drink wine from a plastic cup."

I laughed, squatted down briefly to greet Spoon when he galloped to my side, then let myself into the house to try to locate the glasses. Fortunately, she had several, though they were all mismatched in an artsy sort of way. I grabbed two in one hand and headed back outside.

Now that she'd unloaded her armful of food, I was able to fully appreciate what she was wearing. This dress was a little less retro but no less enticing, a pale green sundress covered in tiny dark green vines and white flowers. It had thin straps and a fitted bodice that displayed more of her curves than any of her previous outfits, though the ruffled skirt fell just past her knees. Her hair tumbled loose in a riot of blonde curls with two small braids pulling the sides away from her face.

"You look like summertime," I said warmly as I joined her in the gazebo.

Her lips quirked upward. "It'll be here soon enough. How's it going at the clinic? You're not bored with our little town, I hope?"

"Not bored in the least," I murmured, letting my gaze stroke over the bare skin of her neck and shoulders.

This dress was definitely more revealing than the last one. While she did look like the perfect embodiment of summer, she also resembled an exquisitely wrapped present. I kept that thought to myself.

For now.

Charlotte met my eyes, her own mossy gaze not just steady, but bold. "My wrist is almost back to normal," she said calmly. "I think it's only fair to warn you that I'm planning to seduce you as soon as it's healed."

Startled by the directness of her proclamation, my lips curved and I gave a slow nod. "Consider me forewarned. Who's going to determine the adequacy of your recovery?"

"Me. My body, my call."

"Very well. I should warn you that I have every intention of succumbing to your seduction attempt," I replied. "But I give no promise that I won't turn the tables on you."

Charlotte's chin lifted slightly, but so did her lips. "It's a deal, then. Let's eat."

"Did you grow up in Spruce Hill?" I asked once we were seated with our plates filled.

"Yup. I went to college here, then did my MLS in Rochester." At my blank look, she added, "Master's in Library Science. What about you, is your family local?"

"In the city, yeah. My parents still live in the house I grew up in. You said your father passed away, what about your mom?"

"She lives in Syracuse now. My dad was pretty much out of the picture when I was a kid," she said quietly. "He was not a great guy."

I paused with a bite of chicken halfway to my mouth. "How so?"

"Not abusive. He'd pop in and out of my life, full of promises that all turned out to be bullshit, then leave my mom to pick up the pieces. She shielded me as much as she could, but it was a lot of disappointment. Every time he showed up, it would seem different, until it was just more of the same old lies. He'd promise to come to important events, then decide not to bother and lie about where he was instead. My mom finally got fed up. That's what led to their divorce."

"Seriously?"

"Yup."

"I'm sorry you were hurt like that." I wanted to rage about what a piece of shit he was, but she was so matter-of-fact about it, I couldn't be sure she'd welcome that.

She shrugged, but her eyes had lost the brightness I'd come to associate with her. "It's over. He's gone."

The man might be dead, but that kind of wound didn't heal easily. I wished he was alive just so I could rip into him for hurting this beauty sitting across from me. Before I could get control enough to not say something stupid, she shook off whatever melancholy had settled over her and spoke again.

"Do you have any siblings?"

"No, you?"

"Just Pen and Grisham. They're enough for me, ridiculous injuries and all," she said, smiling over at me.

In that moment, with the glow of her expression warming me from the inside out, I wanted nothing more than to be enough for her, too.

Chapter Ten

CHARLOTTE

P<small>ART OF ME WONDERED</small> if dinner would lessen my attraction to Sawyer—I'd been on plenty of dates that resulted in my interest taking a nosedive—but it did the opposite. Every moment in his presence only solidified how drawn to him I was, like casual conversation, a friendly meal, and adorable puppy antics were weaving a spell around us both, knitting us together.

I didn't bother fighting it, just let myself sink deeper and deeper into his pull.

He was affectionate and patient with Spoon, charming and sweet with me. Throughout the meal, I caught his gaze lingering on my wrist as we ate, like he was assessing how close to full health I really was.

If the heat sparking in his eyes by the end of the night was anything to go by, he expected my recovery to be complete very soon.

I'd never been so excited to get past an injury as I was then.

Spoon, like his foster mama, was completely enamored with the man, especially when Sawyer spent half an hour after dinner throwing a tennis ball for him to fetch, and that pull between us intensified as I watched him love on the clumsy puppy.

We relaxed for almost two hours under the twinkling gazebo lights after we finished eating, but when I started yawning, he brushed his knuckles along the side of my throat.

"It's a work night. I should let you get to bed," he said reluctantly.

Hearing the word *bed* in that deep timbre immediately woke my entire body anew. I licked my lips and said, "Yeah, I guess."

"Charlotte."

It was a warning, but the kind of warning that lit my nerve endings like fireworks. I wanted him to kiss me again, wanted to spend hours in his arms, and the urgency of that desire was unlike anything I'd experienced.

"Slow," he said finally, drawing the pad of his thumb along my jawline. "We're taking this slow."

"Right. Slow."

"Come on, up you get. I'll help clean up before I go."

He practically had to drag me up from the table, and together we loaded dishes into the dishwasher and put away the leftovers. The puppy eventually collapsed at our feet and fell so deeply asleep that he didn't stir even when I walked Sawyer to the gate.

Before opening it, he tucked a stray curl behind my ear. My lips parted and his gaze dropped to my mouth for a second, then he lowered his head and kissed me. It was no less incendiary than before, no matter how many times I'd told myself that kiss was probably a fluke, and this time he slid a hand to the nape of my neck, tangling his fingers in my hair.

When he released my mouth, he didn't move away. "You mentioned you're a bit injury-prone," he said carefully.

I rolled my eyes. "It's not like it happens on a weekly basis, but the hypermobility leads to rolling my ankles or hurting my wrist doing stupid, normal things like moving furniture. I sprained my shoulder once just lifting a bag of dog food for the rescue."

"Seriously?"

"Yup. Oh, god. Please tell me doctor-patient confidentiality means Libby can't tell you every embarrassing story of my life? Most of the injuries she's treated were attained in extremely humiliating ways."

"Libby hasn't shared, and as your doctor, she won't," he assured me. "But really, has anything been worse than the handcuffs?"

"Well," I hedged. "I jammed my thumb when I jumped up to kill a fly on the ceiling of my office at work. That had to be splinted for months. And I tried to show one of my story hour kids how to do a handstand against a fence when we ran into each other at the park..."

"Jesus." He didn't look amused. "How many other injuries have there been?"

I pursed my lips at him. When his stare intensified, I grudgingly muttered, "A few."

"Has Libby ever suggested it might be something more, like hypermobile Ehlers-Danlos?"

"Yes," I admitted, "but do you know what a nightmare it is, getting in to see a specialist with symptoms that nobody gives a shit about?"

He grimaced. "Unfortunately, yes. And I assume your aversion to doctors means you're not particularly interested in pursuing that?"

"Correct."

"What if I went with you to the appointment, or Libby? I'm sure we could arrange for one of us to take the time off. Whatever makes you more comfortable."

Something warm expanded inside my chest at the offer. "I'll consider it."

"Good," he said, then his gaze locked on mine. "Charlotte, I have the utmost respect for your bodily autonomy, but I would be very grateful if you'd take extra care. For the sake of our future plans, if not your own wellbeing."

A bolt of lust tripped up my spine at the look in his eyes as he said it, the rumble of his voice that I could almost feel trembling in my own chest.

"Yes, I will be careful. Satisfied?"

"I will be," he replied, dropping another soft kiss to my lips. "Sweet dreams, Charlotte."

After latching the gate behind him, I leaned my forehead against the wood, listening to the sound of his footsteps until he was back inside his house.

Between our work schedules and a few evening library events, we couldn't coordinate another get together until Sunday, when Sawyer offered to make us brunch at my house so we didn't have to abandon Spoon for the morning.

Since he refused every offer of help, I sat at the kitchen table while he made us French toast and omelets—at the same time.

"You realize you're spoiling me, right?" I teased, watching the way he moved so comfortably between tasks. "I usually have oatmeal or an English muffin for breakfast."

"If you think spoiling you is some kind of deterrent, let me assure you, it's not."

He threw a smile over his shoulder that kicked my pulse up a notch even as I mumbled, "Oh."

"Has anyone ever spoiled you?"

"I—I don't know," I admitted. "I've been making my own meals since middle school to take some weight off my mom's shoulders, and I don't think I've ever dated anyone who cooks."

Sawyer stayed silent as he plated our meals and brought them to the table, but his solemn expression kept me from immediately digging in. He reached out to tuck a lock of hair behind my ear and studied my features for a long moment.

"Then let me," he said softly. "In whatever form that takes. Let me show you what it's like to be taken care of."

An uneven breath floated past my lips, but I nodded. "Okay. I'll try."

"Good. Now, eat up, then we're going to play Bocce."

"Bocce," I repeated.

"Yes. Have you ever played?"

When I shook my head, he gave me a crash course on the rules and said, "I think we should both play left-handed, so I can test that wrist."

Heat flared in my belly. "Okay, then."

We finished eating, then he jogged back home to grab a black bag housing his own personal set of Bocce balls.

"Are you some kind of Bocce hustler?" I asked as he unpacked them in my yard.

His grin was boyish and utterly charming. "No. If I were going to hustle you, I'd pretend I didn't kick ass at this game."

And kick my ass he did.

After an incredibly humiliating showing with my left hand—not because of my injury, but because I apparently sucked at this game—we switched back to our right hands for a final round. He still won by a mile, but the pleasure in his eyes went deeper than just winning the game.

"Your range of motion is good," he said, examining my wrist after we'd packed up the balls, "but we'll need to rebuild your strength."

I blinked innocently up at him. "I know just the thing."

For a heartbeat, he simply stared at me as the words sank in, then he threw back his head and laughed. "Sometimes I forget what a little temptress you are beneath that prim librarian exterior."

"Don't worry. I'll keep reminding you."

Unfortunately, that would have to wait, because I needed to take Spoon for a home visit to a potential adopter that afternoon.

As had become custom, Sawyer pulled me into a searing kiss before I left. His hands didn't stray, just cradled my hips as his mouth settled over mine. I opened for him immediately and he tilted his head to stroke deeper with his tongue, swallowing my quiet hum of satisfaction until he drew back with an obvious reluctance that made me feel better about my own.

I was ready to move faster. We both wanted this and I was tired of waiting.

By the time I lifted Spoon into the back seat of my car, I was still buzzing with it, still flustered and breathless enough that when I parked in the adopter's driveway, I had to sit there for a few minutes to calm myself down.

No matter what Sawyer seemed to think, he was definitely the dangerous one, and my peace of mind didn't stand a chance against him.

Chapter Eleven

CHARLOTTE

When I finally pulled myself together enough to shove Sawyer and his epic kisses to the back of my mind, the Schroeders greeted me eagerly at the door. Spoon paused to sniff at a bowling bag just inside the door, then he caught sight of the kids and bounded over to them.

Kevin and Ella, their ten-year-old twins, matched Spoon's enthusiasm perfectly. The three of them immediately ran to the living room and dropped to the floor to play.

"Is everything all right?" Mr. Schroeder asked, gesturing back out toward my car. "The kids were watching through the window and said you were out there for a few minutes."

"Just reviewing the paperwork," I said with a bright smile. Either my poker face had improved or it was too boring a lie to garner any attention.

Even Mrs. Schroeder ended up kneeling on the carpet to rub Spoon's belly alongside the kids, but her husband remained on the couch, watching the scene with a blank expression.

"We've been asking for a puppy forever," Ella said, drawing my attention to her brilliant smile.

"Yeah, but Mom said we had to wait," her brother chimed in.

I'd learned not to get too involved in those discussions—adopting a pet was a big responsibility, and I didn't feel right swaying a family into something they might not be ready for—but Mrs. Schroeder gave the twins a soft smile.

"Things were difficult for a while, but we're in a better position to take care of him now, aren't we?"

"That's right," her husband said from the couch, sounding oddly cold still.

I cleared my throat and said, "Well, that's good news for Spoon, isn't it?"

At hearing his name, he perked up and rolled clumsily to his feet, ready for another round of tug with the rope toy I'd had in my purse.

Before I declared it time to head home, though, Mr. Schroeder seemed to warm up to the puppy, petting him any time he came within reach, and Spoon was obviously in love with the entire family.

"I'll get everything processed with the rescue," I told them as I snapped the leash back on. "He has to finish out his antibiotics, but then he'll be ready for you, if you want him."

"We do!" Ella cried, throwing her arms around the exhausted pup.

I looked to her parents, who both nodded. Only Mrs. Schroeder smiled at me, but her husband said, "Absolutely. We'll take him."

"Great. I'll give you a call after the paperwork is sorted and we can set a time for me to bring him to you."

They thanked me again, even Mr. Schroeder, as I headed back to my car.

The rest of the week flew by, but Spoon's imminent adoption threw me for a loop. Thursday morning, after I dropped him off with the Schroeders and rubbed his belly for the last time, I barely managed to save my tears until I was locked in my office at work.

Some dogs just hit me harder than others when they found their forever homes, and Spoon was one of them.

Then my frazzled emotions led to disaster.

During toddler story hour, a kid performed a perfect dive-roll in front of me. I tripped, and in my attempt not to crush his little skull under my knee, I landed hard on both hands against the thin carpet of the library floor.

When my left wrist started to ache more than I could manage with anti-inflammatories, a coworker brought me to the clinic. Both doctors were in with patients, but the nurse, Aaron, led me into a room at the end of the hall and gave me an ice pack.

Unfortunately, we had that particular routine down pat. I waited, trying not to cry, until Libby came in.

"Oh, Charlie," she sighed, but her expression was so full of sympathy that the tears almost escaped. "Let's have a look at you."

She had just slipped out to find an elastic wrap when Sawyer walked by the open door and did a double take.

"Is today my lucky day?" he asked, then his gaze dropped to the ice pack. The question was clear in his eyes when he lifted them back to my face.

"I fell. I'm sorry."

That was all it took—the floodgates opened. I covered my face with my good hand, but Sawyer had me in his arms within seconds. He murmured against my hair, cradled my head against his shoulder, and waited for the tears to subside.

"What happened, angel?"

"A ninja disguised as a toddler threw himself down in front of me after story hour this morning. I had to sacrifice myself to avoid flattening him."

Libby walked in just as Sawyer swept his thumbs across my wet cheeks. "Ah, Dr. Thorne. Would you mind wrapping that wrist for her? I think she just tweaked it, should be right as rain in a few days. In fact, maybe you'd be willing to drive Charlie home? Someone from the library dropped her here. You can take the rest of the afternoon off. There aren't too many appointments left."

"Of course," he said smoothly, taking the elastic bandage from her hand. He waited until she flitted back out the door before his lips twitched. "Charlie?"

I groaned. "No one calls me that anymore."

With a soft laugh, he checked my wrist for tenderness. It wasn't the clinical, impersonal touch from our first meeting—at least, it didn't feel that way to my nervous system, which lit up like a firework display as he ran his fingers over my skin. When he started to wind the bandage around it, though, I had to blink back a new round of tears.

"Does it hurt that much?" he asked gently.

"No." I sniffled pathetically. "I'm just disappointed."

Understanding dawned in his pale eyes, thawing them from ice to a fathomless crystal pool. "There are plenty of things we can do that don't put any pressure on your wrist," he said, his voice low and tempting.

I blinked up at him in surprise. "I thought you said…"

Sawyer sighed as he clasped the bandage, but when he opened his mouth to speak, we heard Libby's laughter from a room down the hall. "We'll talk more when we get home, okay?"

I waited while he gathered his things from the employee locker room, then followed him out the back door to the parking lot behind the clinic. By the time he unlocked and opened the passenger door, my throat was burning again.

"Angel, what else is going on?" he asked, cupping my face in his hands.

Swallowing hard, I managed to say, "Spoon got adopted this morning," before bursting into tears.

For the second time in barely fifteen minutes, Sawyer wrapped his arms around me while I gasped my way through painful, ugly sobs. He held me like he was sheltering me in a storm, like his body would be my shield against the world. Even after I had cried myself out, he didn't let go.

"What a morning," he said, kissing the top of my head. "Have you eaten lunch yet?"

I shook my head. "I should go back to work."

"I'll write you a note. Get in touch with whoever you need to, tell them you have to take the afternoon off. We're going to get some food in you and spend the rest of the day snuggled up on the couch. Doctor's orders. We can have a movie marathon. In light of your injury, I'll even let you pick the first movie."

With a wobbly laugh, I let him usher me into the passenger seat and texted my coworkers. On the way home, Sawyer ran into my favorite sub shop to pick up sandwiches for lunch. It felt like playing hooky, and maybe it was, but I was too grateful to him for suggesting it to argue.

"Your place or mine?" he asked when he pulled into the driveway.

"How comfortable is your couch?" I countered.

He grimaced. "Not terribly."

"Decision made. Comfort is key today and my couch kicks ass."

Sawyer carried our lunches into the house, following along behind me as I trudged slowly up the steps leading to the kitchen. He set the bag down on the counter and took my shoulders in his hands.

"Do you want to change into something cozier?" he asked, his thumb tracing back and forth over my collarbones.

I'd worn pants and a blouse today in anticipation of story hour, and neither piece was particularly suited for lounging on the couch watching movies, so I nodded.

Then my gaze caught on my wrapped wrist and I silently cursed this blouse's tiny buttons. "I think I'll need help," I said quietly. It wasn't meant to be coy or flirtatious, just a statement of fact.

"Lead the way."

A tiny flutter of anxiety took up residence in my belly as I brought him upstairs and into my bedroom for the first time. Though he said nothing, his gaze moved slowly across the four-poster bed, inspiring a whole new host of explicit fantasies that I needed to shut down before I burst out crying again.

Turning away from the bed, I grabbed some yoga pants and an oversized tee from my dresser and set them nearby before the awkwardness of this situation hit me.

"I believe you had a question for me," he said as he strolled my way.

I sucked in a breath when his fingers slipped under the blouse's collar to undo the first button. My brain instantly dissolved, going blank as heat crept along my skin.

"I did?"

"About your injury and my plans for you."

"Oh. Right. I thought you said we weren't doing anything until my wrist was healed," I said in a rush.

"Hmm. I did say that, didn't I? That still holds true for experimenting with any kind of bondage play, if that's something you want to do," he mused as he released the next two buttons.

"It is." My pulse kicked up a notch just thinking about it.

"I thought so. However, one of my ulterior motives was to give you time to change your mind about getting involved with me."

"You thought I'd change my mind?" I frowned at him.

His fingers slowed, knuckles coasting lightly over my skin. "Have you ever slept with a virtual stranger, Charlotte?"

"I—no, I haven't. Have you?" I asked, curious.

"I have. There's nothing wrong with that, as long as everyone is safe and consenting, but I didn't think it seemed like something you were accustomed to," he replied as he released the last two buttons.

"You're not a stranger now."

"No, you're right. Now, we've had some time to get to know each other, but I still don't want you to regret whatever happens between us."

Barely able to get the words out, I asked, "What other ulterior motive did you have?"

"Trust."

The word made me flinch, even spoken in the gentle way he said it, but he waited until I lifted my eyes to his face.

"Do you trust me, Charlotte?"

"Yes."

It slipped out before I could stop it. As I blinked in surprise at the knee-jerk response, his lips twitched.

When he gently parted the halves of the blouse, though, my confusion fell away and I quivered under the heat of his gaze. No matter how many times I wished I'd thrown myself at him that night at the bar, he was right. I'd been so nervous after our conversation about hookups, I thought I might puke.

Without treating me like I didn't know my own mind, Sawyer had managed to reassure me time and again—and it was true. I trusted him. Somehow his patience had eroded my defenses.

You are safe with me. Always.

As he pushed the blouse over my shoulders and carefully down my arms, I held as still as possible, though every inch of me wanted to press closer to him. The fabric floated away, leaving me standing there in just a pink bra with red lipstick kisses printed across it. Sawyer's mouth curved upward as he took in the sight.

"I like this," he said, rubbing one strap between his fingers. My gaze shot from his hand to his face and he shook his head at my unspoken question. "You've had a rough day so far. We've got plenty of time."

I expected him to pull the t-shirt over my head first, but instead he moved to my black dress pants. When his finger hooked through the waistband to unbutton the fly, I almost melted into a puddle on the floor. My lungs stalled as he slowly lowered the zipper, then ran his palms along my stomach to my hips in order to push the pants down. They fell to the floor with a whoosh and I forgot to breathe until he settled one hand at my waist.

"Step out," he ordered.

Oh, shit. Stern Doctor was making an appearance, and this time his command was a low growl, tempered by need. I did as instructed, standing there in my bra and mismatched underwear, feeling more naked than if I'd actually been nude.

Especially when he crouched to pick up the pants and rose slowly, so slowly, as if he wanted to savor the view of every inch of bare skin along the way.

"So very lovely," he breathed.

One hand lifted as though he'd decided to strip me down further, then his fingers curled into a fist and he moved away to grab the change of clothes I'd set down. When he turned back to me, the heat was banked and his movements became almost impersonal as he helped me dress in my more comfortable clothing.

Awash in disappointment that we'd have to delay our sexy time plans yet again, I swallowed back a fresh round of tears and we headed back downstairs.

I'd always been injury-prone, but never before had it interfered so thoroughly with what my heart wanted.

Chapter Twelve

Sawyer

CHARLOTTE WAS *KILLING* ME.

Her admission of trust was headier than I'd expected. I wanted to act on it, seize it and show her it wasn't misplaced. In her bedroom, every instinct I possessed was screaming at me to kiss her, claim her, make her mine like I was a fucking caveman.

The worst part was that I knew the feeling was mutual, but this wasn't the time.

She's hurting, a tiny voice shouted inside my head just before I gave in to the urge to yank her lush body against me. *She's hurting and vulnerable and needs a friend today.*

Now that we were seated on her couch with our lunches spread across the coffee table, all I could think about was what lay underneath the gray t-shirt and black yoga pants I'd helped her into. Velvety skin that tinged pink so readily when she blushed, curves that would fill and overflow my palms. That silly bra I wanted to use as a treasure map, following each lipstick mark with my own mouth.

I hated the disappointment that darkened her eyes when I dressed her in those clothes. I hated that my conscience was telling me not to take advantage of her today, that my own willpower was causing her to look so sad and lost right now as she picked at her lunch and scrolled through our movie options.

Finally, I couldn't stand it any more.

"Put down the remote," I told her, noting the flash of surprise—sharpened by desire—in her eyes as she did so.

I reached over and pulled her onto my lap, careful of her bandaged wrist. Once I arranged her knees on either side of my lap, I sank my fingers into her hair and kissed her until she started to melt against me.

God, she was so warm, so soft. I realized then that some of my reservations were largely because I wasn't sure I'd ever get enough of this woman.

"I want you," I whispered against her jaw. "Don't ever doubt it, angel. That hasn't changed."

"Jesus," she hissed, arching as my tongue traced the delicate bones of her collar.

I nipped at the skin, then soothed it with my mouth. "Do you see why I want you to be one hundred percent ready before we do this?"

"Because you're so intense?" she guessed, gripping my hair with both hands, though her left was not quite as strong as the right. When I nuzzled the upper swell of her breast, she used that hold to lift my head away from her body. "I'm starting to understand, yes. But you missed something."

I gave a slow smile. "I've missed a lot of somethings so far, but we have plenty of time."

"Ah ah ah. Try again," she replied, sounding every inch the scolding librarian.

With a tug, she drew my head back so that my throat was bared, then she trailed hot, open-mouthed kisses along it. My low groan vibrated against her lips and my hands tightened on the swell of her hips. Behind the fly of my jeans, I was already straining against her heat.

"What am I missing, angel?"

Her teeth grazed my Adam's apple before she lifted her head. "I have been *ready* since that first night at the hospital, Dr. Hottie."

A surprised laugh rumbled in my chest. "Is that so?"

"It is. I'll give you a very short reprieve, since you're so worried about taking advantage of me after such a shit day, but it will cost you."

This version of her was new to me, but I realized it had been lurking under the surface all along. "I'll give you anything you want, angel. Tell me, what will it cost?"

She leaned in, her breasts pressing against my chest like temptation personified, and her soft pink lips brushed my earlobe as she whispered, "I want to hear all the things you plan to do with me. In detail."

"Answer one question for me first. The stern doctor thing, you like that? It turns you on, me taking charge, whether there's bondage involved or not?"

"Oh yes," she replied. Another bolt of lust rocketed through me at her confirmation. "I find it very, very hot."

Thank fuck. Between kisses and nips, I gave her exactly what she asked for.

"I want my mouth on every inch of your body, until the taste of your skin is burned into my brain. I want to know exactly how you sound when you come around my fingers and on my tongue, how you look when I finally sink into you, what color your eyes will be when I'm buried deep. Find out how perfect you feel around my cock, hot and tight and wet."

She shivered. "Go on."

"I'm going to fill you up until you're so used to the feeling of me inside you that you miss me the moment I'm gone. Take you again and again until your body is as familiar to me as my own. I'll fulfill every fantasy, play out every dark dream that lurks inside your mind, tie you to that sweet princess bed upstairs and pleasure you until you can't move from that spot."

By the end of it, she was trembling in my arms and I was afraid I might come in my pants.

I brought her carefully back down, reining in my own desire as I murmured how beautiful she was, how clever and bold, how much I enjoyed being around her. Her breathing was still a little shaky, but she slumped against my chest while I stroked my hands along her spine.

"I think you're the dangerous one," she accused, though there was no bite to the words.

I laughed softly. "Maybe we're both dangerous. It's rare for me to be so cautious."

"Why are you, then?" she asked. "Just because I'm friends with your boss? Because we're neighbors?"

"Maybe a little bit of both," I replied, considering it. My fingers sifted through her hair and she nestled closer, practically purring. "The thought of hurting you terrifies me. You're a dream come true, and I'm afraid if I put a foot wrong, I'll ruin that. I don't have a lot of practice with healthy relationships."

"If I had propositioned you that night outside the hospital, would you have been this careful?"

I had to think about that one for a moment, since I didn't want to bullshit her. "It would have been different, Charlotte. In that situation, it would've been a single night, over and done with. That's all I've been able to handle for years."

She lifted her head, her gaze full of questions, but she only said, "And now?"

"I don't think I could ever be satisfied by a single night with you, angel. Is that what you'd want for us? A one-night stand?"

Those long lashes swept downward, shielding her eyes for a moment. "No."

The relief that rushed through me was surprising in its intensity. What was it about her that made me want to break all my own rules? My statement was true—in my old life, I would never have allowed myself more than a night with her. I hadn't been in a long-term relationship in over a decade, not since Veronica ended things.

Charlotte Whitmore, however, made me want to obliterate every rule in the book.

"And that's usually all you have? One-night stands?" she asked. I should have known she couldn't hold back her questions for long.

"Or short-term flings, yes. My last real relationship didn't end well."

"When was that?"

Simple curiosity colored her tone, and though I didn't want to get into the nitty gritty details just yet, I owed her that answer. "Almost twelve years ago."

"That's a long time," she replied softly.

I cupped one hand at the nape of her neck and squeezed her hip with the other. "You're sure you want to get involved with me?"

"Are you trying to warn me away?" she countered.

"I probably should." I sighed, pressing a kiss to her forehead. "But no. I do, however, need a distraction from your delectable self until you're feeling better, so maybe we should finish the movie."

Charlotte drew back and a look of challenge flared in her eyes. "Until I'm better physically or emotionally?"

I snorted. "Both, preferably. The wrist we can work around, but the shit day you've had means the emotional side is more important right now. Let me comfort you without sex this time around, will you? If you can be patient, I'll make it up to you, I promise."

For a minute, I thought she might argue, but then she nodded and swung herself off my lap to nestle beside me instead. "Fine. But now I'll have to make you sit through another *Mission: Impossible* movie with me when this one is over."

"What the lady wants, the lady gets," I conceded.

Though I missed the warmth of her on my lap already, having her tucked against my side was almost as good. Besides, I'd seen these movies before, which meant I had plenty of time to imagine every fantasy I'd described to Charlotte in vivid, delicious detail while we watched.

It was the ultimate test of my self-control.

Chapter Thirteen

CHARLOTTE

Sawyer ended up staying through two more movies after the first ended, then he made us dinner so I wouldn't put any unnecessary strain on my wrist. By the end of the evening, it actually felt much better, but I knew better than to hope he'd dial back his intention to wait. He didn't stay late since I had to work the next morning, just left me with another inflammatory kiss that reiterated all of his promises from earlier in the day.

Friday was even quieter than usual at the library, which suited my daydreaming just fine. One of the volunteers helped me change over the bulletin board for our upcoming events, then I was left with little to do for the remainder of the afternoon.

What better chance to conduct some research to distract myself from thinking about Sawyer?

I left the library in the capable hands of my staff—and while I didn't *lie* to them, I might have let them assume I was off on official business when I slipped away at lunch time, even if this particular venture was anything but.

My first stop was Suds & Fold, which gave me a grand total of zero clues about any link between the fires. It had been part of a historic plaza at the southern edge of town. In its prime, the area had been a bustling business hub close to Oakville, but over the intervening decades, the north-south stretch of Main Street leading toward Lake Ontario had stepped into the spotlight as the center of town and put Spruce Hill on the map.

The plaza was still standing, though every other storefront was now vacant and there was a gaping hole where the laundromat had been. It looked like one of my young readers with a missing front tooth.

Sighing, I headed back toward Al's Discount Warehouse, the most recent fire, hoping I could poke around the area and find some connection to the other two. The discount store had taken residence in an old tobacco warehouse that'd been vacant for years before Old Al bought it when I was a kid, according to my research.

Unfortunately, the block that housed the enormous building and its parking lot were fully blocked off by caution tape and traffic cones.

"Dammit," I muttered, but I wasn't interested in getting arrested for trespassing and I didn't want a ruined building to collapse on my head, so I cut my losses and headed northwest to The Hideaway.

When I was in college, it had been a top pick for boozy nights off campus among other students, the very definition of a dive bar, but I'd never been there. I remembered Pen telling me once that I should avoid any bars I couldn't see into from the outside. They were too sketchy even for her far more intrepid self, so I'd taken that sage advice to heart and never ventured inside.

I parked at the edge of the empty lot and studied the building, which had first been a tavern, then a boarding house, before finally falling into disrepair and being sold at auction. It became The Hideaway sometime before I was born, though I was fairly certain the business had changed hands a number of times.

The building looked desolate, all blackened edges and boarded or broken windows. My mind wandered as I sat there in my car, thinking about generations of people who'd been inside each of those businesses before an act of nature ended that chain.

A knock on the passenger window startled a shriek out of me.

"Charlotte?"

Heart racing, I hit the button to lower the window and managed a shaky smile for the woman standing beside my car. "Hi, sorry! You scared me."

"Sorry, hon," Detective Rose Hanson said, frowning at me. "Are you all right?"

"Yes. Yup. I just pulled over to read a text and got lost in my thoughts," I replied, hoping the quaver in my voice could be passed off as adrenaline from her surprise appearance.

"Is that so?" Rose's skeptical expression didn't change.

Shit. I really needed to practice my poker face. I blinked at her as my mind scrambled for a convincing response. "Um. Yes?"

"Where's your phone then?"

Son of a bitch.

Rose was a little older than Libby, but like I'd told Sawyer, everyone knew everyone in Spruce Hill. Her genre of choice might be romantasy, but I knew better than to try to keep up a lie in the face of her discerning gaze. I offered my brightest smile instead.

"Charlotte." She drew out the word as she bent forward to stare at me through the window. "If you have something to tell me, you better get it over with and tell me right now."

"Nope, nothing. I'm on my lunch hour, so I should really get back to the library."

She narrowed her eyes, but she stepped away from my car without another word. Silently cursing my bad luck, I hurriedly closed the window, shifted my car into gear, and headed back to the library.

When I got inside, I grabbed the folder of return chute items and settled in at the computer in my office, intending to continue my research into the receipt list in case I'd missed some bigger connection, but I was interrupted by Olivia, one of my favorite staff members.

"Oh, Charlotte," she sang, popping her head around the door frame. "There is an absolute stud out front asking for you."

Startled, I rose. As far as I'd gathered from our conversations, Olivia was only interested in women and had been dating someone for a few months now.

"A stud?" I repeated curiously.

She grinned broadly at me. "Oh, I think this level of stud is evident to anyone with eyes. Or ears. God, that voice. I hope you're not going to shoot this one down, Char."

I rolled my eyes and returned the folder to the locked file cabinet in my office before heading to the circulation desk. Olivia had been on my case for the better part of the last year, after I'd gently refused a couple of library patrons who had asked me out.

It wasn't like it happened very often, but those two occasions had been barely a month apart. I was nice about it, I just didn't feel a spark with either of them.

Unlike today's visitor.

There, thumbing through a paperback from a display in front of the desk, stood Dr. Hottie himself. I could see why Olivia had labeled him a stud—he was dressed in dark jeans, a black t-shirt, and his leather jacket. In the afternoon sunlight streaming through the row of windows on one wall, his hair was gilded like flowing gold.

"Hey, you," I said as I reached his side. "Looking for anything in particular?"

His eyes went straight to my unwrapped wrist before returning to my face. "Why, yes, actually. I hoped I might find a gorgeous librarian to invite over for dinner tonight. And maybe a thriller or detective novel, while I'm at it."

"Well, I can certainly help you find all of those things," I replied, smirking at him.

"How's your wrist feeling today?"

The question sounded casual and polite, but the heat in his eyes spoke volumes. I leaned my elbows against the counter, grinning when his gaze dipped to the neckline of my dress. Instead of answering, I lifted my left hand and tipped it forward and back before rotating it in a circle.

"Not even a twinge of pain."

"Excellent news," he replied, his lips curving. When he smiled like that, dark and tempting and so, so hot, I imagined I heard even Olivia swooning behind me.

"I'm clocking out, boss," the younger woman said as she practically danced past us. "Have a beautiful weekend!"

Once she was gone, Sawyer huffed a laugh. "Is that your wingman?"

"She likes to think so," I muttered. We were currently alone in the library, and even though I'd worked here for years, the quiet always made me feel like I needed to speak in a hushed whisper.

"What time are you finished?" he asked.

I checked my watch. "About half an hour."

Sawyer trailed his fingertips from the back of my left hand to the inside of my wrist, leaving goosebumps in his wake. "Well then, maybe you can set this newcomer up with a library card so I can find some books and walk you out."

After entering him in the system and handing him his shiny new card, I left him to browse the stacks while I started my closing routine. When I accidentally-on-purpose brushed my ass against his as I straightened out a shelf, he let loose a low growl that sent tingles throughout my body.

"Careful, angel," he said softly, turning around and capturing my hips with his hands so he could murmur into my ear. "If you want to make it home before I try to get you naked, you'll have to be a very good girl."

Oh, god. In the silence of the library, my ragged breathing sounded extraordinarily loud. I leaned back against him, letting his hips cradle the curve of my ass.

"What will my reward be if I'm very, very good?" I whispered.

His teeth grazed my earlobe. When I gasped, he made a low sound of satisfaction and said, "Anything. Everything."

"And if I choose to be bad?"

He spun us so my back was to the bookshelves, moving so quickly I let out a breathless laugh. That was all I had time for before his mouth was on mine. It was every library fantasy I'd ever had come to life as he crowded me, bracing one arm by my hip and one next to my head.

God, his kisses. Every stroke of his tongue felt expertly designed to drive me wild. I reveled in it—the forbidden nature of the moment as much as Sawyer surrounding me, grinding his hips into mine when I parted my lips. I couldn't wait to tear off our clothes and explore the rest of him. I shifted, wrapping one leg around him as his thick, hard length pressed against my core. A moan slipped from my throat, spurring him to take the kiss deeper.

If we didn't stop soon, I'd lose myself and do something entirely unprofessional.

Fortunately, Sawyer managed to hold onto a thread of control and lifted his head about half a second before I reached for his belt. Both of us panted, staring at one another in a daze, until his lips curved and he dropped his forehead to mine.

"I'm not looking to get you fired if someone walks in here," he said, voice low and rough enough to tighten my nipples into sharp points.

"I'll behave until we get home," I promised in a whisper.

He feathered kisses along my hairline, brushed his thumb over my bottom lip, and nudged me toward the front desk. "Then you'll get your reward."

The rest of my routine was a blur. No one came in during that final half hour, so I was hyperaware of Sawyer's presence for every minute of it. When he sensed me getting a bit frazzled as I tried to make sure everything was done, he caught my hands in his.

"Easy," he said softly. "We're not rushing, angel. Take your time."

It was ridiculous how much those simple reassurances helped. I took a few deep breaths, grounding myself in the feel of his rough fingers against my palms, and nodded.

"Right. Give me two more minutes and we'll be ready to go. Did you drive over?"

"No, I walked. I didn't realize the library was so close to home."

I nodded as I shut down the computers one by one. "Convenient, isn't it? I drove today because of these shoes, so I'll give you a ride home."

"If it's not out of your way," he deadpanned.

"Smartass," I scolded as I skirted around him toward the last computer, but he grabbed me around the waist and dipped me low over the ancient brown carpet.

"I do believe there was a reward at stake for being very good, but I'm just as happy to take you up against one of these nice, sturdy bookshelves."

Air hissed from my lungs. Somehow, he managed to pull every dark fantasy from my head, and we hadn't even slept together yet.

"That's not much of a threat," I said hoarsely.

His lips trailed along my throat and I closed my eyes. Something about this man drew me right out of the tidy little shell I'd been living in for so long. It was as exhilarating as it was disconcerting.

"No, I think you'd quite enjoy it. But if you behave yourself long enough to get home first, I promise I'll make it well worth it. I want to take my time with you, especially the first time."

"Okay." The word trembled with anticipation.

When he drew me back to my feet, his eyes were dark with desire, but there was a soft smile playing across his lips.

"Are you almost finished here?" he asked politely, as if he'd just been standing around waiting for me instead of broadcasting every one of his carnal intentions while I closed up the library.

"Yes. Let's go."

I grabbed my purse from my office, locked the doors behind us, and stepped out into the late afternoon sunlight with this dark prince at my side.

Chapter Fourteen

SAWYER

One of the things that impressed me so much about Charlotte was the way she went from scattered to steady in the span of mere seconds. It was like there was some inner well of strength that she pulled from when she needed to ground herself, no matter how frazzled and distracted I got her.

The temptation to test the limit of that particular skill was almost irresistible.

When we pulled into her driveway, she glanced at me as she turned off the engine. "Are we really having dinner?"

"I wasn't planning to starve you, if that's your concern," I replied, eyeing her carefully. "Your satisfaction is very important to me, after all. Are you hungry now?"

"No," she replied, sounding prim enough that I almost laughed. "I just wondered if I should bring over a change of clothes or something."

Not nervous, I realized, just planning ahead. She was so practical sometimes it floored me.

"I hoped you might spend the night, but it's your choice. If you'd like to, then you're certainly welcome to pack an overnight bag. I doubt you'll need pajamas," I added, just to see her blush.

"Okay, then. I'll be over in a few minutes?"

I caught her chin in my hand before we got out of the car. She looked calm, if a little flushed. Even though she didn't seem to be anxious or second-guessing herself, it wouldn't go amiss to issue a reminder.

"Nothing happens tonight that you don't want. No matter how stern or demanding I might be, you are the one in control, understand?"

Her breasts rose and fell on a rapid breath. "I understand."

"Good. Go get your things. If you're not at my place in ten minutes, I'm coming back for you."

With a mischievous little grin, she bolted out of the car and skipped into the house. I watched until the door closed behind her before heading toward my own, pondering this sweet little librarian and all the steps that had led us to this place. The sheer number of coincidences involved in our first meeting, me getting this new job, unexpectedly ending up renting the house next door—it felt like fate, even if I didn't believe in such things.

Fate, or the interference of a certain mutual acquaintance of ours. I wouldn't quibble.

I had prepared a container of cold pasta salad, some marinating vegetable skewers, and a couple of other options ready to throw on the grill for dinner, figuring it would be quick and easy. If we ended up too distracted by other pleasures, the pasta salad would make a good snack, along with an assortment of fruit I'd picked up earlier.

Charlotte knocked at the side door barely five minutes later. I opened it and ushered her inside, giving her the grand tour.

"This is...nice," she said, her tone carefully diplomatic as she took in the shag carpets and paneled walls when we entered the living room.

"It's wretched," I corrected. "But it'll do. I do have a gorgeous neighbor, at least."

"Gorgeous neighbors are common on this street," she replied with a grin.

As we walked through the house, she touched everything she could reach—running her hand over the back of the couch, rubbing a throw blanket between her thumb and forefinger.

It was erotic as fuck.

Even when I showed her the minuscule kitchen and undecorated spare bedroom, she was still aglow with curiosity, her gaze catching on cabinet pulls and countertops, but as soon as we reached the master bedroom, she went quiet.

"Angel," I began, but she shot me a scowl and brushed past me to enter the room.

I kept my gaze on her, assessing her body language as she set her backpack on a chair and took a slow stroll around the space. The bed, king-sized and framed in solid oak, garnered most of her attention. As her fingers danced over the gleaming wood, my body tightened in anticipation.

Then she turned back to me, her lips curving upward. "So. Did I earn that reward, Doc?"

"Oh, yes," I growled, stalking toward her.

I heard the quick intake of breath, saw the lift of her chin, and fought the urge to pick her up and toss her onto the bed. Circling her, I let my fingers trail up her bare arms and along the back of her neck, stroking one fingertip over the moon tattoo there. She sighed and leaned into my touch. When I reached the zipper at the back of her dress, I paused.

"Unless you have any objections, I'm going to undress you now."

"I have zero objections, in fact," she replied immediately, sounding breathless already. "I'm very much pro-undressing."

I chuckled against her shoulder. "As am I, believe me."

Slowly, so slowly that she bounced impatiently to try to hurry me along, I gathered her hair and draped it over one shoulder before kissing the nape of her neck. A tiny sound slipped from her lips as I caught the zipper pull and drew it downward, following the path with my lips.

I pushed the dress down off her shoulders and over her hips, waiting as she stepped out of it. Today's bra was black, dotted with tiny silver stars, and I grinned at the matching panties.

She threw a sultry look over her shoulder, then I laid the dress carefully over the chair where she'd set her bag down.

"Exquisite," I murmured, circling her again. She was flushed, breathing as raggedly as she had in the library, but even from a short distance, I saw her nipples pebbling against the starry fabric. "I could spend all night just looking at you."

"Please don't," she replied, flashing a grin. "I don't want to expire from sexual frustration."

I laughed as I stopped in front of her, coasted my hands from her hips to her breasts, and teased my thumbs across each nipple as I dropped my head to kiss her. She sighed into it, her hands lifting to my shoulders to steady herself. When I slipped my palms to her back, she made a soft sound of protest at losing them, but then I unclasped the bra and let it fall to the floor. Her eyes darkened even further as my body went still.

"Charlotte," I purred, sweeping my gaze over her. "What have we here?"

Tiny clusters of clear jewels curved along either side of each nipple, highlighting the dusky pink points. The little gemstones twinkled invitingly at me and blood surged to my cock.

"Did I forget to mention I got my nipples pierced last year?"

"You most certainly forgot to mention it." I gave her a stern glare and enjoyed the blush creeping up her neck in response.

"Oops," she said, shrugging.

This woman would be the death of me and I hadn't even been inside her yet.

"I never imagined my sweet librarian was hiding something like this," I mused. "Any other surprises?"

"Nope, just these."

"And they're fully healed? Safe to use my hands? Mouth?"

She bit her lip and nodded. "I haven't been with anyone since I got them done, but they should be fine to play with. I've, um..."

My gaze shot to her face. "You've what?"

"Played with them myself."

Fuck me.

I planned to explore in depth all the advantages to those piercings. For now, I let my thumbs sweep lightly over her nipples, watching as they peaked further between the sparkling gems. Given half a chance, I was sure I could tease them to a deep merlot.

"What convinced you to pierce them?" I asked, my voice hoarse.

"A book. The main character had hers done and I wanted to see what it was like."

Her cheeks grew pinker and I decided then and there that we'd have to play out some scenes from Charlotte's favorite books. I rolled each nipple between a thumb and forefinger, listening to the hitch in her breathing every time I pinched the sensitive buds.

"Did it hurt?"

Her nose wrinkled even as she swayed into my touch. "Like a motherfucker."

I had to choke down a laugh at that word from her pretty lips. "And was it worth the pain? Does this feel good?"

"Fuck, yes," she gasped.

"You are a gift, Charlotte. I've never seen anything quite so lovely."

A soft sigh escaped her lips, drawing my gaze back to her mouth, but she stayed still and silent as I hooked my thumbs in the waistband of her final stitch of clothing.

"Yes?" I asked, waiting until she gave a frantic nod before I dragged them down her legs.

I rose to my feet again, stroking my gaze over all that glorious bare skin until I paused at the curls between her legs, a few shades darker than her hair. For a moment, I looked my fill, but I could see her impatience brimming again.

"Lie on the bed, hands above your head. Don't grab onto the headboard, though. I don't want any pressure on that wrist just yet."

While she climbed onto the mattress and eased herself back onto my pillows, I tossed aside my jacket and t-shirt. Her lips parted when my hands fell to the fly of my jeans, but after easing the zipper down, I left them hanging off my hips.

"That hardly seems fair," she grumbled.

"Do you want your reward or not, angel?" Despite the soft pout on her rosy lips, she nodded. "Then spread your legs. Let me see you."

For a second, I thought this was it—she was going to realize she was in over her head, leap off the bed, and bid me a polite farewell. Instead, her tongue darted out to wet her lower lip and she opened her legs until I could see the glimmer of damp pink flesh peeking out at me.

Calling to me.

"Just beautiful," I whispered, moving to the side of the bed closest to her. "And flexible, aren't you? Don't stress any joints for my sake. Are you comfortable like that?"

"Yes, this is fine. My mom put me in dancing as a kid because I was so clumsy. I kept it up through college," she replied, the blush deepening along her cheekbones.

I reached out and ran one palm from her ankle to her knee, reveling in the softness of her skin. "Now, you'll need to make a choice, angel. Hands, mouth, or cock?"

Charlotte blinked at me like she was in a daze. "I—I don't know. What if I want all three?"

Kneeling on the mattress, I crawled between her legs, stroking my hands along the inside of her thighs. "I suppose it's only fair to let you pick all three. You've been very, very patient, haven't you?"

When I reached the apex of her thighs, parting her folds with my thumbs, she gasped and let her head fall back on the pillows. "Have I?"

I gave a low chuckle as I began to explore her with my fingertips. "Is this why you want me to play the stern doctor role? Because you can't think while I'm doing this and need me to tell you what to do?"

"Yes," she said with a breathless laugh. Her eyes opened again, twinkling at me. "I had a feeling you'd be as overwhelming in the bedroom as you are in regular life."

"Overwhelming in a good way, I hope?" I asked as I let my thumb circle her clit.

A strangled sound escaped her lips, but she nodded vigorously. "Yes. In a very good way."

"Well, since you earned this reward, I'm going to make you come with my hands, then my mouth, then my cock. Sound like a plan?"

This time, her whimpering nod was accompanied by an arch of her back that threw her breasts into sharp relief, the piercings glinting in the light. I leaned down to take one nipple in my mouth, swirling my tongue around the jewelry just as I slipped a finger inside her.

Christ. She was scalding hot and already drenched, her inner muscles clinging to my finger as I moved it slowly in and out. To the rhythm of her gasping breaths, I thrust and circled, suckled and nipped.

"Sawyer," she gasped, her hips rocking against my hand.

One of her hands shifted like she was about to thread her fingers through my hair and I immediately stopped moving, nipping at the side of her breast instead. "What did I say about those hands, angel?"

She made a tortured sound as she shoved her arm back above her head. "Right. Sorry. Fuck, please don't stop."

"Then behave yourself," I warned.

At her frantic nod, I ran my tongue over the pink mark from my teeth, sucked her nipple hard, and flicked my finger over her clit again and again, reveling in every moan and whimpered plea that slipped from her pretty lips.

I didn't stop until she arched with a cry that fell like music around us, then I soothed her back down, and with a final kiss to her breast, I lifted my head.

Her body went limp, her arms still tangled together on the pillows above her head, her eyes half-veiled. Never in my life had I seen anything so beautiful. If I could keep her in my bed like this always, I would die a happy man.

I nuzzled a trail up her throat. Like a sleepy kitten, she lifted her face so I could capture her lips in a slow, languid kiss. When she collapsed back onto the pillow, I grinned down at her.

"One down, angel. Two more to go."

Chapter Fifteen

CHARLOTTE

While I could still think straight, which I was certain was only a temporary reprieve, I considered all the words I'd applied to this man—hot, intense, overwhelming, dominant. At the moment, he was grinning like a schoolboy who'd just won a prize. My heart jolted with an odd rush of tenderness at his expression and I brought my hand down to cup his bristled cheek.

"Ah ah ah," he murmured, nipping my palm as he mimicked my earlier scolding. "You're supposed to keep your hands above your head, my beautiful angel."

Pouting, I tucked it back under my other hand. "I changed my mind. We can just skip ahead to the banging."

Sawyer snorted and said, "We won't be skipping a single damn thing, Charlotte. You might have earned this reward with your patience, but so did I. Just lie back and relax while I finally get a taste of you."

I was laughing until his mouth settled over me, then my amusement morphed into a strangled groan. There wasn't a single part of my body capable of keeping still under the onslaught of his lips and tongue. With one strong forearm banded across my hips and the fingers of his other hand stroking up inside me as he had before, he held me steady no matter how much I wriggled beneath him.

That alone was scorchingly hot.

After the first orgasm, my nerve endings were primed and ready. As he abandoned the teasing swirls of his tongue and sucked hard at my clit, my hips bucked, then when he did it again, my entire body bowed off the bed as a tidal wave of release crashed over me so hard, I thought I'd never recover.

Sawyer gave a few more soft licks, like I was his favorite flavor of lollipop, and planted a kiss to the inside of each thigh. By the time he crawled back up my body, I was shaking like I'd just run a marathon.

"If my heart explodes inside my chest, you'll know what to do, right?" I gasped.

He ran a hand over his mouth and chin as he looked down at my boneless body. "Best part of dating a doctor," he replied with a smirk.

"Is it because you're a doctor that you have such an incredible grasp of human anatomy, or is that just a hobby of yours?"

"Exploring your anatomy is certainly my new favorite hobby," he said as he rolled off the bed.

Unable to move anything but my head just yet, I watched as he shoved his jeans and boxers down over his slim hips. His ass was utter perfection, tight and round, leading down to strong, muscled legs dusted with golden hair. Standing in a swath of sunlight from the bedroom window, he looked like a painting of male virility, all lean muscles and understated strength.

At least, some of it was understated. One particular part was not shy about announcing its presence.

He grabbed a condom from his dresser and tossed it onto the bed before stretching out beside me. "Remember what I said—you're in control here. If you don't like something, if anything doesn't feel good, you tell me and it stops immediately. Got it?"

"Yes, got it. I'm not usually shy about making my likes and dislikes known," I confirmed, mesmerized by the look in his crystalline eyes. That icy blue had gone hot and hungry.

How I'd ever found his gaze cold was beyond me.

"I want things to be clear between us. I promised you were safe with me, and I intend to hold to that." His rough palm cupped my hip before drawing a path of heat up along my ribs to my breast. In a low rumble, he asked, "You want me inside you?"

"Yes. Please, yes."

While his lips curved and his eyes explored my naked body, he tore open the condom and rolled it on. I expected him to issue some sexy order or another, like keeping my hands above my head or spreading my legs wider, but he just tipped his head at me.

"Tell me what positions you enjoy the most. What feels the best to you?"

I blinked for a second. "Oh. Um. From behind, usually, but I trust you to make any position good."

And I did. This was already better than any sexual encounter I'd experienced. I had the utmost faith in him that the rest would be out of this world.

His gaze shot to my wrist, then he reached up and took it in his hand. Pressing gently with his thumb, he worked his way from my palm to my elbow, then zig-zagged back up. "Any pain or discomfort?"

"No," I replied, wondering why this felt so much hotter than the other times he'd checked it.

"I still don't want you putting much pressure on it, but roll onto your stomach, knees tucked under you. Grip your forearms so you're braced on your elbows."

Now, *this* I found almost irrationally hot, this thread of command in his deep, rumbling voice. What I'd told him was true—I wasn't shy about getting my needs met in the bedroom, even when it pissed off the Casanovas who thought they were god's gift to the clitoris. Half of them couldn't find it even with a neon arrow directing them.

Sawyer definitely did not have that issue. He'd made me come twice in a third of the time it usually took me to get to one.

As I settled onto my elbows and knees, Sawyer smoothed his hands over my ass. "So fucking beautiful," he muttered, squeezing the flesh in his palms. "Are you comfortable like this? Wrist is okay?"

"Yes," I gasped as he slipped two fingers inside. As wet as I was, there was no resistance, only sharp pleasure when he pressed his fingertips downward. "Please, Sawyer."

His free hand slid up my spine while the other continued to explore. "Please what, angel?"

"I need you."

The words slipped out on a moan, and to my surprise, he didn't make me wait. As soon as his fingers withdrew, the tip of him pressed against my entrance. He settled his hands on my hips, kneading gently, then he plunged forward in one smooth stroke. When my breath burst from my lungs at the sensation of him filling me, stretching me in the most delicious way imaginable, his grip tightened and he drew back slowly, only to thrust hard once again.

After I adjusted to his size, he settled into a rhythm, slow and then deep, hitting places that sent me spinning into pure bliss, both too much and not enough at the same time. My breathless whimpers must have told him so, because he reached down to palm the inside of my thigh, squeezing and releasing for a moment before his searching fingers reached their destination between my legs.

He leaned forward, his stomach pressed against my lower back, and began stroking over my slick, sensitized flesh before finally circling my clit with his fingertip. Everything inside me quivered at his touch, climbing toward another peak.

"That's it, my angel," he rumbled. "Come for me. Let it go."

With a strangled cry, I did, my arms giving out beneath me as I collapsed forward with my chest against the bedding. Sawyer gave a low chuckle and altered his pace, slowing to a sleek, even glide as I shuddered through the endless waves of the orgasm. He left his hand pressed into my lower stomach, cupping the softness of my belly like he cherished it as much as the rest of my body.

Eventually, I managed to tuck my elbows under me so I could rock back against him with each thrust. That must have been what he was waiting for, because his fingers slipped between my legs again and he moved faster, deeper, until I came one last time with a strangled sob and he followed me over the edge.

I dropped onto my stomach again as he eased out of me, then a second later he was back, pulling me into his arms. Like a rag doll, I lay sprawled across him, listening to the rapid thud of his heart under my ear as I struggled to catch my breath.

"I hope you're comfortable, because I don't think I'll ever be able to move again," I said once my pulse had slowed from a zillion beats per minute to just intense cardio levels.

Maybe I should take a spin class to build my stamina. I had a feeling I'd need it.

Sawyer laughed softly against the top of my head. "I take it that was as good for you as it was for me?"

"Better, I would say, thanks to your little reward system."

"Ah, angel, your pleasure is my responsibility and a reward in itself, as far as I'm concerned."

One of his hands stroked lazily up and down my back while the other rested possessively on the curve of my hip. Though I didn't think his ego needed me to inflate it by saying it aloud, this was by far the best sex of my life. As my pulse slowly returned to normal, I remembered his response when I asked about my heart exploding.

Best part of dating a doctor.

Without lifting my head—I was still too limp for that—I asked, "Are we dating?"

Sawyer's hand stilled for a millisecond before resuming its swirling path. "I'm sorry. I shouldn't have assumed that without discussing it first," he said quietly.

"But that's what you want," I pressed. "To date? Be my boyfriend?"

It was a stupid word when applied to a man who looked like a god among mortals, who knew how to wring pleasure from me like it was his job, but I didn't know what else to call him.

Before answering, he rolled us over so I was flat on my back, staring up at him. His face looked so serious as he searched my expression. Less stern doctor, more concerned partner. Something in my chest thrilled at the word, ridiculous as it seemed.

I hadn't dated in a long time, hadn't really been interested in pursuing anything remotely serious, but I liked the thought of being partnered with this man who could go from drying my tears to caring for my injuries to bringing me so much pleasure I almost burst with it, all in the course of a few days.

"Yes," he replied. The single word rang with conviction.

"Oh, good. I just wanted to be sure we were on the same page."

Sawyer's gaze swept over my features, lingering on the pleased smile that curved my lips, before he dipped his head and kissed me. It was a patient kiss, slow and thorough, but hot enough to send sparks shooting along my veins again. When he lifted his head, his smile burned even hotter.

"Yes, angel, we're on the same page," he whispered as he kissed a path along my neck. "And we're just getting started."

Chapter Sixteen

SAWYER

By the time we took a break for a half-assed dinner of pasta salad straight from the container, followed by a dessert of cubed watermelon that I took great pleasure in placing between her lush lips, I was fully prepared to never leave the bedroom again.

Charlotte was an absolute dream. The things that turned me on set her aflame even more. Underneath that sweet librarian exterior was a beautifully passionate woman who didn't hesitate to make her desires known, though I managed to stay a step ahead, for the most part. She made me feel like I could be myself for the first time in as long as I could remember.

Since my engagement went up in flames, anyway.

I tried my best to keep Veronica out of my head while I was with Charlotte, but the contrast between them threw every memory into sharp relief. Where Charlotte simmered with heat and passion, Veronica had been cold and calculating.

Manipulative, I understood now.

Somehow, she'd been convinced that she could lure me into following my father's footsteps toward neurosurgery. I hadn't seen just how hard she was trying to lead me in one direction until my commitment to my chosen career path finally brought things to a head. My parents, behind the scenes, had apparently been encouraging her in those pursuits long before we got engaged.

Unfortunately for all of them, I accepted a residency position in the emergency department at Eastman Memorial two weeks before the wedding, and that was that.

She broke it off, my parents sided with her, and they'd never forgiven me.

I forced her from my mind and kissed the top of Charlotte's head. "If you're still hungry, I can cook something."

"No," she mumbled into my shoulder. "Let's stay in bed forever."

Laughing, I rolled over so I could kiss the taste of watermelon from her lips. "I won't argue with that."

Neither of us needed to work on Saturday, so we spent the entire night intermittently learning one another and dozing off again, twined together. Though she tended to cocoon herself under the covers after rolling away from me, she was quick to snuggle back into my arms, mumbling sleepily as she nuzzled my throat.

For the night, at least, I set aside all concerns about how things might play out between us in the long run. I was content just to take it a day at a time, to follow her lead and see where this would go. I wanted her too badly to walk away, and too many separate events had conspired to throw her into my arms.

Who was I to question all that?

Sometime past midnight, after Charlotte came so hard against my tongue that she vowed she couldn't take another orgasm before morning, I tucked us under the covers and stroked my hands over her trembling frame until she recovered.

When she didn't fall immediately back to sleep, I asked about her life in Spruce Hill before I showed up. We'd covered the basics, but I felt like I had decades of her life to catch up on.

"I grew up here, but my mom moved in with a boyfriend from Syracuse as soon as I went to college, where I met Penelope. We were dorm roommates and then got an apartment together."

"That's your friend in the city?"

"Yeah, she lives with Grisham now. We met him in college during our senior year. They'd each been living alone after I moved back here, but he went through a bad breakup last year and moved in with Pen temporarily. They get along so well, he just never moved out."

"And Libby was your babysitter?" I asked, sifting my fingers through the thick silk of her hair. "That makes me feel like an old man."

She laughed softly. "You're not that old, but yes, she babysat me every once in a while. Eventually it felt more like hanging out with a cool older sister who'd help with homework and make sure I ate dinner. My mom worked a lot, so it was nice having somebody around instead of being alone all the time."

"I'm glad you had that. She said you knew Mark, too?"

"Mark's family lived next door to me and my mom. He has two brothers, and Libby was always over there, along with their other bestie, Henry. I didn't have a lot of friends as a kid, so watching their crew from afar was like living at the edge of a fairy tale. It was the complete opposite of my life, this big happy family."

"You were a loner?"

"Not really, just different. I wanted to spend my days reading and daydreaming instead of running around outside or riding a bike around the neighborhood with other kids."

She went quiet for a moment, but I didn't interrupt, sensing there was more.

"My life didn't look quite like everyone else's back then—single working mom, latchkey kid who didn't want to play sports. Books were an escape from all that."

I smiled at her. "And now you get to share that with the world."

"Absolutely. At one point in time, I wanted to be a dance teacher. I was always clumsy, but dancing made me feel graceful for once in my life. Then I started helping with baby classes while I was in high school and decided that wasn't for me. I love kids, but I'm less likely to hurt myself if they're sitting on my clock rug at the library instead of twirling around me for an hour. By the time I hit college, my joints started giving me enough trouble to hang up my dance shoes."

"I think you made the safer choice," I teased, "even if your job still clearly carries a risk of injury."

She laughed softly. "Very true. What were you like as a kid?"

"A pain in the ass," I replied, thinking back to all the times my family and I had butted heads. "My father is a neurosurgeon who thinks my career in emergency medicine is a waste of talent and an affront to the family name."

"How could anyone possibly think that?" she replied, scowling.

"They value prestige and reputation. I have no respect for either, which is a serious sin in their eyes."

"They're idiots. You're still saving lives."

Something warm crept through my limbs and settled in my chest, just underneath where Charlotte's head rested. Her defense of me was immediate and instinctive, and I appreciated it more than I could articulate.

When she drifted off, I lay awake for a long time, holding Charlotte in my arms, listening to her soft, even breaths. As I studied the way her lashes fanned over her cheeks, I wondered what this all meant. These feelings, this tug toward her and Spruce Hill. Was I planning to stay here for good? I hadn't thought quite that far ahead when I accepted the job, but I was finding myself pulled deeper into the prospect of making this place my permanent home.

It was far too soon to start working Charlotte into that picture, but even now, it was clear just how deeply I was drawn to her. While my ex-fiancée had pushed me to move more quickly in proposing than I otherwise would have, Charlotte seemed almost like she had no interest in pressuring me to even declare us officially dating—her inquiry earlier had come across more like she was curious if that's how I viewed things.

Just before I fell asleep with her curled into my side, I realized that maybe it wasn't that Charlotte herself was inherently dangerous, only the depth of my attraction to her.

THE WEEKEND PASSED IN much the same vein, though she insisted she needed to go home to throw in a load of laundry before Monday morning rolled around. When I showed up at her door two hours later, she planted her hands on her hips and gave me her sternest glare. It was adorable.

"We cannot spend every minute of every day having sex," she insisted.

I spread my arms in invitation. "I'm open to suggestions. Is there something else you'd like to do this afternoon?"

Surprise flitted across her face and I wondered if she'd been spoiling for a fight—though whether she wanted a reason to slam the door in my face or for me to convince her we could, in fact, spend every minute in bed, I wasn't sure.

"Yes, actually. Do you like ice cream?"

I laughed. "I might be stern sometimes, Charlotte, but I'm not dead. I love ice cream."

She flashed a cheeky grin and grabbed her purse from the hook behind the door. "You've done an awful lot of exercise this weekend," she mused, looking me up and down as she locked the door behind her. "Are you up for a walk? It's only a few blocks."

"I'm not that old, either, brat," I muttered.

Her laughter danced around us and she slipped her hand into mine. This was...new. It had been a long, long time since I'd walked the streets holding hands with a woman, but it felt good. Right.

For the first time since I'd met her, she was dressed in jeans. The t-shirt she'd thrown on boasted a picture of some eighties movie, slipped off one tantalizing shoulder, and lay knotted at her hip. Though she caught me giving the outfit an admiring glance, I kept my mouth shut so she wouldn't accuse me of trying to derail her plans.

The ice cream shop, Caboose Creamery, was located inside a converted train car just outside the park. Charlotte studied the menu board with an expression of such earnest concentration that I couldn't stop myself from kissing her, grinning when she blushed prettily and gave an airy shrug.

"They change up their flavors regularly. It's a very important decision, you know. Whatever you don't choose might not be available next time," she said primly.

An indulgent smile pulled at my lips. "Very good strategy. What would you recommend?"

After another five minutes of discussions on the pros and cons of the offerings, Charlotte settled on Mail Car Mocha and I went with Rocky Railroad. With our cones in hand, we wandered down the sidewalk toward the park rather than straight home.

"How do you feel about geese?" she asked as we reached a tiny pond at the back of the park.

I followed her to an ornate metal bench and stretched my arm along the back when we sat down, curling it behind her shoulders. The way she snuggled right into my side was intensely satisfying, though the hand she rested halfway up my thigh was difficult to ignore.

"In a general sense, or is there something specific I should be considering here?" I queried, inclining my head at the fat Canada geese scattered across the pond.

"In general. I really should have asked you this before I let you in my pants," she replied, "but I guess I was a little distracted."

I pondered what answer she might be looking for. "I...like them?"

"Unconvincing, Doctor."

Dropping my hand to her ribs, I tickled her until she shrieked. "Careful of the ice cream, angel. After all that decision-making, I'd hate for you to drop your cone."

She glared when I replaced my arm along the back of the bench, but I pressed a quick kiss to the corner of her frown before licking away a dot of ice cream from her lip. Those green eyes went a little hazy. I grinned down at her until she made a disgruntled sound and settled back against me.

"Is it safe to assume that you have strong opinions on geese, Charlotte?"

"Yes," she said simply. "They're terrifying, but kind of glorious despite that. I love them for it."

When I laughed, I hoped she wouldn't take it as an insult, but she only peeked over and grinned. "I find you hopelessly charming, inside and out."

A fierce blush crept along her cheeks. "Well, thank you."

We had just finished our cones when a ball of pink tulle came hurtling along the paved path in front of the bench and launched itself into Charlotte's lap. I tried to absorb some of the impact, keeping Charlotte steady so she didn't reinjure her wrist as she caught the child in her arms.

"Miss Charlotte, Miss Charlotte!" the little girl shrieked, bouncing with energy.

Charlotte only laughed. "Miss Emma, Miss Emma! What a lovely surprise."

Emma of the pink tulle bounded back to her feet. "We're going out to dinner but my mom said I could come say hi!"

"I'm so glad you did," Charlotte said with a fond smile. "Emma, this is Dr. Thorne, he's new in town so I'm introducing him to our geese. Dr. Thorne, this is Emma, our reader of the month for April this year."

The little girl held out a tiny hand, which I shook. "It's a pleasure to meet you, Emma."

"Are you Miss Charlotte's boyfriend?" she asked.

"I am," I confirmed, my tone solemn.

Her eyes lit with excitement. "Then you should know that Miss Charlotte doesn't like chocolate candies, but she loves Skittles. The red ones are her favorite. I have to go now. Bye!"

"See you around, Em," Charlotte called as the tutu-clad child disappeared again.

"Skittles, huh?" I shot a glance at Charlotte, who grinned.

"The berry flavors are actually my favorite, but red will do in a pinch."

I leaned back and waited until she snuggled into her spot at my side. "Does anyone in this town *not* adore you?"

"As shocking as it is," she replied, "yes, there are a few people around here who don't like me much."

"Well, Ms. Whitmore, I suppose my devotion will just have to make up for it," I said against her ear, enjoying the shiver that ran through her. "Now that we've enjoyed ice cream, fresh air, and socializing, what do you say we head home and make the most of our remaining weekend hours?"

Chapter Seventeen

CHARLOTTE

WORK HAD NEVER FELT tedious to me, even when certain days moved slowly, but the following week plodded along at a snail's pace. Sawyer respected that I'd rather sleep at home on work nights instead of staying at his place, but he more than made up for it in the evenings. He'd cooked dinner twice, ordered the takeout of my choice another night, and been content just to watch movies together when my period started and I wanted nothing more than to flop on the couch with a hot pack.

Without complaint or condescension, he draped a blanket over me, placed my feet on his lap, and gave me the best foot massage I'd ever experienced.

I suspected he was waiting for me to invite him to spend the night at my house, but he was extraordinarily patient. We both had to work that Saturday, so I texted him mid-morning on Friday when I had a quiet moment to slip into my office.

Pizza night at my place tonight?

I didn't expect an immediate response, since Spruce Hill had jumped on the Dr. Hottie train once word got out he was available for appointments at the clinic, so I settled in to sort through my inbox while I waited. There were a few evening events coming up that I'd need to be here for, but given that I'd had no social life until recently, I was mostly handling them on my own.

Sawyer had just replied to my text with a resounding yes when Olivia poked her head around the door of the office.

"There's someone out here asking for you. It's not the stud, though."

"On my way," I said, pocketing the phone and closing my laptop.

The young man on the other side of the circulation desk looked familiar, but most of the town came into the library at some point or another in their lives. He was in his early twenties, with coal-black hair and blue eyes even lighter than Sawyer's, and I was pretty sure he'd come in with the Schroeder twins for one of our elementary read-a-thons several months ago.

I pasted on my Friendly Librarian smile as I approached.

"Hi there, can I help you with something?" I asked, still wracking my brain to try to place him.

"Hey, Miss Whitmore. I don't know if you remember me, my name is Craig DeWitt. When I was in high school, I returned a book with my mom's check in it and you helped us out," he said shyly.

"Craig! Yes, of course I remember you. How've you been? How's your mom?"

"Good, we're good. Getting by. This is my final semester of college."

"That's fantastic, congratulations. You must be working hard," I said, thinking how fast time flew.

"Yeah, for sure." His smile widened as he dipped his chin, looking both bashful and proud. "I'm still babysitting for the Schroeders, too, so that keeps me busy. The kids told me they adopted their puppy from you."

"Spoon," I murmured, my heart squeezing. "How's he doing?"

"He's great, growing fast though. The kids renamed him Barney."

I hid my cringe behind a forced smile. "That's great. So, what brings you in today?"

His face reddened slightly. "Well, uh, I lost an assignment I was working on. I had a book on electrical engineering checked out that I dropped off earlier this week, so I was hoping maybe the paper was inside. You mentioned back then that you were going to keep a file of stuff that gets returned with library books and I wondered if you still do that?"

"I do, yes. I'll take a look but I don't remember seeing anything like that. I'm happy to ask around among the staff, though. Do you have time to wait a few minutes?"

"Not really," he said, smiling sheepishly. "I need to get to another class, but if you don't mind just checking your folder, that'd be great. I can stop back in the morning if I don't find it at home."

"Sure, be right back," I replied, jogging back into my office as fast as my adorable but impractical new kitten heels would carry me. I unlocked the file cabinet and flipped through my folder of lost items, but engineering homework was not included among the assortment of papers.

When I returned to the circulation desk, I shook my head. "No luck. Sorry, Craig."

"Thanks for checking, Miss Whitmore, I really appreciate it. Have a nice weekend," he said as he pulled on a baseball cap and waved.

Olivia appeared from behind a bookshelf, carrying a basket of toys from the children's section to be wiped down with disinfectant. "That kid has a mad crush on you, boss."

I frowned at her. "He does not. Anyway, if you come across anything that looks like an electrical engineering assignment, set it aside for me, please?"

"Sure. But I'm telling you, that expression was pure hero worship if I ever saw it. Kid thinks you hung the moon."

"I don't even think I've seen him in person since the check incident."

She gave me a skeptical look. "If you say so."

"Besides," I drawled, "I have a boyfriend, apparently."

Her hoot of laughter said my distraction technique worked. "Apparently? You weren't sure?"

"Look, it's been a long time. Let's get these toys cleaned up and talk about the Senior Luncheon next week."

By the end of the day, my feet hurt like the devil and there was a run in my favorite burgundy tights. Olivia stayed to help me close up the library, then bounced her eyebrows dramatically when she told me to enjoy my weekend.

I drove home feeling strangely blah despite her optimism, but when I pulled into my driveway, Sawyer was just lifting his messenger bag from the back seat of his car.

"Well, if you aren't a sight for sore eyes," he said as I locked the car behind me. His gaze sharpened on my face. "Everything okay?"

I walked straight into his arms, pressing my face to his shirt. He always changed his clothes at the clinic after a shift, usually from a button-down and dress pants to jeans and a t-shirt. This one was a blue only slightly darker than his eyes and baby soft against my cheeks.

"Angel, you're worrying me. What's wrong?"

"Long week," I mumbled.

Sawyer cupped his hand at the back of my neck and waited until I lifted my face to look at him. "I'm going to throw my stuff in the house. I want you to go change into something comfortable, then we'll order the pizza. After we eat, I'll give you a massage and you can tell me all about your long week, all right?"

I nodded and trudged into the house, wondering why I felt so low. As I was pulling off my snagged tights in favor of the bamboo pajama shorts I loved, I realized I'd been sleeping like crap since I returned home Sunday night from Sawyer's house. With that knowledge, I came to a decision. I pulled on a sweatshirt and jogged downstairs, feeling renewed.

Sawyer was just coming into the kitchen when I reached the doorway. "You look happier already," he said.

"Just exhausted. I haven't been sleeping well," I replied.

Studying my expression closely, he asked, "Oh? Anything I can help with?"

"That depends," I said as I slipped my arms around his waist. "I know you're working in the morning, but would you be willing to stay the night?"

Joy lit his features like a thousand candles. "I thought you'd never ask," he replied, coasting his lips across my cheeks and the bridge of my nose.

The heaviness of the week dissipated like mist under the warmth of his smile. When we curled up on the couch together to wait for the pizza delivery, he had me sit between his legs so he could work out the knots in my shoulders. Eventually, I relaxed back against his chest, soaking up the feel of his strong arms wrapped around my middle.

The only thing better was taking his hand after dinner and tugging him upstairs with me.

Though he was gone by the time I woke up, I slept better than I had all week long. The clinic opened two hours before the library, but his last appointment slot was at noon, while the library stayed open until three. We hadn't made any explicit plans for the afternoon, but Sawyer came in just after one, holding the books he'd checked out the day he got his library card.

"Well, well, well," I called. "In need of more reading material, Dr. Thorne?"

There was one family over in the children's section, a few scattered students at the computers, and a pair of older gentlemen browsing the nonfiction stacks. Sawyer cast a casual glance around to see if any of them were within earshot before leaning his elbows on the desk and whispering, "Where do you keep the sexy books?"

I slapped my palm over my mouth as I burst out laughing. "I'm afraid you'll need a special card for that."

"Really?" he asked, frowning.

"No." I choked down my laughter. "The romance section is along the far wall. If you need any pointers, I'd be happy to give my personal reviews of the ones I've read."

He looked over at the wall, then back at me, a wicked smile on his lips. "I'm suddenly *very* curious about what kind of naughty books you enjoy, Charlotte."

Right on cue, one of the students appeared at the edge of my vision, fidgeting nervously as he looked back and forth between us. Sawyer winked at me and strolled away—straight toward the romance novels—while I helped the kid find a book for school. To my surprise, though, Sawyer stayed over there well after the kid went back to writing his essay at one of the computers, so I focused on my own work while he read the backs and inspected cover art.

Half an hour later, Sawyer strolled up with an impressive array of books in a variety of romance sub-genres, which I checked out for him, then he flashed a swift grin.

"I have this charity ball thing coming up at the hospital in a few weeks. I thought I might be able to get out of it since I no longer work there, but joke's on me, I guess. My father offered up my attendance to appease the board when he booked a trip to the Bahamas for him and my mom. It's black tie. Can I convince you to go with me?"

I blinked at him for a second. "Black tie. Like, you'll be in a tux?"

"Yes, angel, I'll be in a tux," he replied, smile widening.

"I'll have to find something to wear," I hedged. I was torn between the temptation of seeing him in a tuxedo and the horror of having to rub shoulders with a room full of rich people.

"You'll be the most beautiful woman there, no matter what you wear. Think about it and let me know. You don't have to do anything that makes you uncomfortable, angel. You know that, right?"

I nodded. "Of course."

Sawyer reached over and brushed one knuckle along my cheek. "I'll get out of your hair. Can I make dinner for you tonight?"

"Sure, that'd be great. I'll see you in a bit."

He winked and left the library, unabashedly carrying an armful of books with shirtless men on the covers.

For a long time, I stared after him, my mind whirling with images of getting dolled up for a fancy night out, then I forced my attention back to work just in time for a gaggle of small children to run up to the desk with their finds.

Chapter Eighteen

SAWYER

CHARLOTTE CAME TO TWO important decisions that weekend.

The first was that she wanted to go to the charity ball with me, which was a bigger relief than I'd anticipated. I hated those events with a passion, but having her on my arm would make the entire thing more palatable—especially since I couldn't wait to see her all dressed up. She was outrageously stunning no matter what she was wearing, from work clothes to yoga pants, but something told me whatever she picked out would be mouthwatering.

The second decision was that she no longer wanted to sleep alone. I didn't care whose bed we were in, so I was happy to accept her invitation to spend the nights at her place. Her home was her haven, a sweet little nest she'd built for herself over the years, and mine was an impersonal rental.

In my mind, it was an easy choice.

On Thursday night, I took her out to a sushi restaurant she'd been wanting to try, located at the outer edges of the city. It was closer to Eastman Memorial than it was to Spruce Hill, but I was more than willing to make the drive just to see the blissful smile on her face when she took her first bite.

"I picked a dress for the ball," she told me during dinner. "It's black and a bit retro, but I think it'll be elegant enough as long as no one asks how much I paid for it."

I laughed. "No one will ask, and I'm sure you'll look absolutely divine, angel."

"Pen and Grisham are making me go shopping for accessories next weekend," she added, making a face.

I still hadn't met her friends, though I wasn't sure if it was simply scheduling conflicts or because Charlotte was afraid I thought less of them after their involvement in her injury. Reflecting on their carelessness bothered me a little, but accidents happened—and the course of our relationship might have been very different if we hadn't met that night at the hospital.

Hell, now that I knew what a homebody Charlotte was, even moving into the house next door didn't guarantee she would have spared me a second glance.

"That will be fun," I said, my voice gentle and smile reassuring. I had no desire to alienate her from her friends and even less desire for her to think that I might harbor those intentions.

"Pen has been pushing for a movie night, all four of us. Maybe we can pick a date sometime after the ball?"

I nodded. "Absolutely. Libby also mentioned having us over for dinner sometime. She said if you refused, she'd tell me every embarrassing story she remembers from your childhood."

Charlotte groaned. "She is the worst. Fine, I'll go, but only if you swear you won't believe a word Mark says about me. He's like the big brother I never wanted."

By the end of the meal, Charlotte was happy and relaxed and the slightest bit tipsy. I caught her elbow when she swayed as we stood from the table, but before I could tease her about it, my eyes landed on a dark-eyed brunette seated by the door. Ice flooded my veins, freezing me in place. Even in her distraction, Charlotte caught the way I tensed and followed my line of sight, her green gaze resting solidly on the woman.

My ex-fiancée.

A woman I had managed to avoid for more than ten years, since she called off the wedding days before we were supposed to walk down the aisle together.

"Who's that?" Charlotte asked.

"No one." The lie was a reflex, like some kind of defense mechanism to preserve the bubble of peace we'd created over dinner, and I regretted it practically the moment it slipped out.

"She's pretty."

"Come on, let's get you home," I replied, forcing brightness into my tone.

Charlotte stared back at the woman for a beat before letting me usher her out of the restaurant. When we reached the sidewalk, she said, "Maybe she just thinks you're smoking hot."

I snorted. "Maybe."

"You really are, you know. It's terribly unfair."

Startled, I laughed, then dipped my head to kiss her before I opened the passenger door for her. "I'm not sure why that would be unfair, when you're the most beautiful woman I've ever seen."

Blessedly, she dropped the subject completely during the ride home. Sober, Charlotte could happily go hours without speaking. Tipsy? She became an absolute chatterbox.

For the full forty minute drive, she talked about the charity ball, her upcoming events at the library, and—oddly enough—the time Libby painted Charlotte's finger and toenails with some kind of glitter polish that left her nails sparkling for weeks after she took it off.

Though I managed to carry out my side of the twisting conversation, my gut clenched with guilt over lying to her. I tried to reassure myself that my response was at least partly true.

Veronica was no one to me, not anymore.

Somehow, I didn't think Charlotte would see it that way. I wanted to come clean, but I couldn't bring myself to shatter her happy buzz.

When we got back to Charlotte's house, I helped her undress and tucked her into bed before brushing my teeth with the spare toothbrush she'd added to a little cup on her bathroom sink. I stripped down to my boxers and crawled into bed beside her, tugging her sleepy form into my arms.

This was dangerous territory and completely new to me. I'd never told any of the women I slept with about Veronica because it had never mattered. None of those relationships had any kind of destination aside from an end date.

With Charlotte, everything was different.

She felt like home to me, even more than Spruce Hill did. If we were going to be together for any length of time, she deserved to know the truth.

"Angel?" I whispered, preparing to confess, but there was no response from the woman draped bonelessly against my chest.

I lay awake for a long time, wondering if I could explain my history without her recognizing that the woman in the restaurant was my ex. Even as I berated myself for considering that lie of omission, I suspected with growing dread that Charlotte might hate me for lying to her face when she asked who I was looking at after dinner.

In my attempt not to dampen the glow of a happy evening, I was afraid I'd created a tangled mess of epic proportions.

Though I resolved to discuss my history with Charlotte after work on Friday, that plan was derailed partway through the afternoon when I overheard a patient in the waiting room.

"Did you hear about the break-in at the library?"

My head jerked up, but Libby laid a calming hand on my arm. "It was overnight. Charlotte's fine," she said in a low voice.

"Who breaks into a library?" I whispered back, rubbing a hand over my face. I checked my phone, but I hadn't missed any texts or calls from Charlotte, which surprised me.

Libby gave a one-shouldered shrug. "I'm not sure. Look, after this lot out here, we don't have many appointments left. If you don't mind taking care of Mr. Ankarberg and Mrs. Smithens, you can head out after that, go check on Charlotte."

"Thank you, Libby. I appreciate that."

I sucked in a deep breath before focusing on my patients. Even knowing Charlotte had been safe in my arms when the break-in occurred wasn't enough to completely quell the jolt of fear in my chest.

My remaining two appointments were elderly pillars of the community with common age-related complaints, but nothing serious. I gave each of them my full attention, walked Mrs. Smithens out to where her son waited in his car to take her home, and drove straight to the library.

Charlotte looked exhausted behind the circulation desk, but she offered a weary smile when I walked in. "Sawyer, what are you doing here?"

"You had a break-in?" I scoured her with my gaze to make sure she was really okay.

"Yeah, during the night. No one was here, and nothing was taken. It wasn't a big deal, just a hassle talking to the police all morning. Aren't you supposed to be working?"

I sighed heavily and rubbed my hands over my face. "Libby told me to cut out early. Someone in the waiting room mentioned the break-in and I was worried about you."

She bit her lip. "I'm sorry. It's been so hectic, and I didn't think it was worth interrupting you at work. Everyone's fine, really."

The relief made me dizzy. "No, I'm sorry. I rushed over here like a jackass. I don't know what I was thinking. I'm just glad you're okay," I said quietly.

"Do you want to sit down? You don't look so good," she offered, motioning me to come around the desk. "You can relax in my office for a few minutes, at least. The air conditioning in there is killer. We call it the Ice Box."

I laughed weakly as I followed her around the circulation desk and down a short hallway behind it to her office. Once I was seated in the chair at her desk, she pressed her lips to my forehead and said she had to finish up what she was doing but would check on me soon.

The office itself was small, featuring the desk, a file cabinet, and a couple of bookshelves, but the little personal touches all screamed *Charlotte*. There was even an entire bulletin board covered in artwork and construction paper cards from the youngest of her adoring fans, the drawings ranging from mythical creatures and beloved book characters to flowers and the Spruce Hill Lighthouse—which I'd been meaning to visit but hadn't yet.

After my heart rate slowed, I stood up to go back out front. My gaze landed on a vase of pale pink hyacinths sitting on top of the file cabinet and I wondered if she brought them from her yard.

Then I froze when I noticed scratches around the lock at the corner of the cabinet. I was still studying the marks when Charlotte came back in.

"What is it?"

I pointed to the scratches. "Looks like someone tried to break into this."

She nodded. "Yeah, the police dusted it for prints, I guess. There's nothing valuable inside, though, and based on the security footage, the guy bolted before he even got it open. The cops think he was looking for money."

"Could they identify him from the video?"

"No," she said with a shrug. "He was wearing a ski mask."

I turned to her, frowning. "You don't seem very concerned about this."

"Sawyer, it was the middle of the night. No matter what events we have going on, no one is ever here that late. Something startled the guy and he left without taking a single thing, not even a magazine. The only reason I even knew something was up was that the back door was unlocked."

"Did he pick the lock?" I asked.

"No, he broke a pane of glass."

I heard the frustration creeping into her tone, like she was annoyed by my questions, and forced myself to back off, even though it made no sense to me—why would anyone go to the trouble of breaking in and not take anything? Still, I saw the tightness at the corners of Charlotte's lips. Instead of pressing further, I opened my arms and she practically threw herself into them.

"I'm just glad you're safe," I murmured into her hair.

Despite her apparent nonchalance, she trembled slightly in my arms as she nodded against my chest. I held her until she was steady once more, then she tugged me down for a quick kiss. When her lips lingered, I sank my hand into her hair and kissed her more thoroughly.

"I should get back out there," she said with obvious reluctance when I let go of her. "Do you want to stick around? I'll be closing up soon, but I can just meet you at home if you want."

"If it's not going to drive you up the wall, I'll stay, but I'll keep out of your hair."

A quick grin flashed across her face as she turned to lead us out of the office. Instead of pretending to browse book spines, I grabbed a magazine off a rack by the front desk and planted myself at a small table in the corner, idly flipping pages without glancing down.

Nothing would distract me from my worry, so I didn't bother to pretend.

For the most part, the library remained virtually empty, aside from a couple patrons coming in to pick up their requested items. After tutting about the break-in to Charlotte, they left in a swirl of perfume, leaving just the two of us in the building.

"I'm calling it a day," she whispered loudly when the clock ticked to fifteen minutes before the official closing time.

"Good, the silence is killing me," I replied as I replaced the magazine and leaned against the desk. I waited as she completed her tasks and locked up the office and exterior doors, including the one with a board over the broken pane, then I walked her out to her car.

After the stress of the past hour, I was so eager to get her home where I knew she was safe beside me that I forgot all about my plan to tell her the tale of my broken engagement.

Chapter Nineteen

SAWYER

Just as we sat down at the table for breakfast the next morning, Charlotte's phone vibrated from the pocket of her lounge pants. She pulled it out and frowned as she read the message.

"Chief Roberts wants me to meet him at the library this afternoon to go over everything that's in my office."

"I'll bring you over after you eat. While you're there with him, I can run out for some groceries."

She looked up at me, her expression conflicted. "You don't have to babysit me."

"I know that, angel."

"I really don't think I'm in any danger."

After a calming breath, I stroked my fingers lightly across the back of her hand. "I hope not, but I have nothing else to do today, so I'm happy to drive you. Unless you want me to stay there with you?"

I hadn't wanted to presume or make her feel like I was trying to chaperone her, but I was more than happy to stay by her side as long as she'd let me. The police would ensure her safety, and this *was* Spruce Hill. Even growing up in the city, I remembered a time when Spruce Hill's claim to fame was being voted Safest Town in America.

Though she was silent as she considered it, she ultimately shook her head. "No, I'll be okay. I'll take the ride over, but do what you need to do. I promise I won't walk home before you get back."

I snorted, but I'd been a little worried that she might do just that, so I appreciated the reassurance. "Well then, if you won't let me pamper you anymore, how are we passing the time before you need to meet Roberts?"

"I know just the thing," she said, flashing a radiant smile.

"THIS ISN'T QUITE WHAT I expected to be doing today," I informed her when we pulled up to a small plaza just off of Main Street.

"No, you were probably hoping to tie me to the bed and have your wicked way with me, but you'll have to wait for that," she called as she hopped out of the car and danced around the mostly empty parking lot. "Get a move on, Dr. Hottie!"

I followed at a much slower pace as she practically skipped toward the building. "And you're really not going to tell me why we're here?" I asked, trying to peer through the paper-covered windows.

"Nope. Patience is a virtue, or so I've heard."

"Not one you'd know about," I muttered.

Charlotte turned back with her mouth open wide in an exaggeratedly scandalized expression, then winked and unlocked the door using her own key. I followed her inside, only mildly convinced that she wasn't leading me into some kind of trap, but as soon as the door closed behind us, I heard the sound of joyous barking coming from somewhere in the back.

We strolled down a long corridor with glass-paneled kennels on either side, which Charlotte informed me were for overnight guests. When we finally reached the end of it, the hall opened into a huge room divided into separate play areas, each with wide doors that led to what looked like a little courtyard on either side.

"Hey, Twig! This is Sawyer, who got the Spoon Seal of Approval before his adoption. Sawyer, this is Twig. They run the daycare and volunteer at the library now and then."

I smiled and shook hands with Twig, whose vibrant purple hair was cut into a long shag. "It's nice to meet you, Twig. I can't believe how big this place is inside. From the outside, it looks like a mob front."

Twig threw back their head and laughed. "Don't give away all my secrets, Doc. You two here to meet some of the rescue pups or just to hang out?"

Charlotte hesitated, but I saw the look of longing on her face, so I said, "I'd like to meet some rescue pups, actually."

With a wink, Twig pointed at me. "This is a man who knows what's what, Lottie. Let me go round up a few of them. I'll bring them into the small group section if you want to get set up in there."

I started shaking my head as Charlotte turned around. "Seriously, I am starting to feel left out, here. Does everyone in town have a different nickname for you?"

"You call me 'angel' all the time."

"That doesn't count. It's an endearment. So far I've heard Charlie, Lottie—what else is there?"

"Well, I don't mind the endearment, but the nicknames get old fast. You just keep your mouth shut and maybe you'll live to see another dawn, buster," she warned, but I tickled her ribs as she led the way to a little corral off to one side until she wrapped her hands around mine.

"But there are so many things I can do with my mouth, Charlotte," I murmured into her ear.

"Promises, promises."

I followed her into the sectioned off area, where she promptly sat cross-legged on the floor. "I'm definitely too old for that," I told her as I claimed a folding chair instead.

Those eyes that had snapped at me earlier now twinkled with amusement. "Yes, you're positively ancient, aren't you?"

Twig opened the half door on the opposite wall from where we'd entered and herded a gaggle of stumbling, gamboling puppies into the area with us. After flashing me a wide grin, Twig mimed dramatically from behind Charlotte's head. I assumed they were indicating I should make sure she went home with one of these puppies.

"Why haven't you taken in a new foster pup yet?" I asked as casually as possible.

Fortunately, a little silvery-gray pit mix with brilliant blue eyes had caught her attention, distracting her from my plotting. "I don't know, really. Spoon was one of the special ones. I'm not quite ready yet. Saying goodbye gets hard sometimes," she said with a shrug.

"Maybe it's time to adopt your own."

Her head lifted and her eyes narrowed on my face just as the rest of the herd catapulted onto her lap. Instead of responding, though, she laughed and hugged the crowd of wriggling bodies closer against her own. I wouldn't say this was better than sex, but Christ, it felt good to see her so happy and carefree.

Despite my best intentions, I ended up on the floor with her, my lap covered in three exhausted puppies. One fell fast asleep sprawled across my thighs, and the other two draped themselves over their brother to plaster sloppy kisses across my jaw.

Charlotte's arms were full of the drowsy silver pup, his round little head resting in the curve of her elbow. She gazed down at him with an expression that stalled my breath in my lungs with its sweetness.

"Angel," I said quietly, trying my best not to wake up the sleeping animals.

She met my eyes, her lips quirking upward. "Yes?"

"You are extraordinarily beautiful. And I think that little guy needs you."

"You're a bad influence, Doctor," she replied as she looked down at the bundle in her arms. "You realize you're going to be spending almost as much time with him as I am, right? Puppies are a giant pain in the ass."

"It's a sacrifice I'm willing to make." *One among so many others,* I added silently as I considered all the things I would do to make her happy.

As if summoned by Charlotte's imminent decision, Twig appeared at the wall and smirked at us. "Please tell me he's going home with you. He's the sweetest thing. You know I'll keep cutting you a deal on daycare whenever you need it."

"If I hadn't surprised Sawyer with the trip here, I would accuse the two of you of conspiring against me," Charlotte scolded. When the pup stirred, she rubbed a single finger up his nose, right between his eyes, and he settled again.

"I'll call the foster for you," Twig offered. "Since you're with the rescue, it should be easy as pie to process the adoption. I'll find out when they'll be able to bring him to you."

There was no denying the expression on Charlotte's face—a sweet, wistful sort of yearning. It made my heart clench in my chest.

"Say yes," I prodded gently.

She met my gaze, biting her lip for all of two seconds before she said, "Yes. I want him."

Twig cheered quietly and I couldn't hold back a grin. Careful not to dislodge the crew on my lap, I twisted my wrist to check my watch. "Now that that's settled, we should get you over to the library to meet with Chief Roberts, angel."

Eyes brightening at the endearment, Twig said, "I'll just gather up these ruffians, then. Text me when you're done tonight, why don't you?"

One by one, we surrendered the pups to Twig, saving the little gray guy for last. I helped Charlotte to her feet so she could hold onto him as long as possible, and when she lifted her gaze to mine, her eyes shone through a veil of tears.

"Thank you," she whispered.

"Anything and everything, angel. Someday, I hope you'll believe that."

Chapter Twenty

CHARLOTTE

Under normal circumstances, I would have been an anxious mess after making a huge decision—especially one as important as adopting a dog. Instead, it felt like another little tangle of fate working its way into our lives. Sawyer seemed happy about the turn of events, which was the biggest surprise of the day so far.

"What will you name him?" he asked as we turned back toward the library. "Fork?"

I shot him a blank look. "That's a terrible name for a dog."

His laughter filled the car, settling over me like a warm blanket. "Brat. What, then?"

Tipping my head, I considered it and said, "I'm not sure. He looks like he should be wearing a bowler hat."

"Like Charlie Chaplin? Sadly, I suppose Charlie is off the table. It feels like this town collects nicknames for you."

I grinned. "Maybe I collect them for myself, Dr. Hottie."

Before he could respond, though, we pulled into the library's parking lot. As soon as the engine was off, Sawyer caught my hand in his and squeezed.

"You're absolutely sure you don't want me to stay with you?"

"I'm okay. Go on, do some shopping. I'll text you when we're finished, or feel free to come in and browse if you want, after you're done." I leaned over and kissed him hard before opening the car door. "And think about dog names, for god's sake, because we are getting a real live puppy!"

Sawyer's laughter kept me company as I jogged up the front steps and into the quiet of the library. It always felt like coming home, walking into the place where I'd hidden away for so much of my childhood. Chief Roberts rose from a table by the nonfiction section and shook my hand. I waved at Olivia and the pair of volunteers working today as we passed them.

Roberts hailed from Oakville, but he had joined the police force in Spruce Hill sometime before I was born. I didn't know him as well as I did Rose Hanson, who I suspected would be taking over when the chief finally retired, but he was a jovial kind of guy who liked to read sci-fi on his days off.

I'd been sworn to secrecy about his recent interest in graphic novels, which he claimed were easier on his aging eyes.

"I'm sorry to drag you in here on your day off, Charlotte. Something is lurking at the back of my brain and I just want to make sure we cover all the bases," he said quietly as I led him into the office. "You doing all right?"

"I'm perfectly fine, though Sawyer is on your side in taking this seriously, and believe me, he is the biggest worrywart I've ever met," I told him.

"Good man. I like him already and I haven't met him yet, though I've heard plenty."

"I'm not surprised," I said dryly. News traveled through Spruce Hill at the speed of light. I flipped on the overhead and spread my arms. "Well, this is it. There is nothing valuable anywhere in this room. I don't even know what anyone would be looking for."

Roberts waved a hand back and forth. "What's valuable for one person isn't necessarily valuable for another," he pointed out.

"Fair enough. Where should we start?"

He turned slowly in a circle, scanning the bookshelves. "We know he tried to get into the file cabinet, so let's start with that. What do you keep in there?"

I unlocked it and pulled open the two drawers. "Personnel files, printouts for the occasional board meeting, supply orders, event booking contracts. A large portion of those things are now electronic, but since the average age of the board members is upwards of seventy-two, I try to keep paper copies on hand."

"Sounds about right." He grinned, thumbing through the folders one by one. "Would these personnel files include anything somebody might want to locate?"

Frowning, I opened the folder and spread them out. "They're basically just the staff and volunteer applications on file, so I can't imagine so. No bank info or social security numbers. Finding out where a local lives isn't exactly hard in Spruce Hill. Why break into a building just to find it written down?"

The chief had no answer to that question. None of the folders contained anything that warranted a break-in. Roberts looked as baffled as I felt as we flipped through every single item in the cabinet. When we reached my little lost and found file, he held it up with raised brows.

"What's this?"

"That's just stuff that gets returned by accident. I started keeping it in a folder several years ago, after Craig DeWitt returned a book with his deadbeat dad's very rare child support check inside it. His mom was in a panic. Usually it's grocery lists, sometimes a wallet-sized photo of a grandkid. I'm often able to reunite them with their owner either using my amazing powers of deduction—like in the case of Bernie Hanover's crossword puzzle—or by looking up who checked out that particular book."

"But some things you can't pair with someone?"

I nodded. "The chute isn't terribly high tech. It's basically a mail slot in the outer wall that leads to a bin on the other side. Things fall out of the books on their way down, or papers get caught between a stack of returns rather than inside an individual book's pages. Sometimes kids throw random crap into the chute without a book, though I think Deirdre Collins was the repeat offender, tossing trash, banana peels, that kind of thing. She was grounded for two months after the last incident and it hasn't happened since."

The chief chuckled at that. "Scared straight."

"Or plotting revenge in the form of bubblegum. Anyway, inside the folder is a log of the dates each item came through, but after six months or so, I generally shred anything that wasn't claimed since the last cleanout."

"Right," he said, looking through the small collection of items. "Tell me about these."

"Okay, um. There's a spelling list, probably second or third grade. A love letter to Mikey, which unfortunately is too common a name for me to even guess at its intended recipient. Prescription, practically illegible, so I can't tell you anything except that I know it's not Libby's handwriting." I paused, considering. "Or Sawyer's, for that matter."

Roberts sorted through the rest of the pile, but it was more of the same. He picked up the prescription paper. "This doesn't even look like English. Could it be for a narcotic? Maybe your burglar was an addict trying to get it back?"

"If I can't tell it's a prescription for a narcotic, anyone could have come in and said, 'Gosh, Charlotte, I lost my script for antifungal cream for athlete's foot, can I have it back?' I wouldn't have ever known the difference," I said skeptically.

"I'll see if I can trace the prescriber number, figure out who wrote it."

"Sure," I replied with a shrug. "Do you want to go through the desk, too?"

We spent another half hour rifling through completely useless minutiae of my work life. There were notes from Olivia, book club lists, ideas for displays, required reading for various classes in the school district.

Not a single thing that screamed target for a burglary.

On the bookshelves lining my office walls, the inventory was even more mundane. They housed some books that were pulled out of circulation after sustaining damage, several old day planners because I was obsessed with writing things on calendars only to never look at them again, and half a dozen notebooks and journals I wanted to save for when something worthwhile came to mind but which were too pretty to leave crammed in a corner at home.

The chief and I fanned through the pages of everything, waiting for some clue to drop into our hands, but there was nothing.

Eventually, Roberts leaned back in my desk chair and scrubbed his hands over his face. "This town lives and breathes gossip, Charlotte. Can you think of anything that's come up recently that might be related to the break-in?"

My gaze landed on the folder from the return chute—I'd forgotten all about my research attempt into the businesses. "This receipt was the last thing that I found. A lot of people use them as bookmarks, so it's not all that remarkable, but there's a list on the back."

"A list of what?" Roberts asked, flipping it over.

"Business names. They're not all legible, but I think they're all nearby."

His expression shifted, darkening as he read down the list, but he didn't confirm or deny the connection. "If it's okay with you, Charlotte, I'd like to take this folder back to the station. I'll lock it up for safekeeping, take a closer look at everything with Detective Hanson. If anyone comes looking for anything, you can send them to me."

"Of course."

"You haven't heard any whispers about you, your office, or the library in general that would lead someone to believe there was something here worth stealing?"

"Honestly, no," I said after giving it some thought. "We do occasionally get someone who's upset about a display or the books we have available, but I hosted an info night on book banning last year and that's tapered off since. The last rumor I heard about myself was that Franklin Casey thought I was a frigid bitch when I wouldn't go out with him last summer."

Roberts snorted a laugh. "Believe me, a rumor like that only solidifies the town's good opinion of you, given the source."

"I didn't lose any sleep over it, that's for sure."

When Roberts rose from the chair, I helped him load the items he was taking back to the station into a cardboard box. He was right about Spruce Hill's gossip mill. In fact, word about this stuff being secured at the police station could be all over town before nightfall, depending on who saw him walk out with it.

For a moment, I dared to hope that it was enough to bring this nonsense to an end. Then he turned to me with a sober expression and I knew that bubble was about to burst.

"Charlotte, if whoever's behind this wasn't looking for something of particular value here in your office, I think we need to consider that you, personally, might be the target."

I stared blankly at him before shaking my head. "But I wasn't even here during the break-in."

"People sometimes do weird things to get the attention of someone they've set their sights on. Have there been any other incidents to point toward some kind of stalker? Anyone expressing a particular interest in you, your routines, anything like that?"

"No, not at all." Then I bit my lip and the chief waited patiently for me to continue. "It's probably nothing."

"Tell me anyway."

"Craig, the kid who lost that check, he was in the other day and Olivia said something about hero worship, that's all. I didn't really agree with her interpretation, and I don't think he'd ever break in."

Roberts nodded. "I'm inclined to agree, but it's something to consider. Any relationships gone bad, someone with a grudge?"

"I mean, there's Brent, but it's been four years." Unfortunately, everyone in town knew about that fiasco, including the chief.

"Right, well, I'll check in with him anyway, see where his head's at. I want you to stay vigilant. If you see or hear anything odd, even if you just feel like something's off, I want you to get in touch right away."

"Okay," I agreed, wishing he hadn't planted that seed in my head.

The chief patted my shoulder, apparently satisfied with my agreement. "Not my intention to worry you, Charlotte, but better safe than sorry. If you're ever here alone after hours, I'd appreciate it if you'd give me a head's up so I can have someone keep an eye out."

Sawyer would also appreciate that, so I gave Chief Roberts a tight smile before he carted the box out the front door.

"Fantastic," I muttered, then retreated to my office to wait for Sawyer.

I should have copied down the list from that receipt. This thing with Sawyer had thrown my speculation to the darkest recesses of my brain, and now I couldn't cross-reference in order to perform any further research.

Then again, if The Hideaway's kitchen fire was related to the others, my favorite senior citizens knew *something*, and I wasn't above launching an interrogation the next time they came in.

Chapter Twenty-One

SAWYER

There was an unsettled look in Charlotte's eyes when I walked into the library after my errands, something like worry mixed with a tinge of fear. She tried to cover it with a bright smile when she came around the desk to slip her hand into mine, but the expression lingered. I'd become too attuned to the nuances of her face to miss it.

Once we were back in my car, I angled my body toward her and waited.

She fidgeted with the hem of her shirt, her eyes shifting from the dashboard to the windshield to her lap. We had all afternoon, I supposed, but if she didn't get whatever was bothering her out into the open, she was going to be a mess for the rest of the day.

"Charlotte," I said finally.

Those green eyes snapped to my face. I didn't say anything more, so she let the words out in a rush. "The chief thinks there's a chance I'm the target of whoever broke in."

It was nothing more than I'd already considered, but hearing that the police agreed with me was far from a consolation.

"The chief *thinks*," I repeated. "But he still isn't sure, even after going through your office again today?"

"No. There was nothing obvious in there, and it still doesn't make sense why the guy broke in when no one was around, but...he said it could have been to get my attention." She closed her eyes and dropped her head back against the seat.

I covered her hand with mine, needing that connection, and said, "We'll get through this, angel."

Without opening her eyes, she nodded. "I know we will. I just don't understand any of it."

I leaned over and kissed her, barely brushing my lips over hers, before shifting the car into gear to take us home. Every time I glanced over at her, I could see her mind was a million miles away, trying to explain something inexplicable.

Still, I'd promised her she would be safe with me, and I had no intention of breaking that promise.

When we got home, she came in with me so I could pack enough clothes to get me through the weekend at her place. She made no protest, just smiled and dropped into a recliner in the living room to wait while I gathered my things. Before we left to cross the driveways, I tugged her into my arms and kissed her more thoroughly.

Charlotte Whitmore had an impressively swift recovery time where her mental faculties were concerned, but she was blessedly easy to distract with physical pleasures—at least for as long as they lasted.

Just as we settled down on the couch in her living room, a text came through from Twig, saying that the foster family would bring the puppy over the next morning, along with the adoption paperwork. Thanks to her fostering, Charlotte had everything she needed for his arrival on hand already, so we had nothing left to do in preparation.

"You don't feel like I pressured you into adopting him, do you?" I asked, nuzzling her temple.

She gave a little hum of pleasure as my lip cruised along her hairline. "Not at all. You barely said a word, as I recall."

I laughed and said, "Well, I suppose that's true. So, what would you like to do this evening? Watch a movie? Order takeout?"

"My wrist is fully healed, you know," she murmured. Her eyes had gone sultry, every trace of her earlier concern gone. "I think you should surprise me."

Trying not to let the victorious smile emerge just yet, I stood and held out a hand to her. "I thought you'd never ask."

To say I hadn't been imagining this particular scenario for weeks now would be a lie. Since we were at Charlotte's house instead of my own, I'd have to improvise a bit, but I was up for the challenge. When we reached the bedroom, I brought her to the nearest bedpost and leaned down so my mouth brushed her ear.

"Get undressed, then grab onto that post and close your eyes," I said.

With a shuddering breath, she obeyed. I kept my eyes on her face, flushed with excitement, as she pulled off the t-shirt and leggings, then swept my gaze over her body as she tossed her undergarments aside. For a second, she just stared back at me, lips parted, then she moved to wrap both hands around the post and closed her eyes.

"No peeking, angel," I warned her.

"I wouldn't dare," she replied, though from the smirk on her pretty pink lips, I knew it to be a lie.

I could blindfold her, but those eyes of hers were so expressive, I couldn't bear to miss seeing every sensation broadcasting from them.

Letting her hear my footsteps as I moved around the room, I rifled through her closet until I found a sash from a short cotton robe I'd never seen her wear—we'd have to remedy that in the very near future. I looped the sash around my neck and pulled open the drawer in her bedside table.

From the corner of my eye, I saw her eyebrows shoot up at the sound—though her eyes remained firmly shut, much to my surprise—and I grinned to myself as I inspected the treasure trove I'd just uncovered.

"Well, well, what have we here?" I drawled as I withdrew a variety of sex toys one at a time.

She laughed softly. "I was single for a long time before I met you, what can I say?"

I hummed as I selected a little pink vibrator, though I left a few other options on the edge of the bed, just in case. When I moved to stand behind her, she shifted ever so slightly, like she was seeking the heat of my body against hers. I gathered her hair in one hand and kissed a path along the back of her shoulders, pausing only to trace my tongue over the crescent moon at her neck.

"I think you need something to take your mind off the past few days, hmm?" I whispered, setting my hands on her hips.

After a brief squeeze, I slid them up her ribs until I was cupping her breasts. I swept my thumbs along the edges of the jewelry, then rolled her nipples between my fingers, pinching just hard enough for her to gasp and drop her head back against my shoulder.

"Yes," she said finally. "Yes, please."

I chuckled against her ear. "Then let's play a game, shall we?"

"What kind of game?"

Instead of answering, I threaded the sash carefully between her wrists and tied them to the post. Gently, I guided her back a step so she was leaning forward, still clutching the post, then I nudged her feet apart. Once she was positioned to my liking, I stepped away to admire the view.

"You look exquisite like this. Mine for the taking," I said, moving close again to smooth my hands over her ass and up her back.

"Why, thank you," she replied breathlessly. "What kind of game are we playing, Sawyer?"

"We're going to see just how many orgasms you can take before you beg for mercy."

A tremor made its way up her spine. "Oh," she whispered, squirming under my touch.

I started with just my hands, coasting slowly over her skin, kneading the curve of her bottom before sliding around to the front of her ribcage and up to cup her breasts in my hands. There, I teased her nipples until she was panting and pressing her hips back against mine, then I dropped one hand between her legs and settled in to send her over the edge.

Fortunately, I had devoted a great deal of time to learning just what she needed.

Alternately circling her clit and curling my fingers deep inside her, I wound her tighter and tighter. Those soft, gasping breaths gave way to whimpers and moans until I set my teeth against one shoulder. Her hands squeezed the post with trembling fingers, her back arched, and she gave a guttural cry when the first orgasm swept over her.

Leaning my forehead between her shoulder blades for a second, I said, "That's one."

A shaky laugh was her only reply. I soothed her back down for only a minute, then I trailed my lips along the curve of her ear and whispered dark, dirty promises as my fingers teased her to another peak.

By the time the third shuddered through her body, she was covered in a fine sheen of sweat, the long muscles in her legs visibly trembling.

"Now, open your eyes. I want you to watch this part."

I shifted carefully around her, dropping to my knees between her body and the bedpost. When I glanced up at her flushed face, her eyes were dark, her expression the very picture of temptation.

Then I lowered my head, spread her wide with my thumbs, and devoured her like a starving man. She was always responsive, but now that she was primed by those initial orgasms, every sweep of my tongue made her thighs tighten on either side of my head. Each moan that fell from her lips rained over me, spurring me on until her knees buckled on a strangled groan as she came.

I looped my hands around the backs of her legs to keep her upright, pressed kisses along her hip bones and belly while her breathing slowed, then dove back in again.

"I haven't heard any begging yet," I noted as I ducked under her arms and rose to my feet again after orgasm number six. "I'm impressed."

"My muscles will probably give out before my will, Dr. Hottie," she replied with a grin.

"We can't have that. Don't worry, angel, I won't let you fall."

This time, I moved behind her and squeezed her hips gently, using my knee to widen her stance. I had shed my shirt already, but now I shoved my jeans and boxers to the floor and kicked them aside. I grabbed a condom from the bed and rolled it on.

When I pressed against the cradle of her ass, a soft purr escaped her throat and she rocked her hips backward.

"I think this one might just do it, my sweet angel," I said in a low voice as I eased into her from behind.

Her husky laugh caused her to clench around me. "This one might just kill me."

Deliberately, I kept my pace slow, never quite enough to satisfy her, though a low groan slipped from her lips with each deep thrust. I waited until she was whimpering, the sounds guttural and more than a little frantic, then I hooked my arm around her hip and pressed the pink vibrator between her legs.

"Oh, god," she gasped, jerking as it buzzed against her clit.

"You like that?" I asked, grazing her neck with my teeth as she shuddered before me. I held still for a moment, enjoying the ripples of sensation moving through her. "Do you want me to fuck you while this little toy does its work?"

"Yes, please."

I laughed softly into her shoulder as I resumed thrusting, determined to savor the way she quivered around me. Charlotte might be very quick to ask nicely, but I wasn't sure she was actually capable of begging. Maybe I should have phrased my challenge differently from the start.

Then again, spending all night pleasuring her didn't sound like a bad prospect, either.

As the tempo of her helpless little sounds increased, so did my pace. Her hands still gripped the post, though the sash was tied loosely enough that she could have slipped her wrists out of it without much effort. It was the illusion of ceding control that turned her on even more than usual.

And Christ, that was a gift to us both.

When the orgasm finally ripped through her, forcing mine right along with it, she almost collapsed against the post. I caught her with one arm around her torso as I tossed the vibrator aside, untied the fabric around her wrists, and let it fall to the floor. Then I swept her up in my arms and carried her to the bed.

"Enough?" I asked as I massaged her arms from her fingers all the way to her shoulders. Every inch of her was soft and pliable under my hands.

"Enough," she replied with a sleepy, satisfied smile. "But I might need a doctor's note to take some time off. I don't think I'll be able to move for another week, at least."

Laughing, I pressed a kiss right over her heart. "Ah, but I know you, angel. Give it an hour and you'll be demanding more."

The little brat only smirked at me and draped her limbs across my body, using my chest as a pillow. I stroked my fingers through the long strands of her hair, glinting gold in the evening light, until we both drifted off.

Chapter Twenty-Two

CHARLOTTE

Contrary to Sawyer's assertion, seven intense, outstanding orgasms appeared to be my limit, if only because I fell asleep for a solid ten hours afterward. I woke up far too early, before the sun even rose, and realized I was famished. We hadn't eaten any dinner—maybe it was time to start stocking the bedroom with nutritious snacks for this kind of occasion.

I slipped quietly out of bed, pulled on pajama pants and a tank top, and headed downstairs to find something to eat. My legs still wobbled like jelly, but overall, I felt good. Amazing, even.

Maybe things were looking up after all.

Sawyer hadn't lost his mind when I told him I could be the target. I was adopting a puppy, and even if he'd be coming home to my house, Sawyer had been as involved in the decision as I was.

And now that sleepovers were a regular thing, I went to bed each night utterly sated and woke up feeling rejuvenated.

I had Sawyer to thank for all of it.

For a long moment, I studied the contents of the fridge, reflecting on everything that had changed in the time since I met Dr. Sawyer Thorne. I felt like I'd finally come out of a deep sleep, like finding him had opened my eyes to possibilities I hadn't considered before. He made me happy on a soul-deep level that still surprised me, even after all these weeks.

In the end, I only had enough energy to grab an apple and stare out the kitchen window into the strange light that came just before dawn. Across the driveways, Sawyer's house was dark, not even the exterior lights shining. I was thinking I should thank Libby for suggesting the rental when something caught my eye.

At the back corner of his house, I saw a flash of movement, black on black, a shadow separating from the surrounding darkness.

My heart leapt into my throat. For a split second, I tried to tell myself it was an animal—it wasn't unusual for deer to pass through the yards in this neighborhood. Even a coyote wasn't completely unheard of.

Then the figure stepped further away from the house and I realized it was a person.

One staring straight back at me through my kitchen window.

I patted my hip even though these pants had no pockets and I definitely hadn't thought to bring my phone downstairs. I could scream, but even if Sawyer heard me, the person skulking around outside might hear it as well and flee before we had a chance to call the police.

As the breath stalled in my lungs, I braced to sprint back upstairs, then Sawyer's quiet footsteps padded across the kitchen floor. His phone was against his ear and he was giving my address to someone on the other end. When he joined me by the window and wrapped his arm around my waist, pinning my back to his chest, I was finally able to inhale again.

"The police are sending someone immediately," he murmured into my ear. "I want you to stay here, lock the door behind me."

I jerked in surprise. "What? No! You're not going out there."

"Angel, I don't have time to argue. I promise you I can defend myself if necessary, but I need to know you're safe."

He didn't give me time to process that, just kissed me swiftly and pulled on his shoes. My hands were shaking before he even opened the door, then he was off like a shot. I threw the bolt behind him and ran back to the kitchen to watch through the window.

Sawyer was easier to spot in his white undershirt, until the two of them ran past a motion light in a yard several houses down and I caught a glimpse of the prowler. Dressed all in black, it looked like he had something over his head, a hood maybe.

Or a ski mask.

My pulse skyrocketed. Sawyer had just run headlong into danger without so much as a weapon. What if the prowler was armed? What if Sawyer got shot, or stabbed, or—

"Oh god. Oh god."

On the verge of hyperventilating, my fingers clenched around the window frame. I couldn't make out any discerning features from this distance. The stranger had a head start on Sawyer, whose long legs carried him quickly across the grass, and clearly knew his way around the neighborhood in a way Sawyer did not. As they approached Mrs. Blanchett's six-foot privacy fence, the prowler angled sharply toward the woods at the edge of the property line.

When he disappeared into the shadows between the dense trees, Sawyer stopped running. He bent in half, hands on his knees, then turned back toward the house. I threw open the window and kept watch, in case I needed to shout a warning.

As Sawyer reached the driveway, a police car pulled up out front. There were no sirens or lights, just a pair of sleepy officers who bent their heads toward Sawyer to listen to his description and then set off in the direction the prowler had gone, scanning the ground with high-powered flashlights. I hurried to the side door to let Sawyer back in, trying to control the trembling in my limbs.

Though he was still breathing hard from his run, he pulled me tight against his chest. "He's long gone by now," he said quietly, cradling the back of my head.

"Maybe it was just a burglar?"

"Angel," he replied, sighing. "Look, maybe it was unrelated to what happened at the library, but I don't want you to take any chances with your safety. Please."

To be honest, I'd thought Chief Roberts was overreacting. The break-in had occurred while no one was even at the library, and it seemed unlikely it had anything to do with me. Now, though, as the adrenaline left my system and I clung to Sawyer's solid frame, I wasn't sure what to think.

"How did you know something was up?" I asked suddenly, remembering how he'd appeared at my side like my own terror had summoned him downstairs.

"My woman-shaped blanket slipped out of bed. When you didn't come back, I got up and happened to glance out the window while I was pulling my pants on. I saw him move away from the house and dialed the police."

I shivered. "I was about to run up to get you."

We stayed there by the door until the officers returned, already looking apologetic. It was no less than I'd expected, but my heart sank when I realized that meant whoever had been sneaking around outside our houses was still out there somewhere.

"The chief said he's going to set up a drive by for the next few days, so don't be nervous if you see a car passing the house a few times a day. I don't suppose either of you got a good look at him?" the younger officer, a man named Miller who came into the library with his toddler on occasion, asked.

I shook my head, but Sawyer said, "Probably six inches shorter than me, white. Maybe a bit stockier in build. He had a ski mask on, gloves, all in black."

Surprised, I looked at him. "I can't believe you got all that while you were sprinting after him."

The pair of officers were less impressed. "Next time, just place the call to us, please. He might not have bolted if you had stayed inside."

Sawyer inclined his head. "I apologize. I panicked and acted on instinct."

"Well, you know how to reach us. We'll go take another look around before we go. You see anything else, you call us," Miller's partner said sternly.

"We will. Thank you."

Sawyer released me to walk them out, so I returned to the kitchen to start a pot of coffee. The familiarity of my morning routine, even occurring hours ahead of my normal schedule, was soothing. Before sitting at the kitchen table to wait, though, I closed the curtains in all of the downstairs windows.

When he returned, he planted a kiss on the top of my head and poured our coffee, fixing mine just the way I liked it. I accepted the mug with a smile, but it felt strained. He sat down across from me and studied my face for a long moment.

"Do you want to try to get some more sleep before they bring the puppy over?" he asked finally.

"No, I won't be able to fall asleep now. The coffee will help."

Sawyer leaned back, still watching me like he was waiting for me to fall apart. "Is it overbearing of me to say I don't want you to be alone, especially at night?"

I smirked, though it was a weak attempt. "Is that a way of inviting yourself to spend every night in my bed? Because I already thought that was a standing invitation."

"Look, I'd sleep on the couch if that's what it takes, but I feel better if I'm around in case you need me."

"Will you do what the police asked and refrain from running off after some creeper in the wee hours of the morning?" I asked, taking a sip of my coffee. "Because that was more terrifying than seeing the guy through the window, Sawyer."

He grimaced. "I promise. I don't know what I was thinking, except that I would do anything to protect you, angel."

From the expression on his face, something that looked awfully close to grim determination, I got the impression he was fully prepared to do just that.

Chapter Twenty-Three

SAWYER

By the time Charlotte made me realize that bringing a puppy home meant practicing leash manners on the sidewalk and late night potty trips into the dark yard, it was too late to stray from the course. She was already head over heels in love with the little guy, even when he headbutted her in the jaw five minutes after the foster family left him with us.

"Oh, Christ," she gasped, rubbing at the spot. "He's got a skull like a bowling ball."

I reached over and tipped her chin so I could inspect the injury, then pressed my lips to the edge of her jaw. "I think the prognosis is good this time around. What about Bowler for a name? Bowler hat, bowling ball head."

Her beautiful face lit with excitement. "Yes! That's perfect."

We were seated on the couch with the dog nestled between us, though he had an unnerving tendency to fling himself in unexpected directions. Charlotte insisted he was just a baby and still learning how his own body worked, while I got the impression he was already an expert cock-blocker. Thankfully, the rescue Charlotte worked with believed firmly in crate training, so my anatomy would be safe from his oversized puppy feet when we were in bed, at least.

Ultimately, Bowler fit pretty flawlessly into our lives—almost as flawlessly as Charlotte had slipped into mine. Depending on our schedules for the day, one of us dropped him off at Twig's daycare during the hours we were both at work, and he was already sleeping through the night in his crate.

That part was a relief in more ways than one.

And if I caught Charlotte taking his picture in the back yard next to the hyacinths while he sported a tiny bowler hat and bowtie, well...I couldn't say I blamed her. With his goofy smile and unique coloring, he made an excellent model.

As an added bonus, he already had a deep, scary bark that he let loose anytime the wind blew the wrong way outside. If anyone tried to get into Charlotte's house, we would know about it immediately. Hell, if anyone set foot within a hundred-yard radius, we knew.

Little by little, more of my stuff ended up at her place. I didn't often need to run back over to the rental house, though I had set up a motion light in the yard and on the front of the detached garage. I intended to honor my promise not to go chasing after a potential intruder, but at least we'd be able to see well enough to get a description for the police if it happened again.

The day after Chief Roberts brought up the possibility of Charlotte being the target, he called her to say that her douche ex-boyfriend had a solid alibi for the night of the break-in.

Part of me was relieved, but the rest was still troubled.

Instead of our own emergency, however, I received a midnight call from Libby halfway through the week.

I rolled out of bed carefully to grab my phone off the bedside table. Charlotte lifted her head at the movement, but I still answered as quietly as I could.

"Hey. What's up?"

Libby's voice was muffled for a second. "Sorry to wake you. There's a fire at the corner of Chestnut and River Road, at the bowling alley. The fire department is working on it and they have reason to believe someone might be inside. An ambulance is standing by already, but if there are multiple victims, I might need your help at the scene."

"Christ. Okay. I'll be right there."

"Thanks, Sawyer. See you soon."

Charlotte was wide awake when I started getting dressed. "What's going on?"

"There's a fire at the bowling alley. There might have been someone inside when it started."

Even in the dimness of the room, I saw her go ghostly pale. She scrambled off the bed and started throwing on clothes. "Oh, shit. I'm coming with you."

Since I didn't have time to argue and didn't want her alone here, either, I just nodded as we rushed out to the car. Bowler, fortunately, didn't even stir in his crate, snoring lightly as Charlotte locked the door behind us.

The brief drive was silent, and I was grateful Charlotte was there to navigate along the dark streets at the edge of town. An eerie glow lit the sky as we turned down Chestnut, a combination of flashing emergency lights and the hazy orange of flames licking along the rooftop of the building.

"Oh my god," Charlotte whispered. "How could anyone survive that?"

I hated to admit it, but she was right. The entire place was engulfed—even the steady flow of water from the firetrucks barely seemed to make a dent in the blaze.

"What are the chances of you staying in the car?" I asked as I pulled up beside Libby's blue sedan.

"Zero, but I'll keep out of the way."

It would have to do. We both folded out of the car, clasping hands as we made our way to where Libby and Mark stood.

Without breaking my grasp, Mark hooked Charlotte around the back of the neck and kissed the top of her head. "Hey, kid."

"Hey," she whispered, her features lit by the dancing flames.

"You don't have to be here," he said gently. "I know it's hard for you."

My gaze shot to his face. "What do you mean?"

Libby studied Charlotte for a moment, like she was giving her a chance to speak, then said, "Before she moved in next door to Mark as a kid, Charlie and her parents lived across town. There was a fire and their house was destroyed."

"Christ," I muttered, pressing my lips to the top of Charlotte's head. "Were you home when it happened?"

"No, it was the night of my first dance recital. My dad was at the house, but he got out."

There was more that she wasn't saying, but this wasn't the time or place to push her for information. Instead, I said, "Mark's right. You don't have to be here."

Stubborn as ever, she shook her head firmly. "I'm staying."

I met Libby's gaze and her lips quirked up as she shrugged, clearly used to these kinds of situations. With a sigh, I simply wrapped my arm around Charlotte's waist and looked back toward the burning building.

"Why would anyone be inside the bowling alley in the middle of the night?" I asked Libby.

"A cleaner at the office across the street said the manager sometimes stays after hours. There was a car parked at the edge of the lot when the call came in."

"Shit," I muttered.

Charlotte curled into my side, giving comfort as much as seeking it, and I wrapped my other arm around her as we all stood by, helpless, while the firefighters did their job.

It was almost dawn before the fire was finally contained and the official word came that no one was found inside. My limbs went slack with relief before tightening around the woman at my side, my expression mirroring Libby's over the top of Charlotte's head.

Chief Roberts and a tall Black woman who introduced herself as Detective Rose Hanson approached just as I was about to suggest Charlotte go warm up in my car.

"Doc. Appreciate you both coming out at this time of night," the chief said, shaking my hand after he clasped Libby's.

"I'm just glad there was no one in there," I replied. "Any idea what caused the fire?"

He and Hanson exchanged a glance. "Officially, no."

Charlotte's head jerked up so fast she nearly clocked me in the jaw, but she said nothing, even after Hanson narrowed her eyes in response to the movement.

What did *officially, no* mean? Did they suspect arson?

And why would Charlotte react like that? I wondered about her childhood home, whether that had anything to do with her insistence on coming with me tonight.

Everyone was exhausted, so there was no further small talk, just reiterated thanks and a not-so-subtle prod for us to move along. Once we were ensconced in the car and the heat had kicked on, I raised a brow at Charlotte.

She stared back, wide-eyed but silent.

"What was that look about, with the detective?" When she fidgeted slightly and didn't respond, I lowered my voice to what she liked to call my Stern Doctor tone. "Charlotte."

"There have been a couple other fires," she said quickly. "I overheard a conversation about the most recent one while I was at work."

I scrubbed my hands over my face. "Let me guess, it prodded that insatiable curiosity of yours?"

"Yes."

It was a simple response, but I didn't need any elaboration. If Charlotte set her mind to something, there was no stopping her—not even if it might put her in harm's way.

"Can I convince you to leave the investigation to the police?" I asked anyway.

"I'm not going to be poking around any burnt out buildings," she hedged, "but I want to find out what else my library patrons know about it. It can't be a coincidence."

"Be. Careful."

Her smile was soft and sweet, like she knew my fraying nerves needed the reassurance that she wasn't going to get hurt along the way. "I will. I promise."

I just hoped she knew what she was doing.

Despite our conversation, Charlotte didn't bring up the fires at all in the days that followed. In fact, as we approached the weekend, her anxiety about the charity ball alternately took the form of nervous chatter and utter silence. By Friday night when we sat down to eat takeout from The Mermaid, one of our favorite restaurants in town, I was desperate to reassure her.

"Angel," I said softly, waiting until she met my eyes to go on. "It's going to be fine, I promise you."

She deflated slightly. "Is it that obvious?"

"That you're worried? Yes. Painfully obvious. What is it that you're afraid will happen?"

"I don't know," she said, stabbing her fork into a potato wedge. "That all the hoity-toity guests will wonder what the hell the hottest doctor not-on-staff-anymore is doing with a frumpy librarian from the boonies?"

I swallowed a surprised laugh and laid my hand on the table between us, waiting until she pressed her palm to mine before speaking. "Charlotte Whitmore, you are the farthest thing from frumpy. It will be an honor to have you there with me, and I promise you, I'll be spending the entire evening thinking about all the things I want to do to you when we get home."

Charlotte scoffed, but some of her tension dissipated. "Well, since Twig is keeping Bowler overnight, I guess maybe you'll have time to make those fantasies of yours come true," she mused, tapping her chin with her free hand.

Bowler, asleep at her feet under the table, stirred just enough to peek up at me with one eye before deciding we weren't talking to him. While Charlotte went out shopping with Penelope and Grisham the next day, I would be on puppy duty. It wasn't often that I was in her house without her present, so I hoped to take care of a few things I'd noticed needing attention, like replacing the blown light bulbs she couldn't reach without a stool or reattaching the railing she said she'd pulled off the wall several months ago when she fell down the stairs.

Christ. Just thinking about it made me want to wrap her in a bubble to keep her safe.

Ultimately, I'd learned Charlotte wasn't the kind of person who liked being cared for in obvious ways—she appreciated subtle acts of service over being coddled. She was really quite handy herself, but given her propensity for unlikely injuries, I knew there were things she hadn't wanted to mess with. I was quite thankful for that, actually, since she had been in fine health after her wrist recovered from the second injury.

Struck suddenly by the fact that we hadn't talked about it before, I asked, "How long have you lived in this house?"

Her eyes widened in surprise. "Hmm, almost five years now. I was renting an apartment in town after college, but I started dog-sitting for the old lady who owned this house before me, Mrs. Bakshi. She used to donate boxes full of romance novels to the library, but she'd cross out all the bad words and make little annotations like 'skip to page 137' at the beginning of each sex scene."

"I guess she wasn't aware of your reading habits," I teased.

"I thanked her very politely and never brought it up again." She grinned. "Anyway, she had a little terrier mix who was absolute hell on wheels. All of her kids had flown the nest, so every few months, she'd go visit one of them for a couple weeks. I fell in love with this place the first time I was here. When she decided to move in with her oldest daughter, she offered to sell it to me for a steal."

"Yet another conquest for Miss Charlotte Whitmore," I said, winking at her.

With a haughty lift of her chin, she shrugged. "I can't help it if people adore me. Besides, you should hear all the talk about 'that hot new doctor in town.' I bet half your patients are inventing symptoms just to see you all done up in that lab coat of yours."

"You like the coat, do you?"

"Let's just say when I first saw you in it, I was wondering whether the hospital had a policy against doctors dating patients. After I finished putting my foot in my mouth half a dozen times."

"Dating?" I teased. "I thought you had other things in mind."

She leaned close as she popped a bite of potato between her lips. "You know very well what I mean."

I let a slow smile spread across my face as I finished the last of my meal. "I think it means a certain someone might like to try out a bit of roleplay."

Though she didn't dignify that with a response, the sparkle that appeared in those beautiful green eyes was all the confirmation I needed.

Chapter Twenty-Four

CHARLOTTE

Fortune smiled on me the next morning.

I'd dressed in comfortable clothes, put the dress bag in my car so Pen and Grisham could see it before we headed off on our quest for accessories and shoes, and kissed Sawyer goodbye before stopping at the library to make sure everything was in order.

Olivia and the rest of the staff had it all well under control, but my hope that David and Pop might be there paid off.

The two of them were tucked in armchairs back in one of the reading corners, chatting despite the books open on each of their laps, and they smiled broadly when I headed their way.

"Charlotte, you look lovely today," Pop said.

I dropped into the open chair beside them and leaned forward. "I need details."

His eyes widened, then he said, "Well, that color looks very fetching on you, and I quite like seeing some pep in your step. All thanks to a certain new doctor in town, I expect."

"About the fires," I added.

They both went quiet, glancing at one another before David sighed. "How much do you know, dearest?"

"I know The Hideaway had a kitchen fire over a year ago, the laundromat was so badly damaged it had to be leveled right in the middle of the plaza, Al's burned down recently, and…I think the bowling alley fire is being investigated as arson."

"You've certainly done your research," David said, sounding reluctantly impressed.

"What I don't understand is how it's all connected."

Pop shook his head. "That's the part we're not sure about. They might be entirely unrelated—the first happened quite a while back. As far as we're aware, the bowling alley is the only instance where arson might be suspected, and even that hasn't been confirmed by any official channels."

I flopped back against the seat with a groan. "So we're back to square one."

Their gentle smiles didn't assuage my frustration, so Pop added, "It's all just the speculation of old men, my dear. I'm sure you have better things to do than listen to us invent conspiracy theories."

"Not really," I muttered. "I'm being forced to go shopping so I can attend a charity gala with Sawyer."

David's features lit with amusement, though he coughed hard into his first before commenting, "You make it sound like a punishment."

I wrinkled my nose at him. "It's not often I have to hobnob with the rich and famous, you know."

"Best get used to it. Your young man comes from the tip top of the upper crust."

Pop's words, lighthearted as they were, gave me a second's pause. Though Sawyer had mentioned his parents in passing, along with their disdain for the particular field of medicine he'd chosen, we hadn't discussed his family in any great depth.

"Oh dear," Pop said in an undertone.

"Indeed," David agreed.

My brows furrowed as I focused back on them. "What?"

"A woman in love shouldn't get that expression when her man's family is mentioned, that's all." Pop smiled gently. "I'm sorry I brought them up."

A woman in love.

I blinked at him, ready to protest—or maybe ready to deny—when my phone vibrated with a reminder to get going so I could meet Pen and Grisham.

"Duty calls, dear one. Enjoy your shopping trip and forget about all this. You shouldn't pay us any mind. We're just a pair of biddies chattering in our nest," David said, his tone light and teasing and not nearly enough to distract me from the path my mind had taken.

"If you hear anything else about the fires, I expect you two to keep me in the loop," I warned.

They both smiled and gave their word, but David started coughing again as I stood to leave.

"You should get that checked out," I said, frowning at his pallor.

"I will. Perhaps I'll see your handsome doctor again at the clinic."

I snorted, but I liked the idea of Sawyer being viewed as *mine*. It caused a rich, warm flutter in my stomach. "I'll put in a good word for you."

They each reached out to squeeze my hand, then I said my goodbyes to the staff and headed out to the parking lot, pondering everything I did and didn't know about the man I might or might not be in love with.

At least knowing the previous fires hadn't resulted even in any rumors of arson lifted a weight off my shoulders.

Maybe it really was all just a coincidence.

I met my friends at their apartment in the city, since Grisham insisted that was where the best shopping would be, and the stress brought on by the upcoming event melted away as they exclaimed over my dress and fiddled with my hair to determine if I should wear it up or down before we hit the stores.

"I still can't believe you hooked up with Dr. Hottie," Penelope said, grinning as she gathered my hair on top of my head.

"How am I ever going to introduce you guys if you're still calling him that?"

Grisham drew an X across his heart with one finger. "We can behave, when the situation calls for it."

I wrinkled my nose and said, "No, you really can't."

"What's going on?" Pen demanded, frowning at our reflections in the mirror as she ignored Grisham's assertion. "You have a look on your face."

"What are you talking about? There's no look. This is just my face. I look totally normal."

"Does she?" Pen asked Grisham.

He studied me like an insect under a microscope. "Now that you mention it, she does have a look."

"Oh for fuck's sake," I muttered. "I just—I really like him. And I'm wondering if maybe I don't know him well enough to be feeling that much."

"But you're spending every night with him and now you've adopted a puppy together?"

"Yes, and sort of."

She smirked at me in the mirror. "You're pulling a Penelope Panzetta here, Char. Moving fast, especially for you."

"It doesn't feel fast," I admitted quietly. "It feels…normal. Good."

"I'm happy for you. We're both happy for you. Just guard that big heart of yours, okay? This isn't your usual style."

Grisham tugged a lock of my hair. "What Pen means is we're rooting for you and your hot doctor."

"Of course we are," Penelope soothed. "And I hope you're getting all the scorching sex you dreamed of."

"Can we move on to the shopping portion of the day? I don't want to talk about sex right now."

"Fine, girl, but you can't hold out forever," Grisham replied.

I could hold out for the day, though, and then I'd be in the clear for a while. At least until they came over for a movie night and saw Sawyer up close.

Then they'd catch it in every passing look, every covert touch. I'd never live it down.

Once they'd settled on an up-do and made a mental list of what accessories they felt were needed—half of which I immediately vetoed, because there was no way I'd be wearing a garter belt to this event—we piled into Penelope's car. As usual, Grisham was relegated to the back seat, but he rested his chin beside my headrest.

"I really am sorry about your wrist, Chuckles."

I rolled my eyes. "You're forgiven, as long as you never call me that in front of Sawyer."

He sat back, muttering something about humorless librarians, but Penelope immediately took up the reins of the conversation, moving blissfully away from my relationship and into the mind-numbing territory of gala-appropriate accessories.

Shopping was not one of my favorite activities, but shopping with Penelope and Grisham was a world unto itself. It was like being back in college, letting them drag Pen's shy little roommate to parties and football games and ridiculous Spirit Week activities.

By the time we tracked down undergarments, shoes, a necklace Grisham insisted was the perfect accent to my dress's sweetheart neckline, and jeweled hair combs, I was exhausted and eager to get home to Sawyer and Bowler.

"Look, call me when you're doing your makeup so I can walk you through it," Pen said as I loaded bags into my car.

"And if you have a hard time with the hair, I'll troubleshoot," Grisham added.

Penelope piped up with, "And we'll need a full body shot of the two of you. You know, so we can make sure we succeeded in our best friend duties."

Grisham gave a solemn nod. "And to make sure he's as hot as you say he is. Can't nickname just anyone Dr. Hottie, you know."

I pulled the two of them into a group hug. "You guys are the best. I love you both."

Going home after seeing the pair of them always filled me with an odd combination of emptiness and relief. This time, as I walked into the kitchen and set down my shopping bags, I found Sawyer with a bouquet of blue hyacinths and a box of cupcakes from my favorite bakery food truck.

"You are amazing," I breathed, moving into his arms before he even had a chance to put them down. Bowler ran in excited circles around our legs.

Laughing quietly, Sawyer backed me up until my ass hit the edge of the counter. He pressed one hand against the small of my back and stroked the other up my spine. I nuzzled his throat, breathing in the fresh, clean scent of his skin through his thin cotton tee.

"I missed you today and thought you might enjoy a little something sweet after your excursion. I remembered you had a bouquet in your office and a little vase at home the first time I came over, so I hoped the hyacinths were a safe bet."

"Hyacinths are my favorite so you were absolutely correct, but first I think I need to recharge with a different kind of sweet. Know anybody who could help me out?" I asked, hooking my fingers through his belt loops.

With a devastating smile, he twirled me around and shepherded me toward the stairs. "Do I ever."

Worrying about the past—and the future—would have to wait.

Chapter Twenty-Five

CHARLOTTE

THE WAY MY NERVES threatened to tumble straight out of my throat as we pulled up to the front of the hospital reminded me of that first night when I invited Sawyer over for dessert.

Except much, much worse.

Sawyer nodded at the young valet and circled the car to help me from my seat, looking impeccably gorgeous in his tux. Like he was born to it, which I figured he was, after what Pop said at the library.

"Ready?" he murmured.

"Not even remotely."

His soft laugh eased some of my tension, but not nearly enough. When we walked past the bench where Sawyer had found me the night of my injury, he squeezed my hip.

"I should make a donation so they put a plaque with our names on that bench," he teased. "It saved me from my own stupidity after letting you walk away the first time."

"Why did you?" I asked as we joined the line of donors giving their names at the door.

"You were hurt. No matter how hard I kicked myself for not getting your number or at least giving you mine, the circumstances weren't ideal. I didn't want to sway you when you weren't feeling a hundred percent."

My heart clenched, but there was no time to reply before it was Sawyer's turn to speak to the doormen. Even though he gave his name in an undertone, I saw the immediate flash of recognition in the man holding the clipboard.

Whether it was for Sawyer himself or the father who seemed to instill equal parts respect and distaste among the masses, I wasn't sure.

The charity ball itself was exactly what I would have pictured. Eastman Memorial's cavernous lobby was decorated in shades of blue and gold, filled to the brim with elegant people in extremely expensive clothing brushing elbows among the rest of the elite. It didn't look a thing like the midnight wasteland I'd crossed to go sit in the courtyard after my ER visit.

I would have turned right around and left were it not for Sawyer's hand on my back, its warmth seeping through the fabric of my dress to caress my skin.

During my ridiculous last-minute video call with Penelope and Grisham, Sawyer had accidentally entered the bedroom and been forced to come say hello. They both stared at him like he was some rare and exquisite new species, then after he gave an awkward wave and hightailed it out of the bedroom, the two of them pretended to swoon.

It took another ten minutes to shut them up so I could get ready to leave.

"We don't have to stay long," he said against my ear as we made our way into the lobby.

"Just...don't leave my side, okay?"

His lips brushed over my temple. "I wouldn't dream of it."

There were waiters with trays of champagne and hors d'oeuvres winding among the guests, but I was too nervous to eat anything. Sawyer convinced me to sip at a glass of champagne to try to quell the nerves, but I ended up just holding the glass instead of drinking from it.

For the most part, I did a lot of silent smiling as I was introduced to big donors, board members, and doctors on staff at the hospital as we made our way through the crowd. Sawyer was charm personified, shaking hands and schmoozing with the best of them. I heard at least seventeen times how proud his father must be of him, but the comment always caused an infinitesimal tightening around his eyes.

I was glad I wouldn't have to meet his parents here tonight. This was already overwhelming enough.

"Incoming," I muttered when a gray-haired woman with a sharp bob approached us, a speculative look in her eyes as she took in Sawyer's arm around my waist.

"Dr. Hasselbeck," he said when she held out a bejeweled hand for him to squeeze.

"Dr. Thorne. And who's this?"

"My girlfriend, Charlotte Whitmore."

The woman's blood red lips parted, but she recovered quickly, pasting on a patently fake smile. "Girlfriend, my goodness. Sylvester didn't mention that, but I suppose leaving Eastman Memorial for some backwater clinic makes sense now. You never did have the best interests of your career at heart."

Sawyer's body stiffened beside me. "Turns out there's more to life than just work."

She gave a harsh laugh. "Bought into that dream, did you? I can't imagine what your parents must think of your choices."

"Fortunately," Sawyer drawled, "it's none of their business. Now if you'll excuse us, the chief of surgery wants to speak with me."

He stayed tense as we wove through the crowd toward a slender older man who had, in fact, been waving him over. When I squeezed his arm, he glanced down at me, the clench of his jaw loosening ever so slightly.

"If you need me to get us out of here, I can pretend to swoon."

His lips twitched. "I'll keep that in mind. Should we have a code word?"

"How about *fainting couch?* Think you can work that into a sentence while you're in the middle of a conversation?"

"My gorgeous lady requires a fainting couch, Chief," he intoned, winking at me.

A giggle bubbled out of my throat and he grinned, shifting his hand so his pinky brushed over the curve of my ass. I choked back a startled laugh and finally had to sip at the champagne to try to sooth my throat, all while Sawyer looked on like a man who was utterly smitten.

Flutters rose through my torso and up the warm trail left by the champagne, landing right in the center of my chest.

The chief of surgery didn't have to hide a sneer or force a smile, he simply greeted Sawyer with a blank expression that made me more than a little uncomfortable. I managed a polite greeting despite the calculating look in the man's eyes, then decided to make a break for it.

I touched Sawyer's shoulder and went up on my toes to say into his ear, "I'm going to go find a restroom."

He gestured toward the huge staircase and I nodded gratefully as I slipped through the crowd. It wasn't so much that I felt out of place mingling with the upper crust—even though I *did* despise these icy, surface-level interactions with those who seemed tight with Sawyer's dad. More to the point, I was swiftly losing steam in my socialization reserves, especially in the presence of so many false smiles and underhanded barbs.

Sawyer deserved better than this. Did no one else see how incredible he was?

At the edge of the crowd, I handed my half-empty class to a passing waiter, made my way carefully up the stairs in my heels, and wandered down a hallway until I found the ladies' room. Once the door closed behind me, the sound of the party faded until all I could hear was the hum of the air conditioning. I fought the urge to collapse back against the door and just breathe.

After spending as much time as possible touching up my lip gloss and staring at my reflection, almost unfamiliar under all the makeup and upswept curls, I finally ventured back out into the hallway.

It was quieter up there, giving me a full view of the crowd below. When I moved toward the railing, I spotted Sawyer, still trapped in conversation with a circle of older men, and decided to linger where I was until he was free.

"He seems like quite a catch, doesn't he?"

I turned and almost dropped my clutch purse when I recognized the woman in front of me as the one I'd caught staring at Sawyer across the sushi restaurant. The dark-haired beauty was tall, slim, and wearing a designer dress that Grisham would skin me alive for not recognizing. If ever I had truly felt like a frumpy librarian, it was right then and there.

"I beg your pardon?" I asked, trying desperately to regain my bearings.

"Handsome, charming, successful doctor from a family richer than Midas. It's a shame he's such a disappointment," she said. "I'm afraid Sawyer didn't introduce us a couple weeks back. I'm Veronica, his ex. We were engaged, once upon a time."

Shock ricocheted through me, followed by an almost overwhelming tidal wave of hurt. I tried to keep my expression blank, but I saw a faint tinge of sympathy in her expression and realized I must have failed.

"So nice to meet you," I ground out, "but I should really get back to the party."

Her perfectly manicured hand shot out and caught my arm when I turned to the stairs, stopping me in my tracks. "There are things you should know about him."

"I know everything I need to know, but thanks for your concern." I pulled my arm from her grip and started toward the stairs.

"I thought everything was perfect, you know. He was so attentive and sweet. So driven. He had the potential to be extraordinary, but Sawyer isn't one to count on when the going gets tough," Veronica said coldly. "He'll always run toward whatever shiny thing catches his eye. I learned that the hard way. You should be careful, too."

"Careful," I repeated.

"Surely you know why doctors choose emergency medicine over something like neuro." Her lip curled. "They're the cowboys. The adrenaline junkies. They thrive on that chaos because they can't stand a routine. You really think a small town clinic is going to hold his interest?"

Even as I told myself to keep walking away, I turned slowly back to her. Sawyer seemed happy—with Spruce Hill, with me—but Veronica had thought he was happy, too.

And he'd lied about knowing her. Right to my face.

Still, my heart didn't want to believe this viper knew him better than I did. "You're still angry because he chose his own path instead of the golden road to riches you wanted?"

"He promised me he would make the decision carefully. He knew what this choice would mean for him, for both of us. His father disinherited him. Changed his will and everything."

"How sad," I said quietly.

This wasn't my fight—I had no real quarrel with this woman—but I couldn't bear to let her insults pass, not when I knew he deserved so much better than the hand he'd been dealt, whether he could see it or not.

Veronica nodded. "We were together for almost six years and I had no idea he was so selfish."

I looked her dead in the eyes and replied, "No, I mean it's sad that you were dating all that time and somehow you didn't realize he was forcing himself into a pretty little box just to try to please you."

Even as she jerked back in surprise, I spun and caught sight of Sawyer, frozen at the top of the stairs. From his expression, I knew he'd heard me.

"Charlotte," he said softly, reaching out his hand, but I numbly shook my head.

"I need to go." This place, these people, Veronica's warning—it all had me ready to crawl out of my skin.

"Of course. We can leave right now."

"No. I'm leaving. Alone."

The words tore from my lips as I pushed past him, headed for the opposite hallway upstairs. There wasn't a chance in hell I was venturing back into the fray below. As I hurried away from the pair of them, I texted Penelope.

SOS Code Red. Mulligan St.

I'd never been so thankful for our college shorthand meaning "pick me up right now."

Behind me, Sawyer and Veronica spoke quickly and angrily, then Sawyer's hand caught my shoulder.

Spinning around, I snapped, "Don't you dare touch me right now."

His expression bordered on panic, his pale eyes wide as they searched my face, but he removed his hand. "Charlotte, please, talk to me. I swear to you, I was going to tell you about Veronica, but then with the break-in and the prowler, I forgot all about it. I've been distracted."

I rubbed the bridge of my nose. "Distracted."

"Yes, Charlotte, I swear I—"

"And when I flat out asked you who she was at the restaurant the day before the break-in? You just forgot the two of you were engaged?"

"Angel, please, let me explain," he whispered.

"No." I held up my hand to stop him.

I couldn't bear to hear the words coming from his mouth, but I especially couldn't stand the thought of him touching me just then, and he looked half a second away from pulling me into his arms. More than anything, I was afraid that if he did, I'd melt like I always did and forgive him for breaking the cardinal sin in my life.

"You lied to me." The words came out in a tortured whisper and he flinched.

"I know. I'm sorry. I'm so sorry."

I shook my head, wishing I could erase this entire disaster of an evening. "I told you about my dad, about all the broken promises and the lies. I *told* you."

"You did," he choked out. "Please, I can explain everything."

Maybe I'd want that explanation, once we were beyond the searing pain of this moment in time, but right now?

I needed to get the fuck out of there.

"If you care about me *at all*, you will let me walk out of here, do you understand? I need some space right now."

Pain dulled his eyes as he nodded. "I understand. Please, be safe."

Walking away from him was one of the hardest things I'd ever had to do. I made my way down a quiet stairwell to the opposite side of the building, pulled off my heels, and trudged silently toward a bench down the street. Penelope had texted back immediately that she was on her way, so I sent a quick update with my location to her phone as well as Grisham's.

When her car pulled up to the curb, Grisham jumped out, took one look at my face, and bundled me into the front seat. After the doors were closed and Penelope pulled back into the flow of traffic, every pent-up emotion broke loose from my chest, filling the car with the sound of my sobs.

In that moment, I couldn't tell what was more painful, the fact that Sawyer had lied to my face without batting an eye or the realization that somewhere along the way, I had gone and fallen in love with him.

Chapter Twenty-Six

SAWYER

I LEANED MY FOREHEAD against the cool glass of the windows and watched Charlotte hurry down the street, taking my heart with her. The gaping hole left in my chest ached like someone had taken a sledgehammer to my sternum.

Rubbing at the spot, my gaze remained locked on the woman fleeing from me.

Even when I saw Veronica's reflection appear beside me in the glass, I kept my eyes on the scene below until Charlotte was safely ensconced in her friend's car. My body felt hollow, like the woman disappearing into the night had taken my very soul with her.

"Why didn't you tell her?"

I winced—my ex was the last person I wanted to have this conversation with, but the only person who mattered was gone now.

"Because I'm a fool, is that what you want to hear?"

"She needed to know," Veronica said flatly.

Wearily, I lifted my head. "She did know. She knows everything that matters. She knows me better than anyone."

"But you didn't bother to tell her we were engaged."

I stayed quiet for a minute, still staring out at the street. "There was a time when I was willing to put aside everything for you, Ronni. To ignore my own needs in order to make you happy."

She blew out a breath. "And you don't think that's also a form of lying?"

"Maybe it is," I agreed with a sigh of my own. "I just didn't realize your love was conditional until it was too late."

"I deserved the truth as much as that woman does."

"You're right."

The reflection of her body rocked backward in the window, but she didn't speak.

"I'm sorry I hurt you. It was never my intention. I thought the world of you. I only ever wanted to try to be what you needed, but that wasn't me."

"You're in love with her." Instead of accusation, there was only a thread of surprise in the words.

That surprise amplified within my chest, clanging like a gong as it reverberated through my entire body. I should have seen it sooner, but hearing my ex speak the words aloud made it all glaringly obvious.

"I am very much in love with her," I confirmed, my voice hoarse.

It was a terrible time for such a realization, but I wouldn't deny it. I finally turned to look at the woman I'd once expected to become my wife. It seemed like a lifetime had passed since we'd had a meaningful conversation.

And maybe it had.

Her posture, haughty and tense from the minute I spotted her with Charlotte, softened on a sigh. "Tell me one thing. Were you ever going to follow your father into neurosurgery?"

"I never wanted to," I admitted. "I tried to convince myself I did, but it was his path, not mine. I'm sorry I didn't loop you in sooner."

She gave a humorless laugh. "I would've tried to talk you out of the choice you made."

"I know," I replied.

"It would either have turned out exactly like it did, or you'd have ended up resenting me for the rest of our lives. It worked out for the best," she said, showing me a diamond ring at least triple the size of the one I'd given her.

I tried to hold back the words, but they slipped out anyway. "I can't lose her."

"Then fight for her, Sawyer."

Though my body felt like it weighed a thousand pounds, I managed a tiny smile. "Oh, I will. She's worth fighting for."

"I wasn't." She held up her hand when I opened my mouth. "Because I didn't fight for you either. We just weren't right for each other. That woman...she stuck her neck out for you even when she realized you lied about who I was. Maybe that means she's right for you."

"She is."

For a long moment, we stood there and stared out at the darkness together. It was strange to feel even the tiniest bit of camaraderie from the woman who'd caused my entire world to implode all those years ago, but I'd never hated her for what happened. My parents had borne the brunt of the blame for pulling so many strings behind the scenes, while Veronica had simply been their puppet.

Taking ownership of my choices had been a valuable lesson to learn back then, one that I would need now more than ever.

"I can't say I'm happy to see you, but you look well, Ronni. I hope you've found happiness."

"I have," she replied, nodding to her engagement ring. "We're getting married next month. But look, I'm sorry if I fucked things up for you."

"No. This is on me."

"When you chose that job without even talking to me about it, it was like I was about to marry a stranger. After I saw you two at the restaurant, I overheard her asking about me and you brushing her off. I felt like I needed to pay it forward."

"I should have told her that night. I planned to, afterward, and just...lost my chance."

She was quiet for a second, then said, "But your girl is right. It *was* sad that I never realized you weren't happy."

"People change," I said quietly. "I stopped hiding those parts of myself, but I started hiding others. I haven't been in a real relationship since you called things off. That's why I went about this so wrong. I've never done it before."

Veronica set her hand on my sleeve, the diamond twinkling under the fluorescent lights overhead. "Then tell her that. I think she'll forgive you, if my opinion is worth anything. She's no damsel in distress. She's got claws of her own."

"Yes, she does," I agreed. "I should go."

She nodded, removed her hand, and watched as I jogged down the same stairs Charlotte had taken. Part of me hoped it was the last time I ever saw Veronica, while another part felt strangely better after talking to her.

Even if she'd pulled the trigger tonight in confronting Charlotte, my own omissions had loaded the gun.

I couldn't lay the blame at her feet. No, that was all mine.

Before going home, I drove aimlessly in the direction Charlotte had gone—not with any hope of seeing her, but because the prospect of going home without her filled me with dread. Telling myself she wasn't alone helped soothe that sting, even if I had no way of knowing where Penelope had taken her.

If I couldn't be there for her right now, at least her friends were.

Since Bowler was spending the night with Twig, I walked into my empty house instead of Charlotte's, changed out of the stiff tuxedo I'd always hated, and sat at the kitchen table, feeling utterly numb. As hard as I tried, I couldn't stop remembering Charlotte's expression when she pushed past me or the way her shoulders had curled forward as she walked barefoot along the sidewalk in her haste to get away from me.

But somewhere in the back of my mind, I couldn't stop hearing her sharp words in my defense, either. Until she was willing to speak to me again, I would just have to hope that she believed those things, too.

LIBBY TOOK ONE LOOK at me on Monday morning and shoved me into the staff lunch room, closing the door behind us.

"What's wrong?" she demanded.

"I screwed up. Big time." I rubbed a hand over my jaw, wishing I could wipe away the regrets.

"With a patient?" she asked, surprise evident in her tone.

"No."

She studied me for a minute. "Oh, shit. With Charlotte."

"With Charlotte."

"On a scale of leaving the toilet seat up to sleeping with someone else, how bad is it?"

I scowled at her, but a tiny smile tugged at the corner of her lip as my dreary numbness cracked. "Let's just say I should have told her about something and didn't do it when I had a perfect opportunity. She found out at the charity ball and was ambushed by it instead."

"Ahh. Was it about your engagement?" Libby asked, tilting her head to one side.

I jerked in surprise. "How did you know about it?"

"Sawyer," she said gently, "your father is a surgeon who's literally famous in the medical world. I knew who you were long before you applied for this job, and gossip in those circles has a way of reaching everybody, even out here in Spruce Hill."

I blinked at her for a long, silent moment. "Right."

"Besides, I have a friend at Eastman Memorial and she spills all the tea." She gave me a sheepish grin.

"Oh," I said, feeling as stupid as I was sure I sounded.

"Look, I'm going to put you on inventory this morning. I'll take care of the patients while you get your head together. And Sawyer?"

"Yeah?"

"Charlotte Whitmore is an absolutely amazing human who I love like a sister, but I've known her almost her entire life. She needs time to process things even when other people might not. Give her some space to work through her feelings, then make her listen to you while you beg for forgiveness."

"I lied to her." My voice sounded like I'd swallowed razor blades.

She flinched. "I know. That's going to take some groveling, but I have faith you two will work it out."

I nodded. The relief I felt at knowing Libby thought we could get past this wasn't much, but it was definitely there. "Thank you, Libby."

"She's not unreasonable. Besides, that girl has more love in her heart than anyone I know."

Love.

We hadn't used the word yet, but it hung in the air like a specter, hovering just outside of my reach. Libby was absolutely right about Charlotte and her beautiful heart. I simply wasn't sure I deserved any part of it.

But I wanted to. God, I wanted to deserve it, to earn it, cradle it close and bask in it.

Charlotte asked for space, and if that space allowed her to process the disaster of the gala before she was open to speaking with me again, I had to give it to her. I *would* give it to her. I just hoped it wouldn't result in the decision that she couldn't forgive me for hiding the truth from her when she asked about Veronica that night.

Libby turned to leave, then paused with her hand on the doorknob and looked over her shoulder. "But Sawyer?"

I met her gaze, which was still filled with its usual warmth and humor but sharpened by something else, and tipped my head in question.

"If you ever hurt her for real, I'll break your knees."

My startled laugh seemed to surprise us both, but she flashed a quick grin and disappeared down the hall.

Left to mope freely, I perched on a step stool in the supply closet and let the tediousness of inventory duty attempt to distract me from the shitstorm swirling in my head. I wasn't stupid enough to try to rationalize my prevarication—Charlotte wouldn't accept excuses that didn't get to the heart of the issue.

No, I'd give her everything. Every fear, every hope, every moment that had shaped my reaction to seeing Veronica in the flesh.

I was in love with Charlotte, plain and simple. If that meant laying it all out for her to act as judge and jury, I would do it. If it meant giving her the space she needed to come to a decision about whether she could forgive me or not, no matter how much it pained me, I would do it.

Anything and everything, that's what I'd promised to give her, and that's what I would offer up.

All I could do was hold out hope that she would accept.

Chapter Twenty-Seven

CHARLOTTE

After bawling my eyes out to Penelope and Grisham outside the hospital, I'd convinced Pen to drive me home so I could wallow in peace.

I refused to look toward Sawyer's house as I let myself into my own, but when I accidentally glanced out the window before bed that night, I saw him seated in his kitchen, head in his hands, the very picture of abject misery.

The funny thing was that I was fairly sure I'd already forgiven him by then.

I wasn't happy he'd brushed off my question at the restaurant instead of telling me the truth then and there, but I also believed him when he said he'd been planning to explain. He *had* been extremely freaked out by the break-in, then even more frazzled after chasing down the prowler.

Hell, he'd been even more worried about my safety than I was. I didn't care that he'd been engaged to some woman over ten years ago, especially after hearing the way she spoke about him.

I did care that he'd lied about it, though.

Too much of my childhood had been marred by falsehoods, everything from "of course I'll be there for your birthday" to "I'm going to take you to see this show on Broadway one day." Too many disappointments based on trusting the word of a man who couldn't be bothered to follow through.

Sawyer wasn't like that—I knew it deep down, but it hurt he hadn't trusted me with the truth.

As a result, everything twisted up inside my chest, every emotion tangled and knotted together. For weeks, we'd been practically living together, and suddenly my sweet little haven at home became a beacon of loneliness. Not even Bowler's energetic exploits could fill that gap.

This time, when the work week crawled by, I knew the cause. Every silent moment in my house echoed his name. Sawyer texted me on Monday and left a voicemail Tuesday, each one just to tell me that I was in his thoughts and to reiterate his apology, but otherwise, he'd given me the space I requested.

By Wednesday, I resolved to talk it through with him, to fully forgive him. The fact that Veronica dumped him right before their wedding day because he chose to follow his own path instead of his wallet broke my heart.

He deserved better.

Unfortunately, that evening was an event at the library and I had to stay late with Olivia to make sure everything ran smoothly. It wasn't a large crowd, just fifteen or so people gathering in the meeting room to discuss the graphic novels that were Olivia's one true love.

For the most part, I lingered in my office, stopping in to check that they had everything they needed a few times throughout the night.

"You should join us," Olivia cajoled at one point. "You look like you could use some cheering up."

"Thanks, Liv, but I'm not up for it tonight."

Milo, Mark's youngest brother, stood beside her. He owned the comic shop where Olivia sold some of her artwork, and his steady gray gaze locked on my face for a long moment. He was still older than me, but he'd always treated me more as an equal rather than an annoying kid sister the way his brothers had.

Something in his expression tipped me precariously close to bursting into tears.

"If you need to talk, Chuckie, you know you have friends around who are ready to listen," he said finally.

I nodded, breathing deep to control my reaction, and whispered, "I know."

Before the emotion could burst from my chest, I retreated to the office again and sank down into my chair with a heavy sigh.

The lights of the library were off after hours, so the little Tiffany lamp on my desk illuminated the office rather than the overhead fluorescents. After checking in that Bowler was okay over at Twig's for the night and fiddling with my phone for a few minutes, I sent a text to Sawyer.

Event at the library tonight. Dinner tomorrow?

I sat back in the chair, spinning myself idly back and forth with one foot. When the phone vibrated in my hand, I jolted upright.

Absolutely, angel.

A little bud of warmth bloomed in my chest, twining outward until my whole body glowed with it. I checked the time, wishing this thing was ending an hour earlier than planned. After dwelling for another few minutes on just how happy I was at the prospect of moving forward with Sawyer, I stood and wandered back out into the darkened library.

Olivia and Milo were right. If I let myself get sucked into the animated conversations in the meeting room, the remaining time would pass more quickly.

Just as I turned the corner by the circulation desk, though, a gloved hand wrapped around my throat and slammed me backward against the wall. The impact knocked the wind out of me, then a face covered by a black ski mask leaned in close as the fingers on my neck tightened, cutting off my air supply before I could even refill my lungs.

I struggled against him in an attempt to wriggle free, but he kept me pinned and squeezed tighter. When my vision went hazy around the edges, I grabbed at his wrist with both of my hands, trying to pry his grip loose.

"We're going into your office," the man said, his voice strangely low and gravelly. "And if you do exactly what I tell you, I might let you live."

Oh, god. All I could think was, *Don't let him get you alone,* as though I wasn't alone enough already, trapped out here in the dark while the faint sounds of laughter from Olivia's book club drifted past the closed door of the meeting room.

He kept me up against the wall, unable to draw a breath, so all I managed was a tiny nod. As soon as his grip loosened slightly, I swung my leg as hard as I could, hitting him in the groin with my shin.

The impact caught him off guard and sent him hurtling backward into the magazine rack, which fell over with a loud clang I hoped Olivia's group could hear through the door. Before I could bolt toward the meeting room, though, the man lunged forward and wrapped both hands around my neck, squeezing even harder than before.

I'm going to die.

The thought blinked through my head, reverberating like a cymbal crash, echoing as I struggled against his hold.

A commotion came from somewhere behind me, then I was flung toward the group of people streaming down the short hallway. I didn't even remember hitting the ground, but everything went starkly white.

The next thing I knew, I was lying flat on my back.

"No, no, no, no." Olivia's voice came from miles away. "Please open your eyes, please, Charlotte."

When I managed to peel my eyelids open, I saw not only Olivia but a ring of people in graphic tees from an array of fandoms standing around me like bodyguards. I would have laughed if I'd been sure I could do so without tearing my throat apart.

Someone had turned on every light in the library, blinding me as much as the lack of oxygen had. All I wanted to do was close my eyes again, but Olivia's panicked expression prevented that.

"I'm okay," I said, the words sounding as horrible as they felt coming from my battered throat.

Milo joined the circle, his usually mild expression looking like thunder. "He went out the back door before we could grab him."

Olivia growled, but her focus shot back to me when my eyelids drifted downward. "Charlie, stay awake."

"I'm awake."

"Jesus, Chuck. Stop talking, okay? Just rest your voice for now," Milo said. He looked pained, like hearing my terrible rasp hurt him too.

I nodded in silent agreement.

"We've got James and Tillman on the front doors, Jonesy and Dylan on the back," he told Olivia. "Chief Roberts lives around the corner, so he's on his way."

Another guy who I vaguely recognized added, "I called the clinic's emergency number. The answering service said Dr. Bardot is at the hospital checking on a patient, but they're notifying Dr. Thorne."

Sawyer.

I was barely holding it together, but the thought of him brought the hot sting of tears to my eyes. To stave them off, I struggled to sit up, grateful for every helping hand that guided me so I could lean back against the wall.

"Is he coming?" I asked.

Milo dropped down to sit beside me, wrapping an arm around my shoulders. "He's coming, Chuck. Just hang tight."

I closed my eyes again while Olivia sent a kid in a Nintendo shirt to get me some water.

Chief Roberts arrived before any of his officers. He looked different tonight in jeans and a baseball cap instead of his uniform. When he made his way to my side, the circle of onlookers dispersed—except for Olivia and Milo, who stuck close—as he crouched down to look at me. His gaze moved across my neck and he visibly flinched.

"Should we get an ambulance over here?" he asked gently.

"No." My voice sounded hoarser by the second. "Sawyer is coming."

The chief's expression softened. "Good. As long as he agrees you don't need to go to the hospital, I'll let him take care of you."

I nodded as a cup of water was pressed into my hands. For a few minutes, we just sat there by the wall as I tried to soothe the burning in my throat. A pair of police officers arrived, spoke quietly to Roberts, then went with Olivia to get the security footage.

Hanson strode through the crowd near the front doors just as Roberts pulled over a rolling desk chair and lowered it as far as it would go. When she reached us, the chief said, "I hate to make you speak more than necessary, Charlotte, but can you tell us what happened?"

I ran through it as concisely as possible, every word coming out in a harsh croak no matter how I tried to control it. The fact that it'd been dark and the man's face covered helped, because I had very little to offer. It was only when I said the words *ski mask* that I realized this wasn't a random incident.

"Oh, god. It was the same guy," I whispered.

The chief nodded, obviously having made the connection already. "I know it was dark, Charlotte, but can you tell me anything about the man? Height, eye color, any scars?"

I closed my eyes to summon the image of him. "I couldn't see his eyes in the dark, but I didn't notice any scars. He was taller than me, not as tall as Sawyer. When he leaned in, he was almost eye level with me. But he sounded...weird. Like he was trying to deepen his voice to disguise it."

Roberts nodded, squeezed my hand, and stood just as Sawyer burst through the front doors. I watched his panicked gaze sweep the space before it landed on me, then he sprinted over, dropped to his knees in front of me, and cupped my face in his hands. For a long moment, he just searched my features, then his gaze lowered to my neck and he pulled me into his arms. Dimly, I felt everyone else shift away as I landed on Sawyer's lap.

The tears that had pricked at me moments ago returned in full force, finally bursting free.

As painful sobs shuddered through my frame, Sawyer clasped me to his chest, whispering soft words into my hair and rubbing my back until the tidal wave of emotion gradually receded.

When he finally drew back to tip my chin up and inspect my neck under the light, his lips tightened into a pinched line. I flinched at the delicate press of his fingers against my neck and heard a low growl rumble in his chest in response.

"You're safe now," he said quietly. "I'll take care of you, angel."

It sounded like he needed the reassurance even more than I did, so I just nodded.

"Did you hit your head when you fell?"

"I got woozy when he let go of me, but I don't think so," I replied, reaching up to touch the back of my skull. It had hit the wall when the guy first grabbed me, but there was no lasting pain. My voice sounded foreign even to me, but Sawyer's pale eyes were warm, reassuring.

"She landed on her hands and knees when he shoved her at us," Olivia said as she came over to tell us the police were finished.

Milo joined her. "We caught her, but when it looked like she was going to pass out, we laid her down on her back."

"Good." Sawyer brushed my hair back from my face. "That's good. Thank you."

"I want to go home," I whispered.

His eyes scoured my features before inspecting my neck again. "It might be a good idea to go to the hospital, angel."

"No!"

The word burst from my lips in a terrified squawk and Sawyer immediately tucked me tight against his chest, cradling my head against his throat.

"Okay," he soothed. "Okay, we'll go home."

He helped me to my feet, slipping his arm around my waist for support, and talked to Olivia and Milo for another minute in a low tone as I stared at the magazine rack on the ground, the only visual proof that anything out of the ordinary had occurred.

Well, that and what I imagined must be a gruesome number of bruises around my throat.

A moment later, Olivia came out of my office with my purse and Sawyer guided me into her waiting arms.

"It's going to be okay," she whispered, pulling back to squish my cheeks gently between both of her hands. "I'll lock up with the chief after we get this cleaned up. Your job is to rest and recover, understand?"

I nodded, offered a tiny, wobbly smile when tears hit my eyes again, and met Milo's solemn gaze as he moved in for a hug.

"If you need a hospital and don't go, Libby's going to be pissed," he said against the top of my head. I couldn't see

Sawyer's response with my face pressed to Milo's t-shirt clad chest, but I felt Milo drop one arm to offer his hand. "I'm Milo Davies, Mark's brother."

"Nice to meet you. I should get her home, if you don't mind."

Milo shifted back, still studying my face, but he nodded as Sawyer stepped up beside me again. My knees ached, my throat burned, and my body was so stiff, I could barely move. Sawyer kept his arm around my waist and accommodated each slow, pathetic shuffle as we made our way to the door.

"The police are going to leave a car outside overnight," he said into my ear. "I'm going to take you home, make you some tea and get some ice packs to help your throat, all right?"

I nodded, still not trusting my voice.

The weight of the last few days dragged me down until I was leaning heavily against him. He didn't falter, though, just supported me as we plodded toward his car, illegally parked at the curb by the front doors.

His grip on my waist kept me upright as he opened the passenger door and buckled me inside, running his gaze over my features again like he was searching for confirmation that I was really okay.

With a tenderness that brought tears to my eyes, he pressed his lips to my forehead, then finally stepped away to shut the car door and jog around to his side.

"You're going to be okay," he assured me as he started the engine and directed the heater vents toward me before I even realized I was shivering.

"Okay."

The hoarseness seemed to be getting worse instead of better, and Sawyer flinched before cupping my cheek in one warm palm.

"I'll take care of everything. Anything you need, I'm here."

It was spoken like a vow, encompassing the deepest kind of apology as well as a promise for the future. I leaned my head back against the seat and nodded as a single tear tumbled down to meet the sweet brush of his thumb.

For once in my life, I would gladly let someone else carry the load.

Chapter Twenty-Eight

SAWYER

CHARLOTTE WAS SILENT THE entire way home, but she didn't let go of my hand after I laced our fingers together across the center console. The bruises circling her neck shattered my heart into a thousand pieces. I had to hold myself together for her sake, if not my own.

When we pulled into the driveway, I lifted her hand to my lips. "Are you willing to let me stay with you tonight?"

She nodded, looking pale and drawn and utterly exhausted.

"I need to get some stuff from my house, some cream for the bruises. Do you want to come inside with me or should I get you into bed and run over after?"

"I'll come. I don't want to be alone," she replied, her voice barely above a whisper. My heart broke all over again, but she squeezed my hand and waited until I looked at her again to say, "I'm okay."

"No. You're extraordinary."

A ghost of a smile passed over her lips before we got out of the car. She moved slowly still, like her whole body was stiff, and she didn't brush me off when I came around to take her arm. Olivia had given me a rundown on what happened, but I stopped when we reached the door and looked Charlotte over once more.

"Okay," I said in as measured a tone as possible. "Come on, quick pit stop."

I led her into my living room, but before I could help her into a chair, she dropped her head against my shoulder. "Can we just stay here tonight? I don't know if I'll be able to get up the stairs at my place. Bowler is with Twig until tomorrow morning anyway."

"Of course. Come on then, let's have a look and get you into bed."

I switched on the electric teakettle as we passed through the kitchen. Once we reached the bedroom, I turned on all the lights, grimacing apologetically when she squinted at the brightness. Carefully, I lifted her shirt over her head and laid it aside, then moved to the pinstriped dress pants.

Once she was standing before me in her underwear, I checked her over head to toe. In addition to the blackening fingerprints around her neck, there was one bruise stretching across her shoulder blade marking where she'd been shoved against the wall, plus faint brush burns on her knees and palms from hitting the carpeted floor.

I sat her at the edge of the bed and found the tube of arnica cream I'd been planning to bring over to her house. "This shouldn't sting, but let me know if anything is uncomfortable."

"What is it?"

"Arnica," I said as I surveyed the bruises. "It's an herbal remedy that's supposed to help with pain and swelling. I ran track in high school and a teammate recommended it for muscle strains. My father thought it was quack medicine, so I used it just to spite him, but it seemed effective and meant I wasn't taking so many over-the-counter medications."

As gently as possible, I smoothed the cream over every mark shadowing her silken skin, then applied antibiotic ointment to her hands and knees. When I was done, she stood again, kicked her underpants down her legs, and dropped her bra on the dresser before crawling under the blankets.

I texted Libby with an update, since she'd been frantic with worry from the minute she got that first call, then promised Charlotte I'd be right back and went into the kitchen to make a cup of herbal tea with a hearty dose of honey in it. With that ready, I grabbed an ice pack from the freezer.

Back in the bedroom, I set the mug on the side table, turned off all but the bedside lamp, and stripped down to join her under the covers, sitting with my back against the headboard.

Getting into bed with her held a particularly bittersweet note after our time apart. Stiff as she was, she scooted across the space between us until her head rested in the crook of my shoulder. Carefully, I positioned the ice pack over the worst of the bruises on her neck, ignoring the bite of cold against my bare chest, then wrapped one arm around her and handed her the mug of tea with the other.

Though I didn't want to make her speak any more than necessary, adrenaline still pulsed through my veins. I tried to calm my breathing and hold myself steady for her, but then she whispered, "Tell me."

"What do you want to know?"

"Everything."

She deserved no less, so I nodded against the top of her head. "I'll start at the beginning, then. My parents' families ran in the same circles when they were growing up, even though they weren't what you'd call friends. My father went into med school and my mother was pursuing a degree in English literature when they got married."

"Really?"

"Really. She's not like you, though—I barely remember her ever reading books, even to me as a child. I think it was just an acceptable degree for a wealthy young woman who had no intention of following her heart."

Charlotte sipped her tea and snuggled closer against my side. "That's sad."

"It is," I agreed. "But they got married and she became the perfect hostess, the perfect ornament on my father's arm as he made his way up the food chain. My childhood was...fine. Until

I got older, it was fairly normal, aside from the fancy private schools."

She huffed a laugh.

"But the pressure was there all along, I think. They weren't abusive or cruel, just not really interested in anything I had to say unless it was to parrot their own desires back at them, so I learned to do that. By high school, I knew I'd be going into medicine, and fortunately I did have both the desire and the drive to do so. I'm not sure how it would have played out if I hadn't. I met Veronica for the first time just before I started college, but we didn't start dating until the summer between sophomore and junior year."

"Go on," Charlotte whispered, pressing her lips to my jaw in a show of support I was certain I didn't deserve.

I sucked in a breath and continued. "It was all very polite. I thought I loved her, but the pressure from both our families was intense. At one point, I was convinced she was going to break up with me and all I felt was relief, but then she started dropping hints about engagement rings."

"You're a catch, Dr. Hottie."

If she'd been in top form, I might have tickled her for teasing me as I laid out my sordid history, but the weight of what happened to her still crushed my chest until it was hard to breathe, so I just trailed my lips along her hairline.

"Not enough of one for Veronica Medlock. Maybe part of me knew the job was the dealbreaker. Maybe that's why I chose it."

Charlotte shook her head against my chest. "She didn't deserve you."

In all the years since, I'd never considered that angle. Life wasn't always about who deserved what—I definitely didn't feel I deserved the woman snuggled up at my side, but she wasn't slipping through my fingers again, not if I could help it.

As if she heard those thoughts, she lifted her face, her mouth brushing lightly across mine.

"I'm sorry I hurt you," I whispered against her lips. "Every time I tried to tell you, I let something else get in the way, because I was dreading that conversation. I didn't want to admit that I'd failed you, too. I knew what honesty meant to you and I stumbled at the first hurdle."

"You didn't fail."

"I did. And I'll spend the rest of my life making it up to you if that's what it takes."

I felt her smile more than saw it, those sweet lips curving against mine, then she kissed me in earnest.

Though I tried to keep things gentle, she growled and knotted her fingers in my hair until I took the mostly empty mug from her other hand and set it aside, then I scooted down to stretch out alongside her on the pillows as she tossed the ice pack aside.

For a long time, we just lay there, kissing like we were reacquainting ourselves with one another. I was as careful as possible, conscious of her injuries, but her hands started wandering, seeking, spurring me beyond where I intended to let things go.

"Angel," I murmured, but she shook her head and covered my lips with one finger.

"Please."

That single word, a painfully hoarse whisper in the dimness of the bedroom, obliterated my restraint. I drew her up and over me. And *fuck me,* the sound she made when she straddled my hips and rubbed sinuously along my body, it was indescribably sexy.

I groaned into her mouth, anchoring her to me with my hands on her hips as I tried to slow things down. "Why don't you let me make you feel good, angel? The rest can wait until you recover."

"I need you inside me. Please."

"Let me grab a condom," I managed to gasp when I felt her slick heat sliding along my cock.

She drew back, staring down at me like a queen, teasing, taunting almost. I groaned again when she wrapped her hand around me and said, "IUD."

It took every ounce of willpower to catch her wrist as I met her insistent gaze. "Fuck. Okay. If you're sure, angel."

Instead of answering, she lowered herself slowly, planting her hands on my chest as she welcomed me inside. The expression on her face was sheer bliss, and the only thing that kept it from shredding my self-control was the way she tipped her head back, exposing that circle of bruises. My fingertips tightened into her hips, a visceral echo of the fear that settled in my chest the minute Libby called me.

As if she recognized how the sight affected me, she leaned forward and dipped her chin, pulling at my hands until she could lace her fingers with mine and plant them on either side of my head.

"This is what you need?" I growled into her ear, meeting each roll of her hips with a sharp upward thrust.

On a gasp of pleasure, her mouth settled on mine again. This kiss wasn't gentle or tentative or reassuring. It was pure heat, unadulterated need.

When she released my hands to sit upright again, I grabbed her hips and set a new, more demanding pace. Despite her sore throat, she made helpless little noises, whimpering until I lowered one hand to circle my thumb right where she needed it.

Her back arched as the orgasm took her, tightening her muscles around my cock, then she collapsed forward onto my chest.

I rolled us over, slowing to a careful glide while she recovered. When her legs locked around my waist and she started moving with me again, I followed her lead and thrust deep, hard, until I couldn't stop myself from emptying into her with an intensity that shocked me.

Before I could withdraw, a hoarse laugh slipped past her lips and I groaned at the sensation, which only made her laugh harder. I propped my elbows on either side of her head and gazed down at her, my chest filled with such tenderness that I was sure she could see it written across my face.

"I love you," I whispered before I could think better of it.

Her lips parted in surprise, but her gaze went soft and a smile tugged at her mouth. I dropped my head to kiss each corner of her lips, delighted when the smile widened instead of disappearing as she processed what I'd said.

I kissed her once more before I eased out of her. She flung her arms wide as I moved off the bed, her eyes closed and that sweet smile still on her lips. Even when I returned with a warm washcloth and cleaned her up, she only peeked up at me and grinned. I tossed the cloth into my laundry hamper and switched off the lamp before drawing her back into my arms.

"I don't want you to strain your voice right now, angel, but I want you to know how sorry I am for what happened the other night. I should never have let you be ambushed by that information, no matter the distractions. I wish I could go back in time and fix it, but I can only promise that it will never happen again," I promised against her temple.

"I forgive you," she whispered back. "And I'm sorry she hurt you."

While our breathing slowed and our bodies cooled, I stared into the darkness, thinking about those words. Even after Charlotte slipped off to sleep with her head tucked under my chin, both sentiments circled one another in my mind, over and over.

No matter how fervently I'd hoped that she would forgive me, I never imagined she would apologize for how Veronica had treated *me*. That warm bloom in my chest spread until everything inside me glowed with contentment.

Only then did I follow her into sleep.

Chapter Twenty-Nine

CHARLOTTE

WHEN I OPENED MY eyes, the bedside clock said it was almost ten in the morning. I jolted so quickly, I bashed my head against Sawyer's chin. I was still draped across him, but he'd shifted on the pillows to sit up and read one of the library books he'd checked out. In my distraction, I barely registered that it was a historical romance I'd promoted as a Book of the Month last summer.

"I'm late," I said. My voice still sounded husky, but it was significantly better than the previous night.

Sawyer tutted like a schoolmarm. "You have the rest of the week off. Doctor's orders. Olivia is taking care of everything, and there will be an officer posted at the library around the clock. You, my sweet angel, are spending the day in bed."

I blinked at him. "My throat is sore, that's all. I don't need to stay in bed."

Setting the book aside, he rolled to face me and cupped my cheek in his hand. "You were choked, slammed against a wall, and lost consciousness. While I'd be very happy if you feel that much better this morning, you're not pushing it today."

"I won't push it," I replied quickly.

"If you need other reasons to stay in bed, I can certainly supply them."

My cheeks heated, but I held onto my scowl and replied, "If I want to get up, I'll damn well do so."

"You enjoyed the bondage, didn't you?" he purred into my ear. "I suppose I could tie you to the bed, if you insist."

The scowl evaporated and I laughed, wrapping my arms around him. "You're ridiculous. When you tie me up again, Dr. Hottie, it'll be because I want you to, not because you're being unnecessarily domineering about my recovery."

"I suppose I can agree to that. You can leave the bed, but you'll drink every cup of tea with honey that I make for you today, deal?"

He had started trailing kisses around my neck, but it was a minute before I realized he was following the bruises. I wrinkled my nose as he reached the end of the path. "Deal. Does it look awful?"

"They've faded a bit already. If we keep up with the arnica, I think by the weekend they won't be very noticeable. How does the rest of your body feel?"

I stretched my arms over my head, bounced my knees, and wiggled my hips, which earned me a Stern Doctor glare. "Better than last night."

For a second, he looked uncertain, then he dropped a light kiss to my lips. "All right then, up you get. Let's have some breakfast."

Once I was seated at his kitchen table, he grabbed a small purple gift bag off the counter and set it in front of me. "I'm not sure this is the best thing for your throat, but I was waiting for the chance to give it to you."

I shot him a suspicious look and tugged the layers of lavender tissue paper loose. "What is it?"

"Impatient little thing," he muttered. "Just open it."

Inside the bag was a big glass jar filled with Skittles—not only the berry flavors I'd told him I liked best, but also red ones he must've hand-picked from a dozen packages of the regular flavors.

Tears flooded my eyes as I clutched the jar to my chest. "Sawyer, I—"

The words broke off, but it didn't matter. He squatted beside my chair and wrapped his arms around me like this was a perfectly natural reaction to a jar of candy. It took a few minutes in his embrace, but I managed to pull myself together, gave him a watery smile, and let go of him so he could make us breakfast.

It wasn't *terrible,* being cosseted and fussed over, but by lunchtime, I was done with it. Sawyer had convinced me to take a bath to soak my muscles, which were admittedly still a little sore, so we made the short journey over to my house.

Though I rolled my eyes, he checked through the entire house top to bottom before planting himself on the couch while I ran a bath upstairs.

By the time I came back down, I felt less agitated, even if I was already tired of being cooped up. Twig brought Bowler home while I was in the tub and he was a welcome distraction, but not quite enough to keep me from feeling like I was trapped in the house.

Sawyer, however, forestalled my irritation.

"Penelope and Grisham are coming for dinner, if you're up for it," he said, lips curving like he knew he'd just played his ace.

"Oh," I replied, surprised. They hadn't exactly been informed of our reconciliation. "So, you...you spoke to them?"

He made a face. "I realize they're not my biggest fans right now, but yes, I called Penelope this morning before you woke up to let her know you were okay, in case she heard anything secondhand."

"Oh," I repeated.

"I'm sorry if I overstepped," Sawyer said quickly, looking a little alarmed by my blank expression.

"No, no. It's fine. Pen didn't threaten your life or anything, did she?"

Now he grinned. "Well, she did say that if you gave the signal, she'd—how did she phrase it? Oh, yes, cut off my balls and choke me with them."

I laughed, though it sounded rusty even after the gallons of tea Sawyer had encouraged me to drink, including while I was in the tub. The fact that he'd put himself directly in the line of fire with Penelope meant a great deal to me. I settled myself sideways on his lap, snuggling against him, then Bowler climbed on top of me.

"You not only called her, you also invited her to dinner?" I asked.

He nuzzled under my jaw. "I would do anything for you, angel. Including putting my manhood at risk to make sure your friends know you're safe."

"I appreciate that. More than I can say."

"Anything and everything." He pressed a kiss to the corner of my mouth.

With guests coming, that gave me enough motivation to stop sulking and tidy up downstairs. Sawyer insisted he was cooking as part of his penance toward all three of us, but I'd ignored the house practically since Spoon went home to his new family, so we worked together to get the place ready for guests.

In the middle of Sawyer vacuuming the living room—he'd refused to let me do anything more strenuous than picking up dog toys—something occurred to me. I was cuddling Bowler on the couch to keep him safe from the scary appliance when Sawyer saw me freeze and raised a brow in question.

I stared at him while I gathered my thoughts. Bless the man, he just turned off the vacuum and waited patiently for me to speak.

"The guy disguised his voice. Why would he go to that trouble unless he thought I might recognize it?"

Sawyer's long frame jerked slightly. "I assumed because there was something distinctive about his voice or the way he talks, an accent maybe. Your theory makes more sense, though, especially in a small town where you're a fairly well known figure."

This theory, however logical, was almost more unsettling than the actual assault. The prospect that someone I *knew* was behind these acts made me feel sick to my stomach. I jumped up from my seat so quickly that I dislodged Bowler onto the floor, then swayed.

Sawyer caught me under the elbow. "Easy. Breathe, Charlotte."

I pressed my forehead to the center of his chest and drew several deep breaths before stepping back.

"I'm okay. Thank you," I said, pleased to find my voice sounded steady, if hoarse.

"Don't thank me," he replied quietly. "I wish I had been there. I wish a lot of things. I'm so sorry you were hurt, angel."

I cupped his cheek, shadowed with stubble that made him even more impossibly sexy, and said, "I'm okay, really. That's what matters. Now come help me put the leaf in the dining room table. Pen likes to spread out."

By the time Penelope and Grisham walked in, I was more nervous than Sawyer. I had sent a few text updates myself throughout the afternoon, hoping to ward off the worst of their protectiveness, but there was no telling with Pen.

I'd changed into an emerald green sundress after making Sawyer inspect the bruise on my back under every available light to make sure it wasn't visible, but I had a lightweight scarf covered in Jane Austen quotes coiled around my neck.

Both Penelope's sharp brown gaze and Grisham's baby blues settled on it immediately.

"I'm fine," I said for the first of what was sure to be a dozen times throughout the evening.

Grisham blanched at the remaining rasp in my voice and Penelope threw her arms around me. Sawyer just smiled at us from his spot near the stove.

Suddenly, though, Pen spun around and leveled a finger at him as he blinked in surprise.

"Don't even think that you're off the hook, Dr. Hottie," she snarled. "You hurt our girl *ever* again, you answer to us."

Sawyer bowed his head slightly. "I fucked up big time. Believe me, I know that. I'm just glad Charlotte had the two of you to be there for her."

Grisham hooked his arm around Penelope's waist and dragged her toward the dining room, where Bowler wriggled impatiently in the portable play yard I'd set up to keep him contained.

"And we're very glad you were there to patch her up after *our* big fuckup, aren't we, Pen? C'mon, let's meet this adorable little buddy here."

Though she grumbled under her breath, she did stop glaring after that. Puppies were one of her weaknesses, and Bowler pulled out all the stops in charming her.

Sawyer was a far more creative cook than I, so he knocked dinner right out of the park with homemade tacos seasoned to perfection. I wasn't sure I'd ever be able to go back to the packaged seasonings after that—even Penelope was ready to give Sawyer her blessing by the time she took her first bite.

"When are we going to plan for a movie night, Chuckles?" Grisham asked as he gathered a drooping Pen from where she'd collapsed on the couch after dinner.

"Chuckles?" Sawyer repeated, looking at me curiously.

I rolled my eyes. "Ignore them. My entire youth was full of stupid nicknames."

"I'm starting to think they're just more proof of how loved you truly are." His eyes were warm as he touched a finger to the tip of my nose and leaned down to murmur, "It's the same reason I call you angel."

Even as my cheeks heated, I realized Grisham and Pen were regarding us with unveiled curiosity. Instead of responding, I cleared my throat and followed them to the side door.

"You know you guys could have crashed here if you wanted to," I said, hugging them both at once.

"No, we've got an early morning. We'll get out of your hair," Pen said.

"I love you guys."

"Dr. Hottie's right about one thing, Chuck. You are so loved." She gave me a hard squeeze. "Take care of yourself."

Sawyer set one hand on the small of my back as we said our goodbyes and watched them leave. I turned into him, rubbing my nose along his sternum. As much as I loved spending time with Pen and Grisham, the quiet after their departure was as refreshing as the feel of his arms around me.

"Thank you for tonight."

He kissed the top of my head. "It was my pleasure, angel. It's a blessing to be surrounded by such good friends."

As simple a sentiment as it was, I had to agree.

Chapter Thirty

SAWYER

"YOU ARE A TERRIBLE patient."

The woman in question glared back at me, emerald eyes sparking mutinously. All I'd dared to do was suggest I could bring her breakfast in bed. Apparently, that was enough to unleash the full power of her fury.

"I am not your patient," she said, enunciating each word slowly and clearly, just in case I misunderstood.

I leveled my own glare back at her, though her petulant expression made it difficult for me to hold back a smile. "No, you're the woman I love, which makes your wellbeing even more important to me. Is it really too much to ask you to take it easy for *one more* day?"

"Yes."

Throwing up my hands, I groaned aloud, then picked up the tray from her lap and carried it downstairs. She followed a few seconds later, looking much less triumphant than I'd expected. I set the plate of French toast and fruit on the table, but before I could put the tray back in the cupboard where I'd found it, she burrowed her way under my arms and planted her face against my chest.

"Thank you," she mumbled.

I slipped one finger under her chin and tilted her face up for a kiss. "You're welcome."

"Sawyer," she said when we were finally seated at the table, "I'm serious. I can't stay inside forever. I need to go back to work on Monday. Bowler needs walks. I have a life to live."

While I wished I could argue against every one of those points, she was right. I sighed. "Can we come up with a compromise? I don't think there's any question now that you're a target, and until we know who it is and what the hell he wants, I'm going to be worried sick."

"Okay. Compromise. Let's hear your suggestions."

I eyed her cautiously before venturing into this particular minefield. "Well," I began, "what if we walk Bowler together after work, aside from short trips into the yard?"

Charlotte inclined her head regally. "I can agree to that point. What else?"

This was a trap. I was sure of it. The problem was that I couldn't quite see a clear path before me. After all, I was only barely back in her good graces—one wrong move, and I didn't doubt she'd tell me to go straight to hell.

"Is there any chance I can convince you to let me know if you're going somewhere other than work and back?" I asked, my tone pathetically hopeful.

"Sure," she agreed. Too easily, in my opinion.

"Really?"

"I'm not unreasonable or unintelligent, Sawyer," she replied, eyebrows drawing together. "I understand that there's danger. I have no intention of wandering the streets at midnight by myself."

"I thought I lost you once already through my own stupidity, Charlotte. You're too important for me to risk it happening again."

Slowly, I reached up and cupped her cheek, uncertain whether she'd nuzzle my hand or bite it. Fortunately, she did the former, leaning into the touch. Her eyes softened until those green depths were like the summer grass, sun-warmed and vibrant, and she lifted her hand to cover mine.

"I do love you, you know," she said quietly.

The words hung in the air, a perfume so sweet that for a moment, I could only breathe it in. When I tugged her onto my lap, she came willingly, laughing in that carefree way that made me feel as though I'd won some kind of cosmic prize. I cradled her against my chest and tipped her face up to kiss her.

We didn't break apart until Bowler stood up against our legs and whined pitifully at being left out.

"Get your own girl," I huffed at him, but Charlotte almost tumbled off my lap when she bent forward to scratch his ears.

"So, if you're my bodyguard for the weekend, what should we do?"

I blinked at her. "Do? Well, *you* are supposed to be taking it easy while you recover from being assaulted."

"Isn't it great that I have a doctor to watch over me?" she asked, batting her lashes.

For a solid thirty seconds, I allowed myself to imagine tying her to the bed until Sunday night rolled around, then I said, "Well, what would you normally do with a Friday off? You do know that I'm aware of your homebody tendencies, angel."

She stuck out her tongue at me. "Yeah, yeah. I'd probably take Bowler here to the lake, let him have a good romp, then come home and read a book."

"Perfect. Let's go."

Aside from that visit to the park with Charlotte to see her terrifying geese, I hadn't explored any other town landmarks yet. The little public beach she directed me to was deserted, but beautiful. A tall lighthouse stood at the edge of a rocky outcropping near the water, its gray stone exterior as quaint as the rest of my new hometown.

With a start, I realized that's what Spruce Hill had become. Home.

The lake was still frigidly cold, but the sunshine felt wonderful. While Charlotte laughed at the puppy tiptoeing through water that barely covered his big paws, I watched the breeze lifting and twirling her shimmering blonde locks. For the first time in a week, she looked carefree and content, and I never wanted to ruin that for her again.

The bruises were almost gone, thankfully, but the memory of them would haunt me for the rest of my life. It took intense effort on my part not to picture some stranger gripping her by the throat, squeezing until she passed out, every time I thought about that night.

Here in the sunlight, with her lips curved into a constant smile and her laughter coming easily at Bowler's antics, it was tempting to believe the danger was gone.

Or it might have been, if that smile hadn't faded as she turned to look at me.

"Why would he come back to the library after the files were taken to the station?" she asked.

I should have known it wouldn't be far from her mind, even if she was able to enjoy a brief reprieve. As beloved as she was in Spruce Hill, clearly there was some darker game afoot, one heavily featuring Charlotte herself.

Gesturing to one of the boulders along the shore, I sat and tucked her under my arm when she followed. "Do you remember at the park, I asked if anyone in town didn't adore you?"

She nodded. "Yes, of course."

"You said there were a few people who didn't like you much. Who are they?"

With a sigh, she leaned her head against my shoulder and replied, "A couple of ex-boyfriends. The mean girl squad from high school, though a few of them have moved out of town since then. Maybe one or two potential adopters who got passed over for rescue dogs I was fostering, but that hasn't happened often, and I usually keep working with them afterward to find a dog that's a better fit."

I couldn't picture someone from that last category coming after her so violently. High school seemed like an awfully long time to hold a grudge strong enough for what had happened, too, so I considered the ex-boyfriend angle.

"Tell me more about the exes. How many did you part with on bad terms? How long ago?"

Charlotte gazed at Bowler while he pranced through the surf, now proudly carrying a stick twice as long as his body, then met my eyes. "Only two, really. Brent and I broke up almost four years ago after he got drunk and tried to convince Penelope to sleep with him. Turned out she wasn't the first of my friends he'd propositioned, just the first to refuse."

"You're shitting me," I said, aghast.

"Nope. He slept with three of them in the two years we were together and lied to my face. They all did."

"Christ, angel, I'm sorry." No wonder she had trust issues, and I'd stupidly broken that trust even when I knew how important honesty was to her.

"It's okay," she said softly. "Besides, he had an alibi for the break-in. The chief looked into him."

I frowned but nodded. "Who was the other one?"

"Mike McGinty, last fall." When she hesitated, I lifted a brow. "We hadn't been dating long at all at that point. I never slept with him, thankfully. We got into an argument over something so small, I can't even remember what it was, and he grabbed my arm. Hard."

My jaw tightened. "Hard enough to leave marks?"

"Yes," she said, looking away. "But no, I didn't file a police report. I told him to get the hell out of my house and never come near me again. He hasn't. I haven't seen him in months."

"Now that things have escalated, maybe we should mention him to Chief Roberts," I suggested.

Charlotte shook her head. "I mean, yes, we can tell him, but it wasn't Mike who attacked me. He's even taller than you and lanky as hell. Total stringbean build. The guy who came into the library that night definitely wasn't him."

"He could still be involved, angel."

"Maybe," she said, reaching down to pat Bowler when he came romping toward us. Before I could press any further, though, her phone rang. She made a face and showed me the screen, which read *Chief Roberts*. "His ears must have been burning."

I stayed quiet while she answered the call, but Charlotte's side of the conversation consisted mostly of simple *yes* or *no* responses to whatever he was saying. Her expression didn't betray much until the call ended and she pocketed her phone again with a grimace.

"Well, we're cordially invited to come to the station after we drop Bowler home for a nap. He's got some names for me to look over and says you're welcome to tag along. If I didn't know better, I'd think the two of you had discussed not leaving me on my own," she said, sending a scornful look in my direction.

I held up my hands in a gesture of innocence. "Absolutely not."

The smirk on her lips expressed her doubts, but she clipped Bowler's leash back on and slid her free hand into mine. Before we headed to the car, I tugged her close and kissed her temple.

Even if the chief and I hadn't discussed it in words, it made me happy to know he and I were on the same page.

The sooner we got to the bottom of who was targeting Charlotte, the better.

Chapter Thirty-One

CHARLOTTE

Spruce Hill's police station was almost laughably small, residing in a tidy brick building not far from the library. I remembered touring the station in elementary school—it hadn't seemed quite so tiny back then.

As an adult, walking past the few desks crammed into the main room in order to get to Roberts' office made me feel like Alice in Wonderland. Everything had shrunk down a size or two in the decades since that first visit.

Roberts looked like he hadn't been sleeping well, which I took as a testament to how invested he was in closing the book on this investigation.

"Come in, come in. I'm sorry to make you come over here while you're recovering, Charlotte," he said as he ushered us into the office.

"It's not a problem," I said, waving off his concern. "I feel fine."

His sharp gaze dropped to my neck, which I hadn't bothered to cover up now that the marks had faded to a dingy yellow. "I hope it wasn't a mistake not to send you to the hospital?"

Sawyer smiled and shook his head. "I'm taking good care of her, sir."

"What he means is that I've been fussed over and coddled more at home than I would have at the hospital," I informed him. "But we'd just been talking about you when you called, so it was good timing. Sawyer thought it might be important to mention a possible grudge from another ex of mine, Mike McGinty, even though he definitely could not have been the one who came into the library."

Roberts leaned back in his chair. "McGinty, huh? He lay hands on you, Charlotte?"

I sighed, but Sawyer sent me a stern look, so I said, "Only once. He grabbed my arm last fall, left a couple bruises. We broke up then and there. I haven't really seen him since."

"He's been hauled in here a few times over the years, though nothing recent. I'll do some digging. In the meantime, I've got a list of names here of every man who showed up on library footage from the week before the break-in to the time of the assault," Roberts said, sliding a piece of paper across the table toward me. "Wondered if you could look it over, rule anybody else out based on physical attributes alone."

I scanned the list, then glanced up. The chief handed me a pen before I even asked for it. Looking back at the names, I crossed out a few who I knew were much too tall, several who were far too old. That left quite a few names still on the paper before me. I rubbed my forehead as I tried to picture each of the remaining men.

"It's okay if that's as many as you can eliminate, Charlotte," the chief said gently. "Do you recall anything odd about any of your encounters with the ones left there?"

Just as I started to shake my head, my gaze settled on one name. "Craig DeWitt came in and said he'd lost an assignment. He asked about the lost and found—he was the one who returned a book with his mom's check inside. The homework he was looking for wasn't there, though."

"The hero worship kid?"

I wrinkled my nose as Sawyer and the chief exchanged a look. "Yes, that's him."

"But he specifically asked if you still kept things that came through the chute?" Roberts asked, tapping his fingers against the desk.

"Yes, but...well, I suppose he's the right height for the guy who grabbed me, but he's also very delicate, if you know what I mean. Fine-boned, long pianist fingers, looks like he'd blow away in a stiff wind. I really don't think it could have been him."

Roberts nodded slowly. "I think you're right about the assault, at least, but I'll have a conversation with him. Anyone else standing out from the list?"

"Actually," I said after reading each name again, "Jimmy Anders asked me out last week."

From the corner of my eye, I saw Sawyer straighten in his chair, but the chief held up a hand to him. "I assume you turned him down?"

I laughed. "Yes, I turned him down. He was a good sport about it. For what it's worth, he asked me to be his girlfriend in second grade and I turned him down then, too. I see him a couple times a year around town, but he's not much of a library regular."

Roberts nodded again and accepted the list that I handed back to him. "Thank you, Charlotte. I know it doesn't seem like much, but every little bit helps."

"I'm sorry. I wish I could be more helpful."

The chief waved away my apology. "Oh, I managed to track down the doctor who wrote that prescription. Definitely not narcotics—it was from a dermatologist down in Geneva for a steroid cream."

"Not even athlete's foot," I joked.

Roberts grinned, shook our hands, and sent us back out into the afternoon sun. Much as I hated to admit it, I was exhausted. Sawyer took one look at my face and brushed a gentle kiss to my lips.

"Let's go home, angel. I'll make us some dinner and we'll take it easy for the evening," he said as he tucked a strand of hair behind my ear. "Sound good?"

"Yes," I agreed, leaning into him before sliding into the passenger seat.

My head was a labyrinth of speculation and theories, none of which made any sense. Craig DeWitt was a sweet kid who didn't look like he would hurt a fly—I didn't believe for a second that he was the one who'd grabbed me. Besides, I almost hadn't recognized him when he came in looking for his homework. If he'd wanted to keep a low profile in order to attack me, why march up to the front desk and draw attention to himself?

Bowler barely stirred when we let him out of his crate in the living room, still exhausted from his lakeside romp, so I let Sawyer nudge me toward the couch. I curled up in my favorite corner, picked up the book I'd been reading to try to pass the time when I wasn't speaking to Sawyer, and tried hard to focus on the words. He settled himself at the other end of the couch and started idly rubbing the arch of my foot while he flipped open to the middle of his historical romance.

This, I thought. *This is perfection.*

If someone had asked me months ago whether I could see myself falling in love with a doctor, I would have laughed in their face. I hadn't lived with someone else since I got the job at the library and moved out of Penelope's apartment in order to return to Spruce Hill, but Sawyer had somehow slipped seamlessly into my life.

Like he belonged there. Like that place had been waiting just for him.

And, of course, I wasn't unaware of the little jobs around the house that had suddenly been done, entirely without fanfare. Hell, he'd even secured the railing I tore off the wall and patched the holes from the previous set of screws. Big or small, the projects he took it upon himself to complete were never mentioned unless I was the one who brought it up.

I'd always considered doctors to be pompous, arrogant jerks—Libby being the one exception—but it seemed more like Sawyer tried to avoid accolades.

Even at the charity ball, he had been self-effacing and humble.

"I can see the wheels turning. What are you thinking about over there?" he asked, giving my foot a gentle squeeze.

"Just that I'm really happy I met you."

His smile was slow and sweet, radiating as much warmth as his palm, which slid upward to my knee. "The feeling is mutual, angel."

"I guess being stuck with a bodyguard isn't so bad when he's a total hottie," I mused.

"And I suppose being plastered to an exquisite goddess such as yourself isn't as strenuous as I feared," Sawyer teased back as he stretched out along my body on the couch. His head dropped, nuzzling his way up my torso over my shirt. "Perfectly, decadently, deliciously beautiful."

Just as he reached my collarbone, though, his phone chirped from his pocket. He collapsed onto me with a groan, his fingers clutching and tickling at my sides until I shrieked and tried to squirm free. I shoved at his shoulders but he didn't budge.

"Get off me, you lout!" I grunted, laughing.

Instead, he relaxed, going utterly boneless on top of me as he pulled the phone out. "Libby wants us to come for dinner tomorrow night, if you're feeling well enough."

"Let me guess, she wants to see me for herself instead of trusting your updates?" I asked sweetly.

Sawyer hummed against my sternum. "Yeah, that sounds about right."

"Tell her we'll be there, but we're bringing Bowler."

"You got it."

After typing out his reply with one hand, he dropped the phone on the coffee table, rubbed Bowler's head where he lay on the floor beside the couch, and apparently decided that reading time was over.

Since I hadn't made it through a single chapter since we first sat down, I didn't mind one bit.

Chapter Thirty-Two

SAWYER

During my years at the hospital, I'd gone out of my way to avoid socializing with coworkers unless it was absolutely necessary. For the most part, I hadn't bothered to make friends any more than I'd bothered to actually date instead of engaging in occasional flings.

As we pulled into Libby's driveway, I figured since everything else in my life had turned upside down since moving to Spruce Hill, it stood to reason that this would change, too. The added bonus was that Libby and her husband had known Charlotte her entire life, so I was bound to hear some interesting stories throughout dinner.

Except, of course, the second we walked into the back yard, Charlotte pointed a finger at Libby's husband, Mark, and said, "Start telling tales and I swear that I will eviscerate you in such a way that even these two gorgeous doctors won't be able to save you."

Mark had sun-streaked blond hair and looked like he belonged on a beach in California, though I knew he owned a shop in town that sold organic bath and body products. From what I'd gathered around the clinic, he was utterly devoted to his wife and generally considered an all-around amazing guy.

"What a greeting, Charleston," Mark chided.

My eyebrows shot upwards, but Charlotte's elbow jabbed me preemptively in the ribs. I rubbed at the spot and frowned at her. "Hey! I didn't say a word."

"She's a violent little beastie, isn't she?" Mark said with a grin. "How have you been, Sawyer?"

I carefully sidestepped away from my girlfriend to clasp his hand. "Bit of a shit week, actually, but having a great boss has certainly made things easier."

Mark waited until Charlotte set the puppy down at her feet, then he stepped forward and tipped her chin up with one finger, not to check the bruising on her neck but to study her features so closely, I wondered what he read in her face.

"You hanging in there, kiddo?" he asked quietly, every trace of teasing gone from his expression.

"Doing my best."

He wrapped his arms around her, just as his brother had that night at the library. "When they find the bastard, I want a turn kicking his ass."

Charlotte met my eyes over his shoulder. "You might have to get in line."

"Are those our guests?" Libby called as she popped her head out the back door.

"They are indeed, my love," Mark replied. He released Charlotte, but before she stepped away, he put her in a careful headlock, avoiding any pressure on her neck, and rubbed his knuckles on the top of her head.

"Oh, I am going to annihilate you," she yelped. "Do not mess up my hair!"

Libby practically skipped down the stairs when she caught sight of Bowler. "Hey, you two. Oh my sweet little stud muffin, look at you," she cooed, lifting him into her arms so he could cover her face in sloppy kisses.

Charlotte elbowed Mark in the gut and muttered, "Better make sure she washes her face before kissing you goodnight, Checkmark."

"What is it with this town and nicknames?" I asked.

Wrapping her arms around my waist, Charlotte positioned herself to use me as a shield. "Full of jerks, that's all."

Mark snorted, but Libby pinned the pair of them with a sharp glare. "If you two don't behave, Sawyer here is going to be regaled with embarrassing stories from both of your childhoods, got it?"

To my surprise, they both looked suitably chastened and mumbled, "Got it," in unison.

Libby winked at me before setting Bowler back down. "Good. Charlotte, get over here and let me look at you."

Without complaint—another shock—Charlotte moved to Libby's side and lifted her face to the sky. Libby brushed her fingers gently over the remnants of the bruising, then waited until Charlotte lowered her chin to ask, "Any residual soreness?"

"Not really. I've had enough tea this week to fill a bathtub, thanks to your colleague."

Libby rolled her eyes and pulled Charlotte into a hug. "You take care of yourself, hear me? And let Sawyer help with that, for Christ's sake. I know what an awful patient you are."

Charlotte turned to me with a gasp of outrage, but I shook my head. "Oh, I did *not* tell her that, believe me."

"I somehow doubt she needed to tell him, Charley Horse. You've been a crummy patient since you were four years old and skinned your knee falling off that tiny bike of yours in front of my house," Mark said, tweaking her nose as he walked past. "Not only did she scream bloody murder until I came outside to see what the hell was happening, she refused to keep a bandaid on it and bled all over my favorite shirt."

When she blinked those beautiful eyes up at me in feigned innocence, I leaned down to whisper in her ear, "Truly shocking."

She made an indignant sound in her throat. "I'm allergic to adhesives."

"Are you?" I asked in surprise. "I don't remember seeing that in your chart at the ER."

"I only mention it when someone goes to put a bandaid on, or after blood draws when they try to tape the gauze pad to my elbow." Charlotte shrugged a little and slipped her hand into mine as we started toward the patio table. "If I had some horrific wound and needed a dressing taped over it, I wouldn't want it to stop them from doing it. I just get rashy and it lasts for weeks."

"Huh. Are you allergic to anything else?"

"Lavender," she and Mark said in unison.

I blinked. "Lavender? Like, the flower?"

"Yup. Or the essential oil. I break into giant hives. I tried out one of Mark's first muscle balms when I strained my quad dancing in college. It wasn't pretty. I had to get him to whip up something new just to stop the itching."

"I make sure to keep a separate supply of products with no lavender in them for her," Mark added. "Those hives were the size of dollar bills, I swear."

I rubbed a hand over my jaw. "Good to know. I should've asked sooner."

"I didn't even think to mention it," Charlotte murmured, leaning her head on my shoulder.

"I thought my whole stock of muscle balm was contaminated," Mark said.

Charlotte scowled. "Yeah, he told me he'd send a sample out to be tested for flesh-eating bacteria."

I choked on a laugh. "I'm glad it was nothing so dire."

"Me too. That muscle balm is a bestseller. I could've gone out of business before the shop even had time to get up and running, all because somebody is a delicate little flower," he teased.

"*Allergic* to a delicate little flower, you jerk," Charlotte grumbled.

After rubbing Bowler's belly, Mark said, "Why don't you two go relax? We'll bring dinner out."

I sat down at the table beside Charlotte, running my gaze over her. Despite the banter—or maybe because of it—she looked good. Happy and loved, with only the barest visible reminder of the violence that had been done to her. She was wearing another of her cute, summery dresses, one with a swingy skirt that was a little sweet and a whole lot sexy. With her hair clipped up in a bun, her neck was exposed, but she hadn't covered it up.

"You're staring," she whispered.

I lifted a hand to stroke her cheek and replied, "I'm appreciating."

A blush crept along her cheekbones, warming the skin under my fingertips. There was a certain look that came into her eyes when I touched her like this, a radiance that soaked straight from her body into mine. I could spend hours just looking at her.

Loving her.

I tried to recall my feelings for Veronica all those years ago. We'd said we loved each other and, at the time, I thought it had been true. Now, with Charlotte, it felt different. Less like an expected token in the development of a relationship and more like a connection that tugged me inexorably toward her.

Before Libby and Mark returned, I leaned forward to kiss her softly. "I love you."

Charlotte was not the most talkative person I knew, and that applied to her emotions as much as anything else. Speaking the words aloud seemed difficult for her at times, but the way she softened when I said them made it worth every effort on my part to do so regularly.

This time was no different. A smile tugged at her lips as she dropped her head to my shoulder and snuggled as close as the patio chairs would allow.

Bowler, who'd been busy chasing a butterfly the last time I checked, ambled over and collapsed into a heap underneath us. I trailed my lips across Charlotte's forehead until our hosts pushed through the back door and simultaneously said, "Aww!"

Though her cheeks pinkened even further, Charlotte winked at me as she lifted her head. When Libby rounded our chairs to put a big salad bowl on the table, she squeezed Charlotte's shoulder and smiled down at me with obvious approval. The memory of that night in the bar came rushing back to the forefront of my mind.

"Dr. Bardot," I said slowly, "just how extensively have you been plotting?"

Libby opened her dark eyes wide. "What on earth do you mean?"

"I was just thinking about how quick you were to shoo me in Charlotte's direction when we were supposed to be going out for drinks that night. You were adamant about welcoming me to Spruce Hill before that, and then it was like you couldn't wait to be rid of me. Isn't that strange?"

Charlotte's gaze narrowed on Libby's face. "That *is* strange, Elizabeth."

Mark, wise man that he was, busied himself with serving up dinner to avoid making eye contact with anyone else at the table. His wife managed to hold onto her innocent expression for another minute before melting into a mischievous grin.

"And at our lunch meeting when you offered me the job, you specifically mentioned *quiet neighbors* as a selling point for the rental house," I continued.

Charlotte's mouth dropped open. "You did not."

"Maybe I thought it was an interesting coincidence that you two had already met, and *maybe* I also thought the two of you would be good for each other."

Since I wholeheartedly agreed that Charlotte was good for me—and I liked the idea that I was good for her, too—I smirked. "I suppose I can't complain."

"I can," Charlotte grumbled, scowling in Libby's direction.

"It's not like I set you up on a blind date or something. Besides, there was no way I could miss the way you looked at her when we walked into the restaurant, Dr. Thorne," Libby said with a shrug.

Charlotte muttered something uncomplimentary under her breath, but I couldn't hold back a laugh. There was something reassuring about the fact that my boss, who I respected not only as a brilliant doctor but as a remarkable human being, had seen that same potential for sparks between us.

"Sawyer, can I get you some potato salad?" Mark asked, smoothly breaking the tension with his broad smile.

Grinning back at him, I accepted the container. "So, Mark, tell me about your shop. Aside from non-lavender balms for Charlotte, what else do you make?"

While he gave me the rundown on the store he'd opened to sell his bath and body products, everything from muscle balm to soap, lotions, and shampoo bars, Charlotte leaned against my shoulder. I kissed her temple and watched as the glow of approval lit Libby and Mark's expressions across the table.

By the end of the meal, I felt like these were no longer only Charlotte's friends, but my own as well. There was plenty of gentle teasing, a few stories from their childhoods, and enough love and affection to overflow the yard. Charlotte was sleepy and snuggly at my side as we sat around the firepit after dinner with Bowler sprawled on the ground next to us.

At one point, when Libby and Charlotte had gone inside to debate which wine went best with s'mores, Mark quietly requested a rundown on the investigation. I told him everything we knew, which unfortunately wasn't much, but he asked to be kept in the loop.

"I know both Jimmy Anders and Craig DeWitt, can't say I can picture either of them hurting her like that," he said in a low voice.

"What about the ex?"

"McGinty is bad news but I haven't heard him talk about Charlotte since the month or two after she dumped his ass. Moved on to greener pastures, I guess. I'll keep an ear out, though. People around here do love to gossip. Anyone says anything that might point us toward the guy, I'll let you know."

I nodded my thanks just as the two women came back outside, their heads bent together as they laughed about something. My heart expanded in my chest at the sight of Charlotte's smile. Mark let out a low whistle and shook his head.

"You are in deep, my friend."

"You're right," I replied. "I absolutely am."

And for the first time that I could recall, that realization filled me with joy instead of trepidation.

Chapter Thirty-Three

CHARLOTTE

Bowler slept on my lap during the short drive home, peed in the yard in exchange for a tiny biscuit when we got there, and went into his crate without complaint. Sawyer laughed when I collapsed onto the bed still fully dressed, but I felt like weeks of tension had melted away under the force of friendship, laughter, and wine from Libby's favorite vineyard in the Finger Lakes.

While Sawyer wrestled me into a sitting position so he could unzip my dress, I leaned heavily against him and mumbled, "I love you."

He paused, cupping the back of my neck as he kissed the crown of my head. "And I love you, angel. More than I imagined possible."

Once I'd wriggled free of my dress, I let myself bask in the simple pleasure of Sawyer's hands stroking over my skin. He didn't rush me, not to get ready to sleep and not into anything sexier, just held me tucked against his chest while he rubbed lazy circles across my back.

"What if the police don't catch this guy?" I whispered, suddenly feeling stone-cold sober.

Sawyer let out a slow breath. "They'll find him."

"But what if they *don't?* I can't hide for the rest of my life because some random dude took a shine to me, Sawyer. I won't."

"Angel," he said gently, brushing the hair back from my face, "I would never expect you to hide forever. Laying low for a bit, protecting yourself by letting others watch out for anything unusual, that's not hiding. It's not cowardice."

I sighed. "It feels like it."

"You are the bravest woman I know, Charlotte Whitmore. When I promised to keep you safe, it wasn't because I didn't think you could take care of yourself. You know that, don't you?"

Since I'd assumed that was exactly what he'd meant, I just blinked at him until he cupped my face between both hands. His eyes looked almost silver in the dim light from my bedside lamp as he searched my expression.

"I see I didn't make it clear enough," he muttered.

"Then why?"

"It was because I couldn't fathom a greater honor than giving you everything that you need from me, including the safety to explore your own desires. I know you joked about me acting as your bodyguard, but I swear to you, Charlotte, I never have and never will view you as a damsel in distress," he vowed.

The vise of panic that had clenched around my heart eased at the words, the simple reassurance he offered with such honesty that it soaked into my very bones. I lifted my face to kiss him, wordlessly thanking him for always knowing exactly what to say to soothe my worries.

And then, as he threaded one hand into my hair and unclasped my bra with the other, I was thankful for all the ways he soothed me without any words at all.

AFTER A LAZY SUNDAY spent lounging around the house, working on simple commands with Bowler, and finally having the focus to finish reading the books we'd been working on, returning to work on Monday morning was nerve-wracking, to say the least.

I hadn't had any nightmares after the attack, probably thanks to Sawyer's reassuring presence beside me all night long, but I couldn't quite halt the replay of the attack. Phantom fingers squeezed my throat as I tried to banish the images from my mind.

The library was my refuge, my sanctuary—I refused to let my assailant ruin that, but it was harder than I expected to walk back in there.

Penelope had given me some makeup tips over the weekend so I could go without a scarf, but I waited in the parking lot for Olivia to show up before I went to unlock the door. Though I tried to reply to her steady stream of chatter as naturally as possible, I was on edge, ready to startle at my own shadow.

The day was blessedly quiet, but I brought my laptop out to the circulation desk rather than retreating to my office. It felt a little too closed-in, the air a little too thick to breathe freely. We had a study group coming in later in the afternoon, then no evening events until the following week.

Now, I thought, *if everyone would stop staring at my neck, that'd be great.*

Still, as I greeted regulars and helped kids find a new world to dive into, some of the tension eased. Getting back in the saddle seemed to be exactly what I needed. With each passing hour, each checkout, each book club meeting, I felt more and more like myself again.

Until David and Pop came through the front doors.

They looked entirely different from usual—furious, vengeful, ready to do battle. Their eyes locked on me as they made their way slowly across the library floor and I came around the desk to meet them. David paused to cough into his elbow a few times, then they stood before me like soldiers awaiting marching orders.

My eyes pooled with tears. "I'm okay."

David opened his arms and I walked straight into them. The only thing keeping me from breaking down and sobbing against his chest was the rattle of his breath under my ear.

"Did you go to the doctor?" I asked, not bothering to move away from him.

"We're on our way to an appointment with a certain new physician in town," Pop said from beside us. His hand cupped the back of my head, stroking my hair like I was his own grandchild. "You gave us quite a scare, dearest."

I nodded against David's chest. "I'm sorry. I promise I'm okay."

"You will be. If the police don't get to the bottom of this, we'll take care of it ourselves," David vowed.

"Thank you. Both of you."

For a long moment, I stayed there in our little huddle, then Pop checked his watch and squeezed David's shoulder. "We need to get to your appointment."

"Right," David murmured, then he drew back enough to study the fading bruises on my neck. "I look forward to speaking with your young man again. Gives us a chance to test his mettle now that things are official, hmm?"

I gave a teary laugh. "I'm sure he'll appreciate that."

Pop tugged me in for his own hug, then searched my face intently until he saw whatever it was he'd been looking for. "You take care of yourself, Charlotte. You mean a great deal to a great many people in this town. We won't stand for anyone mistreating you."

Biting my lip, I nodded. It wasn't clear if they'd heard about what happened after the gala—I hadn't given much detail to anyone in town, but the gossip train moved at lightning speed, so I wouldn't have been shocked if it got out—but it certainly felt like he meant something more than just my attacker.

"I appreciate you two more than I can say," I whispered.

They drew me back into a loose group hug before David started rubbing his sternum. I frowned at him, then caught my expression mirrored on Pop's face.

"Tell Sawyer to send you for a chest X-ray, would you?"

At that, Pop winked at me. "We'll make sure he knows the order came from you, dear one."

I stood there in front of the desk as they left through the front doors, wishing I could be a fly on the wall at that appointment, before finally returning to my work. The entire encounter had barely lasted five minutes, but it went a long way toward restoring the peace I usually found in the library.

And when David got confirmation that it was pneumonia, he insisted Sawyer give him my phone number so he could tell me himself.

For the first time since it started, they missed senior activity day that week.

I spent every free moment I could find putting together a care package to send to the two of them, filled with books by their favorite authors, a portable chess set so David wouldn't have to get out of bed to play, and an assortment of teas and cookies. When Pop called to thank me, his voice was thick with tears.

After fighting back my own, I assured him that having each other's backs was all part and parcel of our relationship.

Sawyer had the day off on Thursday and stopped in for a new stack of books, though this time he went with a few classic Agatha Christie novels instead of romance. I was teasing him about trying to impress me with his literary prowess when his phone rang loudly through the quiet space.

"Sorry, angel," he muttered as he silenced the ringer and checked the screen. "It's Libby, I need to take this."

I waved away the apology and turned to help a high schooler find the right version of a Shakespeare play for his literature class while Sawyer hurried out to the front steps to answer his phone. By the time I got the kid situated, Sawyer was jogging back toward the desk.

"There's been an accident. I need to get to the clinic to help Libby. Several cars were involved. They're taking the ones who need it to the hospital but there were a number of other injuries we can deal with at the clinic. I may not be able to reply right away, but text me when you get home, okay? I want to know you're safe."

"Of course," I said quickly. "Go, take care of everyone. Let me know if there's anything I can do to help."

He squeezed my hand and then rushed off. My heart started pounding for no particular reason, like I was the one hurrying to save life and limb instead of standing numbly behind a counter, surrounded by books.

I forced down a few deep breaths, willing myself to be calm.

Olivia came back from shelving returns, took one look at my face, and nudged me into one of the rolling chairs behind the deck.

"What's going on?" she demanded. "Did something happen?"

"No. I mean, yes. Not to me, though. Sawyer just stopped in, but he got a call from Libby that there was a big car accident and she needed him at the clinic. My brain is just whirling, that's all," I said, pressing my hand to my chest to see if my heart was finally slowing.

"We close in half an hour. Do you need me to come home with you?"

"No, Mom, I don't need a babysitter just because Sawyer got called into work." I scowled at her, but Olivia didn't so much as flinch at my caustic tone, just stared steadily back at me until my shoulders drooped in apology. "Ugh, I'm sorry. But no, I'll be fine. I just need to pick up Bowler from daycare and then I'll go straight home."

She squeezed my hand. "Okay, if you're sure. I'm going to clean up the children's section and then I'll help with the closing routine."

We made quick work of shutting down, though we stuck together for much of what would normally be done by one or the other of us. Since our cars were parked side by side, we left at the same time, and I could tell Olivia was killing time by scrolling through social media on her phone until I finally pulled out of the lot.

Though I'd brushed off her concern, I felt the same worry seeping through my veins the further I got from the library. Twig's daycare wasn't that far away—nothing in Spruce Hill was ever really far—but it was in the opposite direction from both home and work.

Halfway there, I passed the clinic, which had an ambulance parked outside with its lights still flashing, and my anxiety doubled.

I took the first turn, feeling a smile tug at my lips when I remembered Sawyer's comment about the exterior of the daycare building. Just as I started to feel a little calmer, I spotted a minivan parked at the side of the road. Peering into the overgrown field like he was searching for something was the man who'd adopted Spoon, though I grimaced at the memory of Craig telling me the kids changed his name to Barney.

"Shit," I muttered as I signaled and pulled over behind his van. I hopped out of my car and called, "Mr. Schroeder, everything okay?"

"Oh, Charlotte, thank god. Barney jumped out of the car and ran off into the grass. I don't know how to get him to come back. I don't have treats or anything," he said, gripping his thinning hair in both hands. "Oh, shit, Kevin and Ella are going to be heartbroken."

"Let's not get ahead of ourselves," I soothed. "I've got treats in my car. Give me a second and we'll find him."

I headed around to my passenger door and opened the glovebox to find Bowler's favorite jerky treats. Just as I stood to tell Mr. Schroeder the good news, pain exploded at the back of my skull and the world went black.

Chapter Thirty-Four

SAWYER

The afternoon passed in a blur as my mind and body settled back into the mode I'd perfected while working in the emergency room—that familiar narrowing of my focus to only the job in front of me, the efficiency of working quickly to get each case treated before moving on to the line of patients still waiting. The worst of the injuries had been transported to Eastman Memorial, and the ambulance out front waited to take anyone else we deemed more critical than we could handle at the clinic.

The rest were ours, and we took care of them all without a break. Libby and I worked steadily through dozens of abrasions, two possible concussions, and eleven lacerations that required stitches.

Fortunately, no one else needed to go to the hospital.

By the time we sent the last of our patients home to recuperate, we'd been at it for over two hours. Libby and I watched them go, then she turned and gave me a weary smile so full of gratitude it nearly knocked me back a step.

"I couldn't have done this without you, Sawyer."

Warmth curled through my chest, though I shook my head. "I don't believe that."

"Fine," she conceded, "but it would have been awful and a whole lot of people would have ended up with bills for an ambulance ride because I couldn't get to them all. I hope you know how much this entire town appreciates you working here. You're making a difference in their lives—for the better."

My breath stalled in my lungs, but I managed a nod. Libby patted my shoulder like she understood the impact of those words, the way they healed something inside me that had been broken far too long, then she moved to the counter to finish her notes.

I took the opportunity to glance down at my phone. Icy dread closed like a fist around my heart when I realized Charlotte had never texted that she made it home safely.

Libby looked up while I was listening to Charlotte's phone ring in my ear, then it went to voicemail.

"Shit," I muttered.

"What is it?"

I swallowed hard. "Charlotte was supposed to text me when she got home from the library. That should've been at least an hour ago. Now she's not answering."

"She could be outside with the puppy," she suggested, but she looked as worried as I felt.

"I'll call Twig. Bowler was at daycare today," I said, scrolling to find their contact number as quickly as I could. Twig picked up right away and I tried to school my voice, to hide my mounting panic. "Hey, Twig, it's Sawyer Thorne. Did Charlotte come to get Bowler?"

"No, actually, I was about to call you. I've still got him here. Is everything okay?"

Shit.

Forgetting to check in with me when she knew I was dealing with an emergency was one thing, but Charlotte would never willingly miss out on time with the puppy after a long day at work. Fear pooled in my gut, heavy as a boulder.

"I don't know. Can you keep him with you until I figure out what's happening? I haven't heard from Charlotte either. If she shows up, tell her to call me right away."

"Of course. I'll take him home with me, he can stay overnight. Jesus, keep me posted if you find Charlotte, okay?" Twig's voice wavered slightly.

"Absolutely. Thanks, Twig." I ended the call and started dialing Chief Roberts when Libby spoke, her phone still against her ear.

"Mark just swung by the house to check for her, but she's not home yet."

I squeezed her shoulder in silent thanks, then the chief answered. "It's Sawyer Thorne. Charlotte is missing," I told him without preamble, already striding out of the clinic toward the parking lot. "I saw her at the library shortly before closing time, but I was called over to the clinic to deal with injuries from the accident. She never picked up Bowler at Twig's daycare, and she's not answering her phone. What do we do?"

Roberts' voice was muffled for a second, then he said, "We found her car by an open field. Someone called it in. The passenger door and glovebox were open. It's parked on the side of the road, phone and purse still inside, keys in the ignition, about half a mile from Twig's place."

I stopped moving, everything in my body frozen in terror.

"What do we *do?*" I asked again. My voice sounded as hoarse as Charlotte's had after the attack, strangled by fear.

"We're investigating, and I promise we're doing all we can. I want you to go home, Sawyer. Stay there in case she shows up. I've got officers checking out her route from the library to the daycare. It was the middle of the afternoon, someone must have seen something. I'll let you know when we learn more."

After hanging up, I took a second to brace my hands on my knees. I felt like I was going to vomit.

"Sawyer," Libby said, her hand on my shoulder. "They'll find her. What can I do?"

"I don't know." I squeezed my eyes shut. "Roberts told me to go home in case she shows up there."

"Mark and I will join the search. Call me if you hear anything."

Not even my gratitude could cut through the worry choking me, but I nodded. It took several heaving breaths before I was steady enough to run to my car and throw it into gear.

I tried to convince myself I would get back home and find her sitting on the front steps of the house in those pinstripe trousers I loved, wearing that satin blouse that turned her eyes rainforest green.

Instead, the house was silent and deserted when I pulled up.

I stepped out of the car, wondering what to do, then I spotted something that didn't belong. Sitting on the steps where I'd envisioned Charlotte was a red shoebox that hadn't been there when I left to go visit her at work.

I debated calling the chief as I slowly approached it, but it was more important that he kept trying to find Charlotte. Instead, I picked up one of Bowler's discarded sticks from the side of the driveway and inched closer, listening carefully for any sounds from inside the box. Everything was quiet, so I used the stick to knock the lid off.

Whatever I'd expected, it wasn't a collection of papers, receipts, and takeout menus thrown haphazardly on top of one another.

Though I caught a faint whiff of some acrid odor, it was washed away with the breeze. After snapping a picture of the contents with my phone, I dialed the police station rather than interrupting Chief Roberts himself.

I wanted his focus on Charlotte.

"This is Sawyer Thorne. The chief told me to come home in case Charlotte Whitmore returned here, but someone left something on her porch. I don't know if it's related to her going missing or to the assault at the library."

"Hold on a second, Dr. Thorne." The operator on the other end spoke in an undertone to whoever was next to them at the station, then someone else picked up the line.

"Doc, this is Detective Hanson. I'll be right there. Please don't touch any part of the box or what's inside."

After offering my word that I wouldn't handle the box or the items within, I ended the call and stared up at Charlotte's house, remembering my initial impression that it was more my style. Now that I knew the beauty within those walls, the peace we'd found together, it rang even more true.

I alternately paced the driveway and drooped against the side of my car until the police cruiser pulled up at the curb. As I straightened, the detective from the bowling alley exited the car.

"Tell me what we're looking at, Dr. Thorne."

"Please, call me Sawyer," I said, gesturing toward the box.

She pulled on a pair of gloves and squatted down in front of it. "The rest of the squad is spread across town looking for Charlotte. You didn't touch anything?"

"No, I opened it with the stick. I wasn't sure what to expect, but I don't even know what I'm looking at."

Hanson poked through the contents. "Let's see here. An old flyer for wing night at The Hideaway, receipt from Pawn Palace on the outskirts of town, a coupon for a laundromat called Suds & Fold, a bar menu from the bowling alley."

"The one that just burned down?" I asked.

"Yeah. The Hideaway and Suds & Fold had fires, too," she said, frowning down at the box as she sifted through the papers. "Pawn Palace as well."

My muscles tensed as she spoke. "Charlotte was looking into that, I think."

"Looking into the fires?" Her gaze shot to mine, the unease lurking in her eyes amplifying my own.

"Yes. She hasn't brought it up lately, but that night we got the call about the bowling alley, she mentioned she'd overheard someone at the library talking about the fires. She—I think her interest was personal."

"Because of the house fire when she was a kid," Hanson muttered. "I should've known."

I watched as she placed the items into small evidence bags. "Why would anybody collect all of this?"

"Good question, Doc." She lifted a scrap of lined paper. "This part gets a little more interesting."

It was a list of those businesses plus a few more, with some big dollar signs next to them. Underneath that, there were a couple of spare keys, a post-it with six digits written on it—which I took to be a passcode—and a list of business hours.

"What were the other businesses that burned down?" I asked, pulling up a search on my phone. As she read off the names, I hit enter and scrolled through the headlines. "Jesus. Charlotte was onto something."

"What?"

I lifted my head to meet the detective's sharp gaze. "These articles referred to each of those businesses as 'local landmarks' as well, all with huge insurance policies."

Hanson pinched the bridge of her nose. "We reopened investigations into the fires weeks ago. Any idea why someone would deliver this to your girlfriend instead of to us?"

"No. Except...everyone in this town seems to love her. Maybe somebody thought they could trust her with this?" I suggested, staring down at the box and the array of clear plastic bags on the driveway.

"Let's hope that's the case, and it's not because word she was investigating the fires on her own got around town."

Fear shivered through my veins like poison. "What if someone found out?"

Sitting back on her heels, Hanson looked at me for a minute. Working and living with brilliant women had made me well aware of the signs of a mind racing through information, so I kept quiet while she was thinking. Then her dark gaze sharpened on my face and she gathered up the evidence.

"If you don't mind, Doc, I think you should come back to the station with me. There's something I need to look into."

Chapter Thirty-Five

CHARLOTTE

I DIDN'T WANT TO open my eyes.

My head pounded like there was a Muppet with a drum kit inside of it. Something bound my wrists to the arms of a hard plastic chair and the smell of manure hung in the air. All I wanted to do was go back to sleep so I could wake up in Sawyer's arms and realize this was all a bad dream.

"I know you're awake. Let's get this over with."

I forced my heavy eyelids to lift and saw Mr. Schroeder standing a couple yards away. He had a gun in one hand, though it was currently pointed at the ground. As I tried to blink him into focus, all I could think about was how terribly I'd misjudged Spoon's adoptive home.

"I don't understand," I said thickly. "Why are you doing this?"

He made a frustrated gesture with the gun. "Because that skinny little shit had to go running to you. Who else knows?"

Oh, god. I was going to die because I had no clue what the hell he was talking about. "Mr. Schroeder, I swear, I don't know what you mean."

"Did you tell that new doctor you're shacking up with? Who else knows, Charlotte?" His voice started rising and fear trickled along my limbs.

"Sawyer doesn't know anything. I don't even know anything, so there was nothing to tell! Please, just let me go home and we can forget all about this," I begged.

Schroeder turned away for a second, like he was gathering his strength, and when he turned back, he leveled the gun at my chest. "The kid told you everything. I know he did. He thought he could cheat me, but I'm smarter than that little prick."

My brain went completely blank as I stared down the barrel of the gun. I didn't understand what the hell was happening, but tiny pieces started sliding into place, even if they didn't seem to make sense. I blinked at him for another few seconds, then shook my head to try to clear the fog.

"You're the one who broke into the library, the one who attacked me," I said slowly. "That's why you disguised your voice. Because I'd just been at your house for the home visit."

When he lowered the gun and started pacing, I almost wept with relief.

It was too early to celebrate, though—I had no idea if anyone was coming for me, no idea where the hell we even were. From the smell and the dim lighting, I gathered we must be in an old barn, which meant probably somewhere outside of town.

Not very helpful. Miles of farmland stretched across the land surrounding Spruce Hill.

I tried to recall any useful information that might've been on the adoption application, but nothing came to mind. He had two young kids, a beautiful stay-at-home wife, and a nice little house with a nice little yard. It had seemed like the perfect family for Spoon. Either I'd been completely fooled or the man in front of me had some reason to go straight off the deep end.

"Mr. Schroeder, please believe me. I don't know who you think told me anything, but I promise you, I don't know whatever it is you think that I know," I said as calmly as possible.

"You know about the fires. Don't deny it."

Of course, then it hit me.

The application had been on file for months now while they waited for a puppy to be available—I'd looked over it a dozen times. Mr. Schroeder's past employment had been listed as proprietor of The Hideaway.

I closed my eyes.

He'd started another job after that, drop-shipping computer parts or something, but until this moment, I'd forgotten all about his connection to the bar that burned down.

People talked about it for weeks when it first happened, because the insurance policy on the place was almost triple what it was worth, but it had been an entire year before any of the other fires.

A local landmark. That was what Pop and David had been discussing that day.

He looked back at me before I could force my features into some semblance of blankness. It still made no sense, except that the receipt must have been what he was after when he broke into the library. I shook my head frantically.

"No, please," I whispered. "You don't have to do this."

"I do. It's the only way."

As he raised the gun once more, I closed my eyes, wishing I'd told Sawyer one last time that I loved him, wishing I'd taken his protectiveness for the gift it had really been. I braced for something—pain, blackness, *anything*—then I heard a voice that confused me even further.

"She's right, Schroeder. It's over. You don't need to hurt her."

When I opened my eyes, the figure who'd entered the barn was backlit by the open door, looking like nothing more than a silhouette until he stepped inside and closed it behind him.

"Craig?" I whispered.

"I'm sorry, Miss Whitmore. I swear I didn't mean to put you in danger," he said, his pale cheeks reddened with shame.

"What are you doing here?" Schroeder demanded. He turned the gun toward Craig and I jerked reflexively against my bindings.

"It's over, Mr. Schroeder. I'm not setting any more fires."

My body went solid, but I kept my mouth shut.

"Who cares? You're not the only one who can light a match, kid. Now I can tie up all the loose ends, can't I?"

Craig shook his head, lifting his hands to show he was unarmed. "No, sir, I'm afraid not. I made sure a box of evidence got to the police about twenty minutes ago. It will tie every single one of the fires right back to you. It's over."

"You'll go down with me," Schroeder growled.

"Yeah, I will. I believed you, at first, when you said there'd be no victims. My mom needed the money you offered, but when you started threatening her life to get me to keep setting the fires, she became a victim. You should have left her out of it," Craig said calmly.

I might have called him delicate, but in that moment, I saw only strength.

The reason I'd started that lost and found file in the first place was because of how upset he'd been as a teenager after losing the check his mother so desperately needed to keep their little family afloat. I still didn't completely understand what arrangement he and Schroeder had come to, but this was a young man who'd do anything to protect his mother.

I just hoped we both survived long enough for him to keep protecting her.

"The police will be here any minute, Mr. Schroeder. If you want to make a run for it, you better get going."

Schroeder paused, glaring at Craig, but he must have seen the truth in the younger man's statement. He shot me a look, then bolted for the door. As soon as he was through it, Craig ran to me and started untying the ropes around my arms. He gave me a quick, shy smile as he freed the first and went to work on the second set of knots.

"Are the police really coming?" I asked.

He nodded, head bent over my arm, then I was free. "Yes, but we should get out of here in case he decides to come back. I'm so sorry, Miss Whitmore."

When I stumbled on my wobbly legs, Craig caught my elbow and helped me to hobble along as fast as I could go. "I'm pretty sure you just saved my life, so I think we can call it even," I replied.

Though it was well into the evening when we stepped outside, the setting sun still felt painfully bright after the darkness of the barn. I squinted and let Craig lead me toward the road where his rusty old sedan was parked. At first, I recognized where we were in only the vaguest sense, maybe a couple miles outside of town, then it hit me.

Montrose Farms.

It looked different without the bustle of apple picking and hayrides.

"Did you really think I'd let you get away with screwing me, you little asshole?" Schroeder yelled from the edge of the cornfield across the street.

We both froze. Craig shifted his body to shield me, but I stepped up beside him. No matter what had happened, all I could picture was that sweet teenager who blamed himself for making what could have been a costly mistake all those years ago. I wouldn't let him trade his life for mine.

"After I kill you two, I'm going for your mommy, kid. Then I think I'll pay a visit to that new doctor, just in case," he taunted.

We were close enough to the car to dive behind it for cover, but that wouldn't protect us for long. I only hoped that Craig was right about the police.

If we were going to survive this, it would take a miracle.

"You're not going anywhere, Mr. Schroeder. Every cop in the county is going to be on your tail," Craig said, shrugging in the casual way of youth.

The sound of an engine reached us all at the same instant. My eyes flew to the line of police cars hurtling down the road just as the sound of a gunshot rang out. I hit the ground beside the car hard enough to see stars and waited for pain to blossom, for blood to soak my skin, but all I felt was the weight of Craig's body curved protectively over my own.

Shouts broke through the stillness that followed the blast. From the corner of my eye, I saw figures streaming around us, racing into the fields after Mr. Schroeder. My ears were still ringing when the chaos faded and Craig rolled off of me. In addition to several police officers in uniform, I spotted Sawyer and Libby in the crowd.

Relief made me limp as Sawyer rushed toward me.

"He's been shot!" I heard someone say.

"Craig?" I whispered, trying to sit up so I could see him. Craig must have thrown himself at me in order to get us to safety behind the car.

"Easy, angel. It's just a graze. Libby's got him," Sawyer said into my ear. "I need you to relax, Charlotte. You're bleeding."

I blinked at him. "I'm bleeding? Are you sure?"

He cupped the back of my head where Schroeder had hit me, parting my hair to look at the wound before smiling gently down at me again. "Just a bit, angel. I don't think you'll need stitches. Everything's going to be fine."

"Fine," I repeated, then Sawyer's face went hazy and my eyes fluttered closed.

Chapter Thirty-Six

SAWYER

Charlotte didn't wake during the ambulance ride to Eastman Memorial, nor for another three hours after we arrived at the hospital. I might not have been on staff there anymore, but nearly everyone we encountered knew me well enough not to bother insisting I leave her side.

For those who didn't know me, my expression said enough.

I held her limp hand in my own, reciting to myself all the reasons why I shouldn't worry. Strong pulse, steady heartbeat. No nausea or memory loss in the few moments she'd been conscious, no evidence of bleeding or swelling in the brain.

All good signs after a head injury.

None of it helped to reassure me. The thought that she might not wake up held me in terrified silence as I waited at her bedside.

Just before midnight, her gorgeous green eyes fluttered open and my lungs loosened enough to finally draw a deep breath again. I swallowed hard around the lump in my throat as I leaned over to smooth her hair back from her forehead.

"Hey," I said hoarsely.

"Hey." She cleared her throat. "How broken am I, Doc?"

A few hours ago, I hadn't been sure I would ever smile again, but I recognized the question as a throwback to our very first meeting in this same hospital and let out a strangled laugh.

When her lips curved upward, I was certain there was no more beautiful sight on earth.

"Somehow, you managed to get out of that mess with a mild concussion, a half inch long laceration on your scalp, and probably some bruises from hitting the ground. The prognosis is excellent, now that you're awake."

"Not as funny a story as jamming my thumb trying to kill a fly or spraining my wrist on fuzzy pink handcuffs." Her eyelids dipped for a second before she forced them up again.

I blinked back the relief flooding my chest and kissed her forehead, then her cheeks, then her lips. "You're alive to tell the story, that's all that matters to me."

"Have I told you how much I hate hospitals?" she whispered as she closed her eyes.

"I thought it was only doctors you hated. Now you're holding a grudge against the poor building? Might I remind you that this is where we met?" My heart lifted at the sight of her smiling as I stroked her hair.

A soft laugh drifted past her lips. "A good tale to tell the grandkids, but not a romantic destination to come back to visit on anniversaries."

"You're thinking about anniversaries and grandchildren, huh?"

"Yeah," she whispered. "I want it all."

"Does that mean you're planning to keep me around?"

"We adopted a puppy together, Dr. Hottie. I think that means you're stuck with both of us."

Before I could get control of myself enough to reply, she slipped back into sleep. The fact that she'd awoken would have been enough to reassure me of her wellbeing, but the rest of the conversation finally managed to ease the riot of emotions I'd experienced since that first moment after checking my phone at the clinic.

She was alive and well. More importantly, she was mine.

Just as I was hers.

Though she'd slept fitfully in the narrow hospital bed, Charlotte woke up around eight the next morning clearly ready to go home. Her color was good, her vitals perfect, and her disdain for hospitals evident in full force.

Instead of apologizing for my hellion of a girlfriend, I just grinned when she snapped at the doctors on staff, pleased her ire wasn't directed at me.

We got word that Craig would pull through the ordeal just fine after surgery, though he was facing a number of criminal charges. Roberts seemed confident he'd be given a lighter sentence in exchange for testifying against Bert Schroeder, who'd been picked up by police within half an hour of trying to flee, as well as the other business owners who'd received colossal insurance payouts after the fires.

Between the box of evidence Craig had collected, the young man's own testimony, and the recordings Craig said he had taken during some of their meetings, Schroeder would be going away for a long time.

"He saved my life," Charlotte said quietly, her eyes a little misty.

I brought her knuckles to my lips. "Then I owe him a great debt."

"How did you know where to find us?" she asked suddenly. "Craig said the police were on their way, that was all. I thought he was bluffing."

Every terrifying moment of the evening was still crystal clear in my mind. "He left a box on your doorstep, filled with information on all the businesses that were destroyed by fires in the last few years. Each one received a huge insurance payout on the property."

"The businesses from the list that came through the return chute?"

"Yup. The owners of all of them met years ago in a bowling league at the alley we were called to that night and came up with the insurance fraud plan. There was also a map in there to a place called Montrose Farms, which was circled on the original list."

Charlotte's lips parted in surprise. "So all of the fires were arson after all. I wondered how they were connected. The farm made no sense, though—it shut down years ago, but they used to host field trips, hayrides and stuff. I think it's been vacant ever since."

"Apparently that's where Schroeder often met with Craig. Secluded and far enough outside of town not to attract any notice. Detective Hanson recognized the information in the box as matching the list from the library. Since the farm wasn't operational anymore and didn't have the same astronomical insurance policy as the rest, she guessed that it must be important for some other reason, probably as a meeting place. We were already on our way out there when Craig sent a text to the police emergency line with the location."

"I still can't believe it," she said softly. "He's so young. From everything the two of them said, Schroeder played him, then started threatening Craig's mom to make sure he cooperated. She's been sick for years, so I'm sure he felt responsible for taking care of her."

I nodded. "Craig was working on a degree in electrical engineering. I don't know how he and Schroeder connected to begin with—"

"Babysitting," Charlotte cut in. "Craig babysat the twins, I think for the last several years at least. He mentioned it when he came into the library and I remembered him bringing them to some of our events."

"Well, when Schroeder learned Craig had the skills to cause an electrical fire that looked like an accident? He couldn't pass that up."

She opened her mouth to respond, but a tentative knock drew our attention to the open door, and I was struck silent for a stunned second.

"Sawyer," my mother said softly, then her gaze moved to Charlotte. "I heard you were here and I wanted to meet your young lady."

Charlotte's eyebrows shot high on her forehead as I squeezed her hand. "Mom, this is Charlotte Whitmore. Charlotte, my mother, Cynthia Thorne."

"Nice to meet you, Mrs. Thorne," Charlotte said immediately, smiling politely.

My mother took a few steps closer to the bed, her eyes filling with tears behind the professional makeup job she was never without. "I'm so sorry to hear you were hurt."

"Who told you we were here?" I asked. It was an effort to keep my voice calm and even, and I wasn't sure I succeeded, since her gaze flew to mine.

"Your father was working last night."

Charlotte's fingers flexed within my grip, but she stayed silent, letting me process the fact that he knew I was here with my unconscious girlfriend who'd been kidnapped—and that he chose not to come check on us himself.

But just as I opened my mouth to say something that would undoubtedly upset both the women in the room, Dr. Sylvester Thorne himself walked in.

"Ah, she's awake. Good."

Charlotte made a sound that might have been a strangled laugh. My mother smiled at him like this was an everyday occurrence, and my father held out his hand toward the hospital bed for Charlotte to shake. She glanced at me before peeling her hand from my own to clasp his.

"Sylvester Thorne, since my son's clearly forgotten his manners."

My temper simmered, but Charlotte gave a tight smile and said, "I think that can be excused, given the circumstances."

Deep within my chest, something shifted, and my frustration with my father faded into the background. For the first time ever, someone was on my side, ready to throw down with the high and mighty Dr. Thorne on my behalf.

It felt glorious, especially when the skin around his eyes tightened ever so slightly.

I caught my mother's smile from the corner of my eye as she nodded at Charlotte and the tension that sprang up the minute my father entered the room faded even further.

Ignoring him, I tucked a lock of hair behind Charlotte's ear and waited until her gaze focused on me to say, "Your discharge paperwork should be finished any minute. We'll get you home so you can rest."

Mom moved around the bed and bent to kiss my cheek. "I'll leave you to it. Charlotte, I hope to see you again soon. If you two need anything, please let me know."

"Thank you, Mrs. Thorne." Charlotte's eyes twinkled as she offered a more genuine smile this time.

"Thanks, Mom," I replied.

She bustled out of the room without a word to my father, leaving me to wonder what exactly had happened after I left Eastman. I studied the man still standing on the other side of the bed and waited for him to either storm out or say whatever he'd come here to say.

We didn't have to wait long.

"Veronica spoke very highly of Miss Whitmore when we met her and Bill for dinner," he said stiffly.

Again, I got the impression Charlotte was choking down laughter as she shot me a sly look from beneath her lashes.

"I—okay," I muttered.

There was a long beat of silence before he continued. "I'm glad to hear you'll make a full recovery, Miss Whitmore."

"Thank you," she managed to reply with a straight face.

Christ, twelve hours ago, I'd been afraid I might never hear her voice or see that beautiful smile of hers, and now I wondered if she was going to burst out laughing in the face of my father's awkward-as-fuck pseudo-apology.

"Sawyer," he said quietly, "I truly do hope you've found what you were looking for."

Gazing at the woman I'd fallen head over heels in love with, I replied, "I have."

A nurse appeared in the doorway, looking half-ready to bolt at the sight of my father standing in the room, but he waved her in and nodded toward me and Charlotte.

"Take care, both of you."

Before we could reply—not that I knew what to say—he strode out into the hall and Charlotte let out a giggle that made the nurse widen her eyes at us both.

I leaned down and pressed my lips to Charlotte's temple. "You," I whispered, "are a troublemaker through and through. I can't believe you almost laughed in his face."

She gave an airy shrug, grinning at me. "He's not as scary as I expected. I can't wait to get out of here."

When I pulled some strings to get Charlotte's discharge paperwork taken care of more quickly, she dragged me close enough to whisper several dirty promises to be fulfilled once she had fully recovered. I winked at her and managed to commandeer a set of scrubs so she wouldn't have to ride home in her bloodstained clothes from the day before, which had taken a serious hit during the ordeal.

Once I'd helped her change into the blue scrubs, I lifted a brow. "You know, I don't remember any such offers when I treated your wrist *and* gave you my jacket after your friends forgot about you."

"Only because you're not a mind-reader," she replied, smirking at me.

"Remind me again why I didn't get your phone number that night?"

She batted her lashes. "Because I'm worth the wait?"

"Fuck yes, you are," I whispered, cupping her face gently so I could kiss her. By the time I pulled back, a flush had banished the pallor in her cheeks and her eyes sparkled at me.

I convinced the discharge nurse to let me be the one to wheel Charlotte to the exit, mostly for the man's own protection. Her dislike of medical professionals and facilities also extended to hospital policies that were, as she called them, "utterly ridiculous."

In turn, I whispered a few dirty promises of my own to persuade her not to make a fuss on the way out.

Since Charlotte's eyes had filled with tears when I told her Twig kept Bowler overnight for us, I'd quietly arranged for Mark to pick the puppy up from Twig once we were on our way home. After our conversation when she first woke up the night before, I'd started to see Bowler as a symbol of what lay between us, the proof that we were inextricably bound together.

The two of them were my family now, though it was becoming more and more obvious that our little family included a great many of the friends surrounding us.

Though Libby had offered to bring my car to the hospital the night before, Penelope insisted she and Grisham would drive the two of us home to Spruce Hill as soon as Charlotte was released. They'd been so grateful for my updates last night that it seemed only fair to give them a chance to see Charlotte was safe and well with their own eyes.

Both of them jumped out of the car to envelope Charlotte in a hug as soon as she stood up from the wheelchair. I passed it back to the discharge nurse, who winked at me, then I stood back to watch the three of them embracing, crying, and chattering all at the same time.

Before I could fully appreciate the sight, Grisham reached over and caught the back of my neck, drawing me into the circle.

"Thank you," Penelope mouthed at me over Charlotte's head.

I nodded back at her, unable to wipe the smile from my face. It only grew wider when Charlotte drew back and muttered, "That's enough of that. Let's get the hell out of here."

The two of us climbed into the back seat, holding hands during the drive home. As we left the city and drove past broad swaths of farmland, Charlotte turned her face away from the window, citing the passing landscape making her dizzy, but I suspected it was too soon for the reminder of her ordeal. I glanced out at the dilapidated barns dotting the fields outside of Spruce Hill and squeezed her hand in silent support.

For a long time, she stayed quiet, leaning her head against my shoulder. When she peeked up at me, I kissed her forehead.

Processing it all would take time, as would accepting that this nightmare was finally over.

However long it took, I intended to be beside her every step of the way.

Chapter Thirty-Seven

CHARLOTTE

Though I was sore, overtired, and emotionally fragile after all that had happened in less than twenty-four hours, it was pulling into the driveway at home to find Mark holding Bowler's leash that tipped me straight over the edge. I burst into tears, burying my face against Sawyer's chest as he unbuckled our seatbelts and tugged me onto his lap. He murmured soft, comforting words into the top of my head while sobs wracked my body.

Penelope and Grisham got out and closed their doors behind them, though whether to give us privacy or because they wanted to play with our adorable puppy, I wasn't sure. In truth, I didn't care. I just needed to release the pressure of everything that had transpired, to feel Sawyer's solid arms around me and his heart thumping steadily under my ear.

"I thought I'd never see you again," I wailed into his throat.

Though I had no idea how long Mr. Schroeder had me in that barn, every second from the moment I opened my eyes until Craig and I ran out of there weighed on my heart, the remnants of my own panic pummeling me like blows. It shuddered through my ribcage and poured itself out of me in hot, relentless tears, soaking Sawyer's shirt.

"Let it out, angel. I've got you." His hands were strong and soothing as he stroked up and down my spine. "You're safe now. I'm here."

"I love you."

It was barely more than a hiccuping whimper, but I felt his lips curve against my temple as he trailed soft kisses across my forehead. "And I love you. Always."

I cried harder, burrowing into him like he could shield me from the world.

Several minutes later, when the tears finally slowed, I realized that he could. He would stand between me and anything that might hurt me, again and again. This stern doctor had morphed into a protective lover—and he was mine.

Mine to love. Mine to keep.

"I adore you," I whispered. "Thank you for coming for me."

His lips coasted along my hairline, trailing down my temple and across my wet cheeks. "I will always come for you, angel, and I'll do everything in my power to keep you safe. Everything is going to be fine."

I nodded, my grip on his shirt tight enough to leave wrinkles when I finally sat back and met his calm blue gaze.

"There's no rush," he said gently, brushing his thumb over my cheekbone. "We can sit here as long as you need to."

"No, I'm okay. I'm ready."

I drew one shaky breath, but the next came easier. Sawyer pressed a firm kiss to my forehead, then shifted me off his lap so he could open the door.

When we finally climbed out of the car, Bowler stood up on his back legs and barked so excitedly that we all laughed, then he immediately dropped to the grass and rolled over. I wasn't in any shape to fall to my knees on the driveway, so I held onto Sawyer's arm for support and bent down to rub Bowler's belly.

By the time I straightened—which took so long, I felt like I was ninety years old—Mark was smiling gently. I tried to smile back, but the tears started up again.

Mark handed the leash to Sawyer and wrapped me in the kind of big brother bear hug he'd perfected decades ago. "Hey, kiddo, it's okay. You're home and safe. If you stop crying, I'll let you use the nickname."

My head lifted as I dashed the wetness from my cheeks. "For how long?"

"You people and your nicknames," Sawyer muttered, but I caught sight of the grin creeping across his face.

"Two weeks?" Mark offered.

It took another second to get a hold of myself, then I held out my hand. "Deal. I love you, Marky Mark."

He groaned, but he pulled me back into his chest and kissed the top of my head. "I love you, Charlatan."

Sawyer huffed a laugh behind me and suddenly I was ensconced in an even bigger group hug than when we left the hospital. Caught in the middle of it, I had to close my eyes and breathe deeply to keep myself from crying again. Even Bowler wriggled his little body into the huddle, plopping his behind down on my foot so he could lean against my legs.

And right there, surrounded by so much love, the memory of that barn faded away.

When they finally drew back, Sawyer's arm slipped around my waist and Penelope gave me a teary smile.

"Both of you better promise to keep me posted on your recovery," she said, raising a threatening finger in our direction. "And I'll bring your favorite sushi to movie night as soon as you're up for it."

"I love you," I whispered.

She wiped away the shadow of mascara beneath her wet lashes, gathering herself before replying, "I love you, too, babe."

Grisham nudged her out of the way and kissed my forehead, then turned around and planted one on Sawyer's. "Take care of our girl."

"You know I will," Sawyer vowed.

"Dr. Hottie's a winner, Chuck." Grisham winked and threaded his arm through Penelope's as they headed back toward the car.

Mark moved in to kiss my temple. "Libby will want to check up on you later, kid. Sawyer, I trust you'll keep us in the loop."

"I will. Thank you for bringing Bowler home."

As Mark jogged toward his car, Sawyer unlocked the side door and tried to keep Bowler from tripping me while we went inside. I desperately needed to shower and get into something more comfortable than borrowed scrubs, but I lowered myself carefully onto the couch while Sawyer started a pot of coffee. Bowler backed up a few steps, then managed to hurl his clumsy body up onto the cushions beside me after a running start.

"What a smart boy," I told him, perfectly content to have him flop across my lap, his weight warm and comforting. I rubbed his ears as he turned his pretty blue eyes on me. "You take after your daddy."

Sawyer snorted as he brought two mugs of coffee over and set them carefully out of range of the puppy. "Is that a reference to our eye color or the fact that we're both utterly devoted to you?"

I laughed, but as I stroked Bowler's head, I asked the question that had been weighing on me since I realized the truth about Mr. Schroeder. "What do you think will happen to Spoon?"

"Well," Sawyer said gently, laying his arm along the cushion behind me so I could nestle into his side, "I guess it depends. If Mrs. Schroeder was involved, I'm sure the police will find that out. Will the rescue step in to take him back if that's the case?"

"I would think so. And if she had no idea what her husband was up to, she and the kids may need him more than ever. What a mess."

"After the gala, Libby said you have more love in your heart than anyone she knows," he said softly. "It's true. It shines on all of us like the sun. Everyone around you can't help but lean into that warmth."

I bit my lip, determined not to burst into tears yet again, but he knew what I was thinking. Sawyer always knew.

He tugged me into his arms, leaning his cheek against the top of my head as he laid his other hand on the puppy's belly. For a while, we stayed just like that, with the sounds of the quiet house and Bowler's happy snores surrounding us. I still had a residual headache and a million questions buzzing through my brain, but as I relaxed against Sawyer's side, it all gradually dissipated.

After several long moments, I said, "Would you...I mean, if you want to..."

"Yes, angel?" Sawyer prompted gently after the words trailed into silence.

"Do you want to move in with me? For real, I mean." When he didn't respond immediately, a flush of embarrassment heated my skin. "You don't have to. I just thought since you're staying here at night anyway, we could make it official and—"

"Yes. Absolutely, yes."

I peeked up at him to find his lips curved into an expression of pure joy. "Really?"

"Of course. I don't want to lose another minute with you, Charlotte. Not if I can help it."

"I love you," I whispered.

"And I love you," he whispered back, kissing me so sweetly that my eyes flooded all over again. "Charlotte, angel, you are my heart. I never thought I'd find this kind of happiness, but you see me in a way no one else ever has. Beside you is exactly where I'm meant to be. Always."

When the tears spilled over my cheeks, Sawyer was right there to brush them away with his thumbs, then he kissed the trails they left behind. After letting his lips ghost over mine, he tipped my head up and kissed me properly.

There was nothing in the world like kissing this man. He made me feel like everything around us disappeared into the background, leaving only our two bodies in sharp focus.

Once he drew back, his crystal blue gaze swept over my features like he was cherishing every nuance, every freckle. In this topsy-turvy world, teetering around us, Sawyer had become my rock, an anchor in the storm.

I remembered the words spoken so long ago, words I didn't understand the meaning of at the time, words that now encircled my heart and protected it.

You are safe with me. Always.

Now, finally, I believed it with my whole heart.

Epilogue

SAWYER: SOME MONTHS LATER

THE YARD WAS AWASH with laughter. Though the hyacinths had faded, the rose bushes along the back fence were in full bloom, their perfume prominent even beneath the aroma of the burgers cooking in front of me.

We'd decked out Charlotte's gazebo for the party, draping additional curtains of fairy lights around the outer walls and installing an overhead fan to circulate the late summer air. Mark stood near the table, where he introduced his friends Henry and Juliet to Penelope and Grisham. Henry's Border Collie raced around the yard with Bowler, who'd practically doubled in size over the last few months, along with two terrier mixes Twig had brought. Libby, Olivia, and Twig brought dish after dish from the kitchen out to the folding tables set up along the fence.

I'd been assigned to man the grill, which gave me a perfect view of our little gathering. This was the exact type of event I had avoided like the plague once upon a time, but now?

I couldn't hide the smile continuously pulling at my lips.

"What are you grinning about?" Charlotte asked as she appeared at my side. "You're ruining your stern doctor image in front of all our friends."

"Now, angel, you know the stern doctor is reserved for your personal pleasure," I said in the low voice that always caused her to shiver a little in anticipation.

"How long is this shindig? Maybe Mark can take over for you here while we, um, go fix a small plumbing problem upstairs. I'm sure they won't miss us."

"Brat. This 'shindig' was your idea, so you'll have to keep your panties on until everyone goes home. Then I'll check your plumbing for as long as you want," I muttered, bouncing my eyebrows at her.

She grinned up at me, those green eyes gleaming emerald in the summer sun, then she leaned in close to my ear and whispered, "Who says I'm wearing panties?"

I growled as she flounced away, but I kept a close eye on the ruffled skirt of her sundress, wondering if she was serious. Even after officially living together for nearly four months, she was still full of surprises. Just before she reached Libby's side, she turned and winked at me over her shoulder.

Oh, she was *definitely* serious.

Turning back to the grill, I dreamed up a dozen scenarios to play out after our guests finally went home. None of them would keep Charlotte from playing with fire in the future, but we'd both enjoy ourselves in the process.

In fact, it had been altogether too long since I'd had her tied up in that sweet princess bed upstairs—*our* bed—and the little tease had definitely earned herself pleasurable retribution.

When dinner was ready, we sat around the table, Charlotte on my right and Grisham on my left. I would have been content to let the tide of conversation sweep me along, but instead, I was drawn in, as though I'd been friends with this crowd my entire life.

Something new had started the minute I moved to Spruce Hill, extending far beyond a new job and a new girlfriend.

Somehow, somewhere along the way, I'd become part of a family.

Of course, some family members were more annoying than others. I was reminded of that fact when I placed my hand on Charlotte's leg under the table to see just how far I could creep up under her skirt before she stopped me.

"Dirty birdy," Grisham whispered in my direction.

I laughed and started to remove my hand, but Charlotte caught it in hers, lacing our fingers together.

As she smiled up at me, all I could think was that everything I needed was right here. With the woman I loved at my side, surrounded by all the people who cared about us both, life was sweeter than I'd ever dreamed possible.

I hadn't been looking for love or family when I set out on this adventure, but I was grateful every day that I'd found both.

Also by

RACHEL FITZJAMES

Keep in touch! Sign up for Rachel's newsletter at https://rachelfitzjames.com/ for a FREE bonus epilogue, sneak peeks, sales, and news about upcoming releases!

SPRUCE HILL SERIES

Unpacking Secrets

A Lonely Road

Canvas of Lies

Crumbling Truth

Playing for Paradise

Sinister Returns

Treasured Legacy
Coming May 2026

Acknowledgements

First and foremost, immense thanks to those who've stuck with this series, as well as those who've just happened to stumble upon it. I didn't set out to create a town with this many books (or crimes...) but here we are. To my ARC readers who jumped at the chance to read these books, it means the world to me, so thank you!

As always, to my family for sticking by me through rounds of drafting and revisions and renaming and reordering, I love you. Thanks for making Charlotte into the fullest (and blondest) version of herself, and for suggesting insurance fraud as a suspense element, because I would never have been able to plan that out on my own.

Christina Brennan, Tobie Carter, Lindsay Barrett, Anne Knight, Briana Newstead, and Sia Williams, thank you so much for turning this book into something worthwhile. Your input was absolutely golden and I hope the final version honors all your insights!

To my CPs, Christie Curry, Christina Brennan, and Briana Newstead, thank you for putting up with me while I tried (and failed) to Frankenstein this manuscript from two separate books into a single cohesive plot, and then sticking by me as I made myself rewrite the entire thing from scratch without looking at either of those documents. As always, you are the guardians of my sanity, and I appreciate that to no end.

About the author

Rachel Fitzjames is the author of a contemporary romantic suspense series set in the fictional town of Spruce Hill, NY. She started writing on her brother's ancient computer back in the early 90s and never looked back, though her first short story about an underground cat thievery ring was sadly lost. With a degree in geography inspired by wanderlust, Rachel has a keen appreciation for the escape that the romance genre allows. She is a lifelong resident of Western NY and created Spruce Hill in order to give a little bit of home to all of her characters.

Connect with Rachel at her website, https://rachelfitzjames.com/, or on Instagram and Threads at @rachelfitzjames.

www.ingramcontent.com/pod-product-compliance
Lightning Source LLC
LaVergne TN
LVHW041742060526
838201LV00046B/877